S g

& Sweet

Stories from

Granbury

Writers Bloc

www.GranburyWritersBloc.com

i

ii

# Strange

# & Sweet

Stories from the Granbury Writers' Bloc

# ACKNOWLEDGEMENTS

The publishing team thanks the contributors and members of Granbury Writers' Bloc for their talented efforts that made this book possible.

We give special thanks and recognition to Tina Vanderburg for her creative efforts formatting pages and text, designing the cover, and providing professional technical support. Her experience and enthusiasm created a book that makes us proud.

We appreciate those authors, John M. Floyd, Charlaine Harris and James Scott Bell, who graciously offered comments for the back cover.

We also recognize the following hard-working team members for their editing, publishing and marketing skills.

Editing Team:  Brian Condike and Donna Pierce

Publishing Team: Dan Vanderburg, Gary Christenson, and Peggy Purser Freeman

Marketing Team: Mary Lou Condike, Connie Lewis Leonard, Beverly Harrison and Holli Harrison.

# INTRODUCTION

*Strange & Sweet* short stories and poetry entice you to grab your pipe and magnifying glass and dive into these twisted tales of mystery and suspense. Prepare for a good belly-laugh as humorous stories unfold. Sneak into the unknown, spooky or just plain weird as you read the paranormal or fantasy tales. Teleport into a sci-fi world, launch into an action/adventure, and mosey into a western. To round out your reading choices, *Strange and Sweet* includes several entertaining short stories in the non-fiction literary and young adult categories. Don't overlook the thought-provoking poems.

About the Authors: Curl up with *Strange & Sweet*, and enjoy the latest offerings from the Granbury Writers' Bloc. Many of these talented authors have received awards from prestigious writing contests such as The Writer's Digest Short Story Contest, 2019 OWFI Writing Contest, Austin (Texas) League Children's Book Teddy Award, Greater Dallas Area Writers Contest, The Writers Guild of Texas Kathryn McClatchy Flash Fiction Contest, Johnson County Writers, and the Granbury Writers' Bloc Buster Challenge Short Story Contest.

# CONTENTS

**MYSTERY/SUSPENSE/THRILLER**      1

Sharp Money – BJ Condike      3

Lilly – Gary Christenson      9

Death Diary – Meg Arlen      13

Mystery in Granny's Attic – Gail Armstrong      19

Retribution Day – Gary Christenson      25

Gringo – BJ Condike      31

Nowhere Diner – Gail Armstrong      37

96 Stories – Gary Christenson      43

**ACTION/ADVENTURE/WESTERN**      47

Any Dang Fool – BJ Condike      49

Richard of Lewis Castle –
Connie Lewis Leonard      53

Spirit Pouch – Donna Pierce      61

Crossing the Line – BJ Condike      63

North Ridge – Donna Pierce      69

**SCI-FI/PARANORMAL/FANTASY**      75

Franklin's Secret Garden – Robert C. Taylor      77

Santa Duty – Gary Christenson      83

Prophecy – BJ Condike      87

A Question of Heritage –
William 'Bud' Humble      95

Ghola – William 'Bud' Humble      109

**YOUNG ADULT/WOMEN'S FICTION**      135

A Purple Lizard – ML Condike      137

The Yellow Shoes – Robert C. Taylor      143

Ruth's Friend Jake –
    Peggy Purser Freeman      149

Hershey Remembers The Fire –
    Robert C. Taylor      155

LITERARY      159

Naked Reflection – Meg Arlen      161

Unforgiveness – Donna Pierce      165

Micro – H.M. Harrison      167

A Cruel and Unusual Place – ML Condike      173

The Dream Snatcher – Robert C. Taylor      179

Seven – ML Condike      181

The Ballet – Dan Vanderburg      189

Dark Chocolate – Kathryn McClatchy      193

It Ain't Heavy—It's My Ladder –
    Gail Armstrong      201

Reunion – Rick Anderson      207

HUMOR      217

Handcuffs – ML Condike      219

Another Day with Bubba – Dan Vanderburg      223

A Guy Walks Into a Bar... – R.L. Sykes      237

Lucky Underwear – ML Condike      241

Playa – Rick Anderson      247

Old Gus – Dan Vanderburg      257

NON-FICTION      263

The Tube of Torture –
    Connie Lewis Leonard      265

Reflections on my Thirteenth Year –
   Robert C. Taylor                                      269

The Phantom – Beverly Harrison                           273

Why's That Dog on the Bus? –
   Kathryn McClatchy                                     277

Four Guys in a Boardinghouse –
   Barna A. Richards, M.D.                               281

POETRY                                                   293

   The Old Home Place – Dan Vanderburg                   295

   A, B, C, D – Connie Lewis Leonard                     301

   What Have You Done? – Donna Pierce                    303

   The Pageturner's Pen – Jonathan Mathews               305

   Grampaw, Was That You? –
      Dan Vanderburg                                     307

   Perspicere – Jonathan Mathews                         309

   Friendship – Donna Pierce                             311

   The Last Dance – Dan Vanderburg                       313

AUTHORS                                                  315

# MYSTERY/SUSPENSE/THRILLER

# Sharp Money

## by BJ Condike

"Hit him again."

The roundhouse blow exploded on my jawbone. Cold pain radiated to my eye and neck. I hung my head, drool and blood dripping from swollen lips. Gasping and spitting, I probed teeth with my tongue, ensuring all were present. So far only one felt loose.

Borislav grabbed my hair and yanked my head up. "I want my money."

I blinked the sweat from my eyes. "I told you I don't have it. Tuesday. I'll have it Tuesday." I whined like Wimpy from a Popeye cartoon.

The rotund Russian let go, and waved at his weasel-faced henchman. The next punch landed in my gut. Spasms gripped my diaphragm, stealing my breath, and the room began to darken. A certain amount of pain was inherent in the role I played, but I didn't have to like it. Finally I caught some air, wheezed a few short lungfuls, and the space around me came back into focus.

A bare bulb lit the small concrete room. A low doorway revealed rough stairs leading up into darkness. Wan light from a basement window dribbled down a blackened sheet metal chute. A mound of coal rested at the foot of the metal spillway. Fist-sized lumps of anthracite littered the dirt floor. My wallet, keys, and ballcap lay in a pile at my feet.

Borislav and his flunky had duct-taped me to a chair. I was bruised and bloody and had peed myself, but so far they hadn't cut me. I had the Russian mobster just where I wanted him.

"Where'd you get the new goon, Boris— Thugs 'R' Us?" I said, nodding at his stooge. "May I call you Boris? I feel like we've gotten to know each other so much better these past few hours." I spit out some more blood. "Say, whatever happened to Ratcliff and his toady sidekick, anyway? Now Rat could throw a punch—not like this lightweight."

Boris glared at me. "Rat disappeared."

"Oh, yeah? That's too bad. What about the rest of your little army?"

The fat Russian scowled, and not for the first time. "Crew gone. All gone."

I knew they were gone—I had seen to that a few days earlier. It hadn't been easy, but they didn't call me for the easy jobs.

Weasel-face gut-punched me again. He was short, but muscular. I had called him a lightweight, but if he hit me any harder I'd have to increase his weight class.

Boris lifted my chin with his thumb and forefinger. "Who do you think you are, McGinn, blowing into town, taking my money, and not paying me back? I can't have *mudaks* like you disrespecting me. I got to make an example." Boris reached under his suitcoat and pulled out a shiny revolver.

"Hey, hey, hey, let's not get hasty, Borya." The mobster stiffened at the use of his diminutive name. It was like calling Charles Bronson 'Chucky.' "Did I say Tuesday? What was I thinking? Of course I meant today. That's right, I can have your money today."

"How? You got no money." He pointed one of his chins at my wallet.

"Look again. I got plastic. Expensive plastic."

Weasel-face picked up my wallet and extracted a wad of credit cards. He fanned them out like a multi-colored bridge hand and displayed them for his boss. I hoped he handled them carefully.

Boris sniffed and wrinkled his nose. His gravelly skin reminded me of a dirt parking lot. "They're not worth enough. You owe me ten large—fifteen with the vig."

"That's where you're wrong. Those are gold and

platinum. I can get two or three G's cash advance on each one."

Boris took the cards and peered at them closely. "They're not yours. How're you gonna cash 'em?

"Of course they're not mine. I'm a thief. I lifted them at the airport yesterday and bought the passwords on the dark web. I was saving them for a rainy day." I eyeballed the revolver. "I see lightning on the horizon, so I guess today's the rainy day."

The corpulent loan shark stared at the credit cards in one hand, and twirled the revolver with the other.

"Why don't you send your gorilla friend here to an ATM and get the cash?" I said, nudging him in the right direction while trying to sound desperate. "I'll give him the passwords. There's a machine over on Seventh."

This is where it got sticky. My employers had squeezed the fat Russian for money, and he was anxious to collect my debt. I had eliminated Boris' band of ruffians, and had counted on him being alone. I hadn't figured on him hiring outside help. Weasel-face was just one hoodlum, but he complicated matters.

What they call 'sharp money' in Las Vegas is a side bet. My side bet was that Boris wouldn't trust an underling with all that cash. Certainly not one he just hired, someone he didn't know. He couldn't take the slightest chance of losing the money. Not when he needed it so badly.

I needed Boris alone and unprotected. I prayed he would make the right choice.

The fat man gestured at me. "No. I'll take you, and you'll get me the money." He thrust the gun in my direction for emphasis. "And no tricks." He spoke to Weasel-face out the side of his mouth. "Cut him loose."

The goon did as he was told, and Boris herded me out the door with the revolver and up the stairs. I grabbed my ballcap on the way out.

I squinted in the harsh sunlight as I drove the fat Russian's Cadillac to the walk-up ATM on Seventh. The street held several boarded-up stores, and the rest had bars on the windows. In that part of town I could depend upon deaf and blind witnesses, if there were any at all.

We exited the car. The gun barrel deformed Boris' suitcoat pocket, but it wasn't because he was happy.

I flipped my sweatshirt's hood over my head and held up my hand.

"You might want to stay behind me." I pointed to the small lens over the cash machine. "Camera."

Boris pulled the brim of his fedora down and kept a half step to my rear.

I shuffled the credit cards until I had the order I wanted. I dutifully pumped the cards into the ATM and repeatedly withdrew money. Fifteen thousand in twenties is 750 bills, too much to hold all at once. Twice I handed thick stacks of cash to Boris, and returned to the machine.

"Here's the last of it." I turned, and Boris reached for the remaining bills. I let one drop, and the overweight money lender instinctively bent to grab it. I swung my left arm in a sweeping arc, tightly grasping the last credit card, the special one I had prepared that morning.

The razor-sharp PVC corner sliced through the mobster's neck with little resistance. He stood up abruptly, dropped the bills, and clamped his hand on his throat with a surprised look. Blood spurted and oozed through his fingers in unrelenting streams. He fell heavily to his knees, croaking and gasping, incapable of speech.

I sidestepped the blood and calmly plucked the handkerchief from his breast pocket, using it to wipe the ATM keyboard of any fingerprints.

"Next time don't skim from the mob," I said. "Oh, that's right—there won't be a next time."

The life faded from his eyes, his skin sagged, and the

body collapsed on the sidewalk. A rivulet of blood inched its way toward the gutter. An empty paper cup skittered across the otherwise silent street, pushed by a rogue gust of wind.

I walked away and dodged down the first alley I came to.

My employers would be pleased. I had completed the assignment in a short time, and it hadn't cost them anything extra. I would give them the money I had borrowed from Boris. Since he worked for them, it was their money in the first place. They owed me my fee, which was substantial, but that was the cost of doing business.

The mob had wanted a public statement—steal from them, and pay the price. I had given them one. I had cut down Boris in broad daylight in front of an ATM, his pockets stuffed with cash, loose bills scattered around his body, soaking up his life's blood.

Boris had placed a side bet, a wager that the mob wouldn't miss some skim off the top of his loan sharking. The sharp money had cut him. Actually it wasn't money, only a credit card. But it had cut him dead just the same.

7

# Lilly

## by Gary Christenson

Gone? Where was Lilly? At seven, Lilly had been the light of my life since my wife died. With a sweet disposition and beautiful eyes, she brought joy to my saddened world. Just minutes ago she and I had been playing catch in the backyard. Then I took a phone call in the house. Now she was missing.

In my frantic worry I almost missed the large envelope standing up in the grass. Someone had pasted "Lilly" in crude letters on the front. I ripped it open. The letter inside was pasted words.

*If your girl is important to you, wait by the phone.*

I couldn't stop pacing around the living room. I felt like I might explode. The phone call came several hours later.

"My name is Smith. Shall we talk about Lilly?"

"What have you done with Lilly?" I yelled. "What do you want?"

Smith's voice sounded cold and brutal. "We want cash. If your girl is important to you, gather one hundred thousand bucks in large bills and follow directions. Don't contact the police. We'll know if you do. Your only concerns are gathering the money and following directions."

I clenched a fist wanting to reach through the phone lines, grab his throat and strangle him. Instead, I calmed myself with deep breathing. "I understand. I'll do whatever you ask."

He cleared his throat and added, "We know your net worth, liquid capital and reputation as a 'can-do' type of guy. Don't go all Green Beret on us. We'll crush you and kill Lilly.

Do as you're told, pay us a fraction of the money you've accumulated, and she comes home. We'll be out of your life forever."

Smith said, "Drive north tomorrow on highway two-seventy-eight from Eureka in the Nevada desert. Twelve miles down that road you'll come to a sign pointing to a ghost town on the right. Take the dirt road and continue until you see broken-down houses and businesses. A huge white 'X' painted on the dirt road is your transfer point. Arrive around noon. We'll take a while to confirm you're alone and there's no surveillance."

Smith's voice hardened as he said, "Don't get any ideas. A trained sniper will hold a scope on you the whole time. If you do anything but what you've been told, he puts a bullet in your head, we take the money, and Lilly dies. Got it?"

The next day I removed a stack of hundred-dollar bills from my safe deposit box, placed them in a briefcase and drove toward the transfer point.

I'm a retired professional soldier trained to manage my emotions and react proactively in difficult circumstances. But now as I drove north, my stomach churned. The lightweight briefcase lay on the front seat beside me.

Following directions, I parked my car, grabbed a bottle of water and my case, and stood on the large white "X." They watched everything. I repressed my anger

After a while I glanced at my watch. Twenty-three minutes had passed, and nothing moved except a black crow hopping in the weeds between abandoned houses. The ghost town was two hundred yards down the road. My watch read three minutes before noon.

I looked around thinking I might spot the sun reflecting off a rifle scope. No reflection, nothing. Two buzzards circled in the sky. The sun burned down upon the landscape.

After standing on the "X" for over an hour, a faint buzzing sound came from the west. Several minutes later a huge, black, eight-propeller drone hovered in front of me. A tiny video camera focused on me and Smith's voice emanated from the miniature helicopter, "Open the briefcase so we can view the contents."

The drone circled the briefcase. A moment later he said, "A cell phone hangs from the underside of the drone. Unhook the phone and connect the briefcase handle."

After exchanging the case with the phone, the drone ascended beyond my reach. Smith's voice told me, "There are two keys taped to the phone. One key opens the door to the building where we're holding her. The other key unlocks her prison cell. She's healthy and unharmed. After we've examined your payment, we'll direct you to her."

The drone rose and flew west.

The cell phone rang twenty minutes later. "So far so good. Drive down the road toward the abandoned church and turn left. Behind the church you'll find a building secured with a new padlock. Open it with the silver key. Inside you'll find Lilly. The blue key will unlock her cell."

He disconnected and I prayed he had told me the truth.

The weather-beaten and damaged front door of the run-down church creaked in the wind. Someone had repaired the building behind it. The large padlock and new hardware contrasted with the dilapidated condition of everything else in the ghost town. I opened the door and spotted Lilly. She jumped with excitement when she saw me.

The blue key opened the lock. Lilly kissed my face. "How's my best girl?" I hugged her and retrieved two of her favorite treats from my shirt pocket. She wolfed them down. Lilly, my honey-colored cocker spaniel, was unharmed, and I rejoiced.

She jumped into my car and yelped. I rolled down the window so she could stick her nose into the wind as we drove.

Back home I fed Lilly and played her favorite game of fetch until she tired. An hour later we relaxed on the couch. I smiled and savored the complex flavors in a glass of wine while Lilly snuggled against me.

I paid $100,000 to rescue Lilly because she was more important than any human in my world.

The transmitter I had implanted in the briefcase might help the police apprehend Smith and his crew. I had set it for a delayed broadcast because I didn't want the bad-guys detecting a transmission while they examined the cash.

"We know what's important, don't we, Lilly? You're home and that's all that matters."

# Death Diary

## by Meg Arlen

The dimly lit closet seemed to shrink around me. I struggled with the cold clothes bar clicking it in place. That should have been fixed before I moved in. Joe had pleaded with me to delay my move until after our wedding, which I had once more postponed.

The secluded country home offered me a sanctuary to work on my looming deadline and finish my latest Gothic novel. Deadlines had become the crushing pressures in my life. Always the publishers pushed. Write! Faster! More!

I stooped to pick up the clothes scattered at my feet. A brown piece of leather caught my eye. The shelf gaped away from the wall revealing the dog-eared-corner of a book. Moments later I had the leather-bound volume in my hands. A diary, not as old as my creative imagination would have preferred, but still interesting. I flipped the musty pages and stepped out into the bedroom. The bay windows offered a shaft of rain-filtered light to aid in my introduction to Laura.

She crept off the first few pages in a shy, insecure way, grasping at the brief moments of happiness her marriage of necessity had given her. Outside of her pregnancy that began in the back seat of a '57 Ford, she had led a boring life. A brief account of her wedding night convinced me tears had caused the smudges on the page.

A snapshot, yellowed with age, slipped from the pages and fell to the carpet, face up. She was as I had imagined, frail with large brown eyes that pleaded with me through space and time. Ronald, the reluctant groom was handsome and arrogant-looking.

Rationalizing it as a character study of a repressed personality, by nightfall I had read all her joys and sorrows that spanned seven years—more sorrows than joys triggered by her husband's infidelity. His cruelty. His ultimate weapon scarring Laura's spirit was blaming her for their daughter's death. Symptoms of mental illness and potential suicide sprang from the page. In a pathetic scratch that bore no resemblance to the writing contained on the first hopeful pages, she confessed her plan. The entry ended abruptly, as if the torrent of words had raced to the rim of a high edifice and teetered on the edge.

I cried. Cried for Laura, for everyone alone, without hope. I cried for a soul so lovely as to create, and yet so lost that she would terminate that loveliness.

I couldn't read the final page, not yet. I was too involved. I saved it for the last moments of my day to allow it to filter through my mind as I dropped off to sleep.

A light supper, a hot bath, a cup of herbal tea, and I snuggled into the covers on the four-poster bed. Deep in the downy-filled comforter I contemplated the day.

The pieces fit. Now I understood why the house had been vacant all these months, why no one locally had wanted to purchase it even at such a reasonable price.

"Ghost!" I smirked. I picked up what I knew would be the end of Laura.

She wrote.

*"I had planned to free myself from pain today. Now, I know it will be done for me. I heard Ronald tell her, his new young one. It's a relief to know I'm not crazy. He's been giving me a drug. For the first time in a long time, I desperately want to live. I have to get away. If there was just someone, anyone. But there's only you, a book, a blank page, a void where no one will hear and no one will answer."*

Terror swept up my spine and lifted each hair follicle. He killed her. It wasn't suicide.

"This is stupid!" I spoke aloud in hopes my voice would startle the ghost that chilled my bones. "I'm intelligent. I write of villains and things that go bump in the night, but I don't believe in them." I continued reassuring myself as I fluffed my pillows and turned out the light. In the future I

14

resolved to finish all diaries in the safety of the afternoon sunlight wrapped in Joe's arms.

Rain pelting the windows beside my bed woke me. I was cold. My vaporous imaginings of the night before should have dissipated with the light of day. But I knew Laura's reality wasn't imagination. As I poured my first cup of coffee, I admitted it. The authorities, the town—they all accepted it as suicide. Just me. I knew the truth. Me—and Ronald.

Reaching for my phone to call the sheriff, I remembered my internet service wouldn't be turned on for another week. And this far out offered no cell service. Still, I had to get this settled.

A few days later I stared out the window, watching, waiting, for what? Laura? I needed to get busy. My writing suffered and it wouldn't get better until I acted on Laura's behalf. I grabbed some stationery and rummaged every drawer for a stamp, every pocket and compartment of each purse. No stamps, only an old postcard. I wrote:

*"Please contact me about a crime that may have occurred recently at Applegate Farm."*

Now I could ignore Laura's nagging presence. Her life, her creativity, would be avenged. I walked the half-mile to mail the postcard, and then rushed back to my study where my writing flowed in spasmodic waves. Hours later when gray light turned to dusk and dark, I took a break, walked to the window, and glanced out. Car lights rounded the drive, casting long beams through the premature darkness. An angry blast of thunder chased a streak of lightening across the sky, illuminating a dark form that moved toward the door. I waited for a knock and then jumped when it came.

"Who's there?" I asked.

"This is Sheriff Jones." A voice boomed like the storm's thunder. "Ms. Mackenzie?"

I breathed a sigh of relief. Holding the door wide I took his dripping raincoat and spread it to dry.

"It's really awful out. Isn't it?"

"Yes, Ms. Mackenzie, but we learn to work in all weather." He was every inch of the height his voice suggested.

"I thought that motto was for the post office not the Sheriff's Department." I turned toward him. His arrogant smile froze my heart. Fear struck and buckled my knees. This face was the other half of Laura's picture.

Pulling an expressionless mask over my fear, I walked to the den and offered him a seat.

"Would you join me for a cup of coffee?" I said, thinking of the back door and escape. As I entered the kitchen, I remembered the keys in my purse beside the couch, beside Ronald.

The back door was within my reach. The cool air hit my face where beads of liquid fear had formed. Its sobering effect halted my steps. When I raised my eyes to the horizon, a feeling of complete isolation swept over me. Four barren miles to my nearest neighbor. The kitchen once cozy was now stifling and oppressive. What would my heroine do? Hide? Where could I hide in a house the murderer knew better than I?

I did the one thing you do in a crisis—I boiled water.

If I couldn't hide or get away, I could manage a little insurance. I raced up the back stairs and grabbed the diary. The only place it would be safe was where it had lain, unseen for months. I pushed and shoved, only to pull the tattered journal out and try once more. Like the ghost of its author, the diary refused to return to its grave.

My ears strained for any movement below. I forced the book in and down. An envelope slipped into my grasp.

Pills! That's how Laura had planned to end her life. Now, the capsules just might rescue mine. I clutched the envelope and ran back to the kitchen. The tablets dropped into the cup on the right just as the door squeaked and opened. Startled, I turned to find Ronald's dark eyes searching mine.

"You're just in time." I offered the tray.

Seated across from him I felt the heat of his eyes and understood Laura's crumbling beneath his hypnotic sensuality.

"Now, where is this evidence?" He took his coffee.

"Tell me a little about the Applegate case." I sighed in relief as he took his second sip without detecting the drug.

"There's not much to tell. I doubt there's any evidence that could change the case." He smiled, much like a crocodile just before he snaps. "She locked herself in the upstairs bathroom and slashed her wrist." His voice sounded calm and cold.

I felt the color rush from my face. I could see Laura lying there, her blood on the white tile.

"After reading the diary again I realized she was depressed enough to take her life." I stammered. "I've wasted your time, Sheriff."

A muscle twitched at the corner of his mouth.

"More coffee?" I asked as I reached for his cup. His hand covered the rim.

"Are you cold?" He patronized me as he stared at the goose-bumps on my arm.

"Not really."

His fingers curved sadistically around the arm of the wing-back chair.

He suspected! I had to move. "I shouldn't have bothered you." I walked closer to the door, desperately hoping the drug would claim its victim. "I can get rather fanciful when I write."

"You know, Sloan—" he used my first name as if it were painted in red neon over a bar door. "—you shouldn't put private information on post cards. You never know who will read them—the postman, the murderer." He followed me.

"Being postmaster has numerous benefits."

My eyes flashed to the door knob.

"Don't try it!" he threatened.

A cry escaped from my trembling lips and I lunged toward the staircase.

"There's no need to run, Sloan." His breath was coming faster, his voice slower.

I ran up to the study and locked the door.

"Be a little more creative, my dear. This is where Laura hid." His steps slowed and stopped. "Her ghost still walks this hall."

I fortified the door with furniture.

A bump on the wall was followed by silence. "You know, you want my happiness." He mumbled. "Laura!" With a thick tongue, he spoke again. "Laura, it won't hurt to die." His body hit the floor with a loud thump.

An agony of time passed. No sound came from the other side. I moved the furniture and listened again. I cracked open the door.

Ronald lay still. He seemed even more sinister without his beguiling smile. I stepped over him. A steel hand grabbed my foot. Terror enveloped me. Ronald pulled himself up, crushing me to the floor. With his left hand on my arm, he lunged for my neck. I ducked. He teetered on the stairs and hurled downward, where he lay twisted on the marble floor below. A trickle of blood seeped from his head. His eyes stared into the void of Laura's house.

In the face of death, I realized I had only written about life, but never lived it. I packed a bag and drove to the city, a new deadline on my calendar. There in the safety of Joe's arms, I would ask him to marry me—tomorrow.

# Mystery in Granny's Attic

## by Gail Armstrong

*Ring! Ring!*

"Throw the damn phone!" a voice in her head screamed, as the young girl sighed and tugged the warm blanket over her long tangled blonde hair.

"Ummm...six o'clock," Darcy quietly moaned. *Who would be calling me on my day off and at this early hour?* "Oh, no. It has to be her. Just because she's my older sister, she thinks we're tied at the hips."

She grudgingly turned over and grabbed the obnoxious phone.

"Morning, this is—"

"Never mind, I know who would be rude enough to call me on a Saturday. What do you want, Big Sister?"

"I know it's Saturday," Sophie said. "I'm a working girl and this is my day off too—and you know why I'm calling."

"Oh, yeah, we're supposed to be rummaging through Granny's attic looking for lost or buried treasures, right?" Darcy was waking up to a reality and she didn't like it.

"I remember. We made a promise to dear Mom that we would look into her stuff in the attic and see if there was anything worth saving before the house goes on the market."

"I guess I'll have to wake up and become more human-like, won't I? —as you would say sweet sister. Good grief. She just died last week. Don't you think we could wait a little longer? Her body is probably still warm."

"Darcy. That's awful! You're cruel!"

"I know, and the time is now, so I'll get up, clean up, and come over to the house and I'll try to bring a happy face."

"Please do."

\* \* \*

Darcy arrived late. "Let's get this over with, Miss Bossy," she said with an attitude.

"Good. Let's get this show on the road, Grumpy."

The two headed up the old dusty pine stairs right off the back, north bedroom. What would they find in Granny's attic after they went up those creaky stairs?

The door was always locked.

"The attic is off limits until Grandpa and I are dead and buried." No one challenged the feisty little matriarch further. Even though she was only five feet tall, she was a force to reckon with. She knew who she was, and she ruled her house. Darcy liked that about her old grandmother. Boy, did she have spunk.

Today they would find out what mystery awaited them in the dark attic.

They had the key.

"Oh, it's dark and it smells like dust," Darcy said as she grabbed sticky cobwebs that caught up in her hair, and quickly pulled them off from across her unsmiling face.

A light switch on the wall caught her eye. She turned it on.

"I hope we don't regret this. It feels like intruding."

Sophie agreed.

Feeling impatient, Darcy shrugged her shoulders, and as she pumped her arms in the air, she sighed and said, "Well I'm not looking forward to this, but let's get it done."

Only a couple of old books were scattered on the floor, and vintage, worn Christmas decorations hanging from large hooks on the wall were depressing and belied the fact that people had lived here.

"Why would she have been so against us or anyone coming up here, do you think?" Darcy asked.

Sophie shrugged her shoulders. "I have no idea."

"Maybe there's something of sentimental value here, hiding somewhere," Darcy said. She was beginning to think it was a waste of time when some boxes in a dark corner caught her eye. A small shelf jutted out near them. Two giant steps brought her staring into a small cubby, and on a stack of papers was a Macy's credit card.

"What the—"

"—Don't say that word Darcy. You know I hate it."

"What the—heck is all this?" she said, as both sisters' eyes widened.

"And I wonder what those papers are with it?" They were engaged and alert.

"They're bills," Darcy said. "Paid to Macy's for clothes. No, not just clothes, gowns. Why gowns? What would Granny be doing with gowns? They never went to dances, they hardly entertained or went anywhere."

"And where are the gowns?" The two looked at each other in puzzlement.

With pulse racing, Darcy slowly put her hand on a small white knob of what looked to be a built-in closet that took up a large portion of one side of the attic.

"Let's see what's in here Big Sis." She abruptly pried open the creaky wooden door, her heart beating faster.  In the dim light she saw a string hanging from a lightbulb. She pulled the string, and bright, glaring light filled the compartment. Their eyes bulged and they blinked, and for the first time in a long time neither one could speak. The sight before their eyes made them both quiet as they looked at several rows of racks, loaded with gowns on hangers. White, black, red, blue, yellow, silver, gold. Beautiful gowns in different styles and colors all hidden from view in a private room of Granny's forbidden attic.

"They look new. Like they've never been worn. How many are there, I wonder?"

"There's a big mirror behind them."

"This must have been a private, special room for her. A dressing room where she came up to try on gowns when Grandpa was away. She came up here and admired herself in the mirror. It made her feel special."

"Her 'mirror of fantasies.' Oh my God." Darcy cried out as she counted 30 gowns, each in a clear plastic bag with a pair of glamorous silver three-inch heels on the floor. A big pair.

"Look, on the end is her wedding dress. It probably started this whole thing."

"It's beautiful. It's all amazingly cool." Darcy's grumpiness was now gone. "And look here. A box full of wigs. Blonde, red, black." They were both puzzled.

"Wait Sis. What is this next to the shoes?"

Darcy picked up a photo album. "It's filled with pictures of—of—oh no! I don't believe my eyes. It's full of pictures of Grandpa in, in—oh no, this is awful. I can't believe it." She started to cry.

"For Pete's sake. What could be so bad to make you, cry? Let me see."

There in living color were pictures not of Granny, but of Grandpa in, of all things, the gowns, and the big shoes, and different wigs. The gowns were his!

"No wonder no one was allowed up here," Sophie said. "She was embarrassed and wanted to keep his 'side' life a secret." Their sweet grandparents were gone now and the secret was out. Sophie felt nauseous.

"Do we really ever know the people we love?" Darcy asked sadly.

"Apparently not." Her sister looked perplexed.

"Hey, let's call Mom. I don't think we should tell her though, do you?" Darcy was beside herself with what she had seen and what was the right thing to do now.

"The gowns are all like new and someone will appreciate them," Sophie the responsible one replied, trying her best to be calm and think of a good plan. "We'll bring them home and give them to charity."

"Sounds like the best thing to do, and no, let's not tell Mom. She should be able to have her own memories of her dad. Maybe she knew. How could you not know something like that when you lived here most of your life? Anyhow, we should not be the ones to tell her."

"I agree."

"Unexpected things can come up with people we love. What matters is we loved them both and I think our grandparents loved each other, which is the only thing that counts or works."

"She kept his secret because she loved him and respected her husband for who he was to her and to his family. Who cared what clothes he put on? She didn't care. That's pretty cool. What harm did it do? None that I can tell."

Darcy felt sad that she had to discover his secret this way. She would always remember her Grandpa with thoughts of love and respect. He deserved it.

Her sister agreed, and they both left the attic with some of the gowns and would come back for the rest later in the day. What an interesting day it had been, filled with mystery and surprise.

"I guess being sisters ain't so bad" Sophie said as she put her arm around her younger sister. "We're different, but we still love each other as sisters, in spite of that."

"Yeah, most of the time it's not too bad, except in the early morning hours when one of us—is not respecting the other." Although said with a hint of annoyance, her head down, she looked up with smiling eyes that took off the edge.

"And the best part? It's nice to know my younger sister can be sensitive after all."

# Retribution Day

## by Gary Christenson

They found my baby girl's body.

"Dad, I saw Alice." John called three nights after my only granddaughter, Alice, disappeared on her way to visit me. His voice broke into heaving sobs.

In my heart I knew. "Tell me."

Between bouts of crying he explained. "They found her body. She had car trouble driving to your house, walked toward a roadhouse to use the phone, and ran into a biker gang. The police said they raped and killed her. Her injuries showed that she fought them."

The arteries in my throat pounded. I gripped the phone and squeaked out, "Are you sure it's our Alice?"

"I'm at the morgue. It's her. I saw the birthmark." He broke down. Choking sounds overwhelmed his voice.

I pounded my fist into the wall by the phone. Sweet Alice. Gone at eighteen. My throat locked up.

After several deep breaths, I asked, "Did they get the bastards who did it?"

"The cops arrested five guys, but they claim they're innocent. They lawyered up with a high-priced shyster out of Dallas." Contempt made his voice hard and bitter.

I asked, "How are you and Tammy holding up?"

"Tammy is in terrible shape and I'm crazy with grief. Moments later he said, "They should execute the bastards." His voice sounded like dry leaves blowing in a stiff wind.

"Her funeral is two weeks away. Tammy and I hope you'll feel up to it." His voice broke when he said 'funeral.'

After a few moments I said, "Yeah, I'll be there. I'll take my meds so I won't cause a scene."

"I'm sorry to give you such bad news. We know how much you loved Alice."

He hung up, and I drank myself into oblivion. My gut hurt worse than usual during the following days.

\* \* \*

A week after the funeral, the police released the five alleged murderers citing an improper search warrant. I wondered how much drug money the attorney paid the judge. I watched the television news and fumed.

"My clients were falsely accused of a heinous crime. Justice was served by releasing them." Their attorney pontificated from the Dallas courthouse steps into a dozen microphones. The video showed him acting smug and superior.

My head throbbed and my hands shook with rage. The doc had told me months ago, 'It's just a matter of time before the cancer gets you.' I doubled over with gut pain and gobbled a handful of pills.

The next morning my gut was on fire. After my morning pain pills took the edge off, I decided to finish this while I still could. Pictures of the five killers were posted on-line. I memorized their faces and planned retribution.

Seven days later I knew the roadhouse where they drank, their bikes and colors, and the drugs they sold in a three-state area. Online news stories confirmed Alice was the latest victim in a dozen or more rapes and deaths connected with the gang. Witnesses died or disappeared, but they never testified.

The more I discovered, the more I hated these animals. I shadowed them for two days and found a concealed location beside the highway where I could observe their favorite roadhouse. The hunter in me took charge. The stench of impending death filled my nostrils. I savored it.

My son accepted what they did to Alice as God's will, but I was built differently. I would balance the scales like we did in 'Nam.

The poker game happened without me, but the other six players, all ex-military buddies, would testify I played in the game for over five hours, and left when the game finished.

Instead of playing poker, I waited about four hundred yards down the road from their favorite watering hole beside a little-used road. The killers rushed inside after parking their Harleys in the front lot. Minutes later I drilled the closest bike with a .308 sniper round. Gasoline poured on the ground but didn't ignite.

I blasted a second round into another Harley. The third blew a front tire with a loud bang. A black-clad figure emerged and yelled. His face, purple with rage, filled my scope.

The other four killers ran outside, examined their bikes, searched for the shooter and screamed obscenities.

I shot a bullet into the forehead of the first. He dropped like a bag of cow manure. The second collapsed when I slammed a 168-grain slug into his wide-open mouth. The pungent smell of gunpowder enveloped me.

After seeing two of his buddies drop, the third killer ducked behind a Harley for cover. The others scrambled toward shelter. I took one down with a shot to his chest as he ran and nailed the other as he reached the front door. The rifle was my instrument of retribution.

The last one stood and raised his hands. He waved a white handkerchief to surrender. I whispered, "You get the same consideration you gave my Alice." I shot him between the eyes. He crumpled where he stood.

The five killers lay in the parking lot. I put two rounds into the front door to discourage other drinkers from investigating. Brass casings lay in the surrounding dirt. I retrieved them and minutes later I drove my truck toward home.

I hated to dump a good sniper rifle, but I wouldn't need it again. The rifle sank to the bottom of a lake.

* * *

As expected, the cops arrived to question me the next day. "Mister Cramer, we understand Alice Cramer was your granddaughter. We're sorry for your loss."

The older one played bad cop. "We charged five individuals with her murder, but Judge Johnson released them on a technicality. Someone killed them yesterday around four p.m. from a considerable distance. You served as a Marine sniper in Vietnam. Is that correct?" His voice was hard.

I stared at them, face blank. "Yes."

"And you've had a few scrapes with the law?"

"Ancient history." I coughed up blood and spit into a tissue.

Both cops frowned and glanced at each other. "Where were you yesterday between three and five in the afternoon?"

"Playing in my regular poker game at a buddy's house." I smiled through the pain.

"We'll need their names and addresses." The senior cop's beady eyes missed nothing.

Convincing him I played in the poker game on the day of retribution was as insignificant as a fart in a thunderstorm.

"Someone shot those bikers with a .308 round, a favorite of Marine snipers. May we see your rifle?" His words sounded polite but his eyes bored holes in my face.

"Sorry. I sold it at a gun show years ago. I have no use for a rifle these days." I was certain he knew I lied.

They left with names and numbers jotted in their notebooks. I shut the door and swallowed pain pills.

*** 

The next morning my gut hurt worse than usual. The blood in my stool looked like I had butchered a chicken in the toilet. It smelled worse than I felt. My check-out date was close.

I loaded a handgun and drove to Dallas to reckon with the attorney who for years had helped the killers escape prosecution. Those predators should have rotted in prison. Instead, he enabled them to terrorize and kill innocents like my beloved granddaughter. He was no better than the killers he protected.

An avenging spirit surged through my body as I walked into the shyster's office building to balance the scales of justice. The attorney's mouth fell open when I terminated his law practice with a .45 caliber retribution. The blood dripping from the hole in his forehead spattered on his pin-striped suit before he crumpled to the floor.

I walked out knowing I had corrected the injustice done to my granddaughter. What happened next hardly mattered.

# Gringo

## by BJ Condike

A loud noise shattered the sultry afternoon.

I spun around, scanning the parking lot. Twenty yards away a white pickup truck stood at an awkward angle, its nose mashed into a black SUV. Steam rose lazily from the pickup's hood. Glass shards sparkled on the blacktop. A tall man in a white polo shirt stood at the driver's side of the pickup. He calmly raised his arm and fired several pistol rounds into the open window of the passenger compartment. Two silhouetted figures jerked, and then slumped in the truck, their red auras dripping down the windows. A sardonic smile twisted the gunman's swarthy face.

The gunman tore off his blood-stained shirt, using it to wipe red splatter off his arms and face. A bushy mustache matched a full head of jet-black hair. His muscular frame glistened in the sun. A snake tattoo slithered from one wrist up over his shoulders and down to the other.

The tattooed man barked Spanish to two shorter men, one skinny, one burly. The skinny one ran to the SUV and returned with another shirt for the gunman. The burly one opened the pickup door, pushed the bodies aside, and drove in my direction.

Dazed, I fell to the ground behind the car, my heart pounding, my breath short. Voices speaking Spanish approached. The acrid odor of gun smoke snapped me alert like a smelling salt. I scurried away between the vehicles, crouching low, moving as quickly as I could.

I had to find her. I had to find her fast.

Halfway to the mall, I spied my quarry, a tall brunette pushing an overloaded shopping cart. Her long curls bobbed in time to the *clickety-click* of her spiked heels.

"Hey!" I called softly. "Connie! Over here!"

The woman slowed her pace, searching the sea of vehicles. She was two cars away, at the end of the row where I squatted.

"Connie! Down here!" I waved my hand frantically.

The woman glanced down and did a double-take. "Bill? What are you doing? Are you all right?" She stepped toward me, and I scuttled over to her.

"Quick! Duck down!" I said, and reached for her.

She drew her hand away. "What? No! I'm wearing a skirt. What's the matter? Are you hurt?" Her brows wrinkled.

"Just get down!" I grabbed her hand and pulled her onto the blacktop. Her perfume wafted over me, overwhelming the aromatic fumes of sunbaked asphalt.

"Ow! Now look what you did!" She stared at her knees. "You ruined my new tights. What is wrong with you?"

"Where have you been?" I hissed.

"Clothes shopping. I said I'd meet you at the car. Why are you whispering?"

"Shhh! He might hear you."

"Who might hear me?" she whispered back. "What are you talking about? What the hell is going on, Bill?"

"*El Serpiente*. I just saw him shoot someone in the parking lot. Actually two someones."

An odd look flickered across her face at the mention of his name, her expression quickly transforming into a frown.

"*El Serpiente*? Are you sure?" She was silent for a moment as the name of the drug kingpin hung in the humid air. "Who did he shoot?"

"I don't know! What does it matter? He's a drug lord for Chrissakes! And yes, I'm sure. I saw the tattoo. All that matters is that he killed two people and I saw it."

"This is bad, Bill, real bad." Her eyes widened. "Omigod! Did he see you? Does he know you saw him?"

"I don't think so. Not unless one of his flunkies saw me."

"That would be Arturo and Miguel. They follow him like remora on a shark."

We all knew of *El Serpiente*. You couldn't live in Laredo and not know. But Connie seemed to know more than I did. That wasn't surprising, since she grew up there and I didn't.

"We have to get out of here, Connie. Now. Before he figures out what I saw."

"Okay. Let me get my cart."

"Do we have to? It'll slow us down."

"Yes, we have to! I spent hours shopping for those clothes! Think of the money I spent! Besides—" She wagged her finger at me. "I've known Juan Pablo my whole life, and he is not stupid. He knows I would never leave the mall without buying something."

This was the first I had heard Connie personally knew Juan Pablo, the one known as *El Serpiente*.

"All right," I said. I didn't ask how she knew a drug lord. She knew everyone.

As we approached Connie's Miata, I could see Juan Pablo and his skinny friend examining the damage to the black SUV. We loaded up the car. We almost got away unnoticed, but not quite. As I backed out of my spot, the well-built Hispanic and his skinny sidekick sauntered over to our vehicle, he to my side, and the skinny one to Connie's. We opened the windows to the Texas heat, and I began to sweat.

"Hey, *Amigo. ¿Que pasa?*" Juan Pablo possessed an easygoing, confidant manner, exuding power like Italians ooze garlic. A drop of blood dripped from the snake's mouth on his wrist. The blood looked real.

He tipped an imaginary hat at Connie saying, "*Signorita*," and winked. She nodded and smiled in return. Skinny leaned his arms onto Connie's windowsill and leered at her voluptuous body. She ignored him.

Juan Pablo directed his attention to me.

"Did either of you hear any loud noises a few minutes ago? Some *estupido* ran into my new Escalade." He gestured toward the damaged SUV.

"No, sorry. We just got here." Perspiration burned hot trails down my face. "We were shopping." I waved my hand at the packages in the back seat.

Juan Pablo stared at me for what seemed like a long time. He glanced at the packages, and then at Connie's legs, one eyebrow wrinkling. Suddenly he shrugged and slapped his hand on the car. I flinched.

"Hokay," he said. "*Hasta la vista, gringo.*" He flashed me a toothy grin.

I waved and drove off, slowly.

"He noticed your tights," I said, clenching the wheel. "The holes in your knees."

"I don't think so," she said. "Keep going." She craned her neck, looking back.

In my rearview mirror I saw Juan Pablo's burly companion run up to him. As I reached the street, the two henchmen were gesticulating and pointing at us. Juan Pablo's head snapped in our direction, staring at us as I turned right onto the main road.

"Shit. The short one must have seen me." I sped up.

"*Mierda!*" She turned around. "Where are you going? Home is the other way."

"The bank. We need travel money. And our passports are in the safety deposit box."

"What are you talking about?"

"We're leaving the country."

"I can't leave! I have a job. My family is here."

"Listen to me, Consuela! This is serious! As in life and death serious—mostly death. Your friend Juan Pablo won't let us live if he even suspects I saw him murder those two men. You know his reputation."

"Don't Consuela me, William! I don't think he does know. And he doesn't just go around killing people. And he's not my friend, not exactly."

"Except that he already did. Kill people. Two of them. In the parking lot, remember?"

"I am not leaving!"

"Oh, yes you are! We're a couple, and you'll go where I go. I'll—I'll marry you if I have to."

"Oh, you will, will you? Now, after all this time? How very generous of you. How gallant. How chivalrous."

"Don't start with the feminist stuff." I pulled up to the bank. "I'll be right back."

Connie fumed in steamy silence as I left the car.

When I returned with the passports and cash, she was holding her phone.

"That reminds me," I said. "We have to destroy our phones so he can't track us. And our credit cards. We'll use cash for everything."

"What do you mean, 'we,' *gringo?*"

"Come on, Consuela! Don't play the ethnic card on me. Not now."

"This is more than that, Bill. This is about family. My family. Blood."

"What are you talking about?"

"I'm not the one who saw something. He's after you. *El Serpiente* won't hurt me."

"Of course he will! You've heard the stories. He leaves no witnesses. You're in danger as much as I am."

"No, I'm not." She smiled. "Juan Pablo's my uncle. In fact, he's my godfather."

A black Escalade screeched to a stop in front of us. Juan Pablo and his two thugs leaped out and headed our way, brandishing pistols.

I watched in horror. "Oh, no. Connie, what have you done?"

"I sent him a text," she said, as she exited the car. "He's family. Blood. *Hasta la vista, gringo.*" She slammed the door and walked away.

The men raised their arms, pointing their guns at me.

A loud noise shattered the sultry afternoon.

# Nowhere Diner

## by Gail Armstrong

With bold red fingernails, bright red lips, and brassy blonde hair in a style fit for a poodle, Stella wore a look suggesting she had been around the block a few times.

She watched the man eat like a ravished dog. Food at the Nowhere Diner was regular food—it filled the stomach, doing its job well. People came to talk and share a few jokes. In a small town with nothing to do, you went there to connect as much as to eat.

The man fidgeted as he glared suspiciously around the small room. As he nervously approached the woman behind the counter, he fumbled to get his wallet from under his coat. After a short struggle, the wallet was out.

His wrinkled clothes smelled of cigarettes and cheap hotels. Several days of black stubble stood out on his burly face. As he sidled up to the counter, he nervously jerked down the brim of his dingy hat. It barely covered his scraggly brown hair. The aging waitress caught a glimpse of shifty eyes and shivered.

"That'll be fifteen forty-eight, sir," she said in a forced upbeat tone.

His hands visibly shook as he removed a twenty-dollar bill, dropping his wallet. He stooped to pick it up and maintained his gaze around the room. He shoved the bill on the counter.

"I hope everything was to your liking sir. What brings you to Hollow Creek?"

He glared at her.

"Business," he said, with no hint of friendliness.

Yeah, monkey business, Stella thought.

She gave him change, put the twenty into the drawer

and closed it. He watched every move she took, and turned to leave.

"Whoa, no tip today?"

He turned back, sneered, and left.

"Yeah you have a good day too," she said, sarcasm in her voice.

Stella had never met a customer she had taken such an immediate dislike to as this character.

After 25 years at the Nowhere Diner, the boss made Stella manager. It was more money, more responsibilities.

"Expect to take on problems when I'm not there. Act like it's your place," the owner told her. The promotion was challenging, but Stella was ready. She had always lived frugally with only a few dollars left over. She welcomed the extra money.

"Someone watch the front. I need a break," she called. "I can't believe he didn't leave a tip, even after I asked for one," she muttered as she sauntered to the back room for a smoke.

When Stella returned, something shiny on the floor caught her eye. A Visa credit card. "It must have fallen out when that creep dropped his wallet." She swooped it up, put it in the cash register drawer, and called the sheriff. "He can take it from here. More his job."

The sheriff read the name off the card. "Mmmm... Alfred Hicks." He called his deputy to put the name through their computer. "Bingo! On the run. Robbed a gas station at gunpoint up in Flagstaff last week."

"Holy crap!" Stella yelled. "I could've been killed!"

"He hasn't killed anyone yet. He did rob them—a definite badass. He's scared and running. We need to stay alert and use good sense. He won't go far. He'll return. He wants that credit card.

"When he comes back, and he will, be cool. Stella, can we expect some help from you? You will be safe. My deputy and I will be right outside, out of sight and ready for him. We're here for you Stella. It's a lot to ask, but you can do it."

"Easy to say when you're the sheriff with a gun." Stella moaned.

Stella had a feeling of uneasiness she couldn't shake. The owner's words echoed in her mind. 'Act like it's your place.' She knew she had to protect the owner's money and perhaps her job.

"When he comes back what should I do?" Her brown eyes pleaded for help as she looked at the sheriff.

"Whatever he wants. He has a gun."

"Oh God, a gun, a real gun, with bullets. Oh God." Stella felt like a scared kid.

The sheriff directed everyone to leave. With the owner away, this fell on Stella.

It was closing time. Alone, Stella was to do her usual thing, and she hoped she was ready. The sheriff didn't want to tip this crook off. Her hands shook and her heart pounded even with the sheriff right outside.

*Why should I worry, right? Everything was planned.*

She counted the money and put it in the money bag, when she froze to the sound of footsteps. *The door!* In her stressed state of mind, she'd forgotten to lock the door. The number one rule when counting money—lock the damn door. *How dumb!* She hoped the sheriff had seen him. She began to tremble, and slowly turned to look into the glaring, unfriendly eyes of Alfred Hicks. How could she not have noticed how dark and sinister his eyes were?

"Oh, uhh...Mr...."

"Forget my name. Where's my credit card? Give it to me. Now."

"Right away. Mr. Hicks, right?"

"Give me my damn card, and now, if you know what's good for you." He shoved his ugly face right up to hers.

Stella's legs turned wooden, her stomach ached, and her hands were damp and clammy. Could she open the cash register? It opened. He shoved her aside and stuck his grubby hand in the drawer His odor turned her stomach.

"What? No money?" He saw his card, grabbed it and turned, his red face glaring.

She felt his knife-like glare shoot shocks through her body.

"Where the hell's the money?" From under his long raincoat he drew a big, black gun. "Don't play cute with me." He pointed the gun at her.

His coat. A raincoat on a sunny day? Who wears a raincoat when it's not raining? Someone who carries a gun, that's who, and someone who plans to use it.

"Oh God." Stella muttered softly.

She reached under the counter for the bulky black moneybag filled with the day's receipts. 748 dollars— enough to keep any robber happy for a day or two. *That's dozens of fried eggs, donuts and burgers sold. The owner would not be happy!*

"Here, take it." She shoved the bag in his surprised face. "It's yours, all yours. Please, please Mister, don't hurt me. Just take the money and go."

With a creepy smile, he laughed and as he looked into the bag, his smile widened.

Hah! He can smile when he wants to, Stella thought.

He shoved the bag and gun under his raincoat and turned to leave.

Stella looked up. In the doorway as big as life was the sheriff and his deputy, both standing tall with legs parted and feet firmly planted with incredibly big guns drawn. The guns were beautiful indeed.

"Hands behind your head boy. You're under arrest." The sheriff grabbed him, while the deputy took away his gun and handcuffed him. They put him into the sheriff's car and took him to jail.

I never did get that tip, she thought.

The next day at the diner, Stella was the center of attention. People kept her busy all day relating her terrifying ordeal. The money was safe, she was safe. She was a hero.

As one gentleman rose to leave, he put down a generous tip for Stella.

Stella stared with disbelief. Ten 100-dollar bills. A thousand dollars? "Why?" Stella asked, with her middle-aged hands on her hips and a look of bewilderment.

"My only daughter worked in a small restaurant to help put herself through college," he replied. "One night, robbers hit the restaurant and shot several people. Two died. My daughter was one of them."

"I'm so sorry. What an awful, sad thing. You must miss her terribly." Stella felt a sudden compassion for this man she hardly knew.

"After my daughter died," he continued, "I put some money aside for people who could use a little assistance in her name. Michelle. Her name was Michelle. It made me feel better. It makes me feel better to help you, Stella. That is if you could use a thousand dollars"

"Sir, use a thousand dollars? I sure could! Thank you! You're a good man. I'll never forget you and your sweet Michelle.

"You deserve a real tip Stella."

"I did yesterday." A warm tear trickled down her rouge-painted cheek as she shoved the money in her pocket.

This makes up for the one I didn't get yesterday, she thought.

# 96 Stories

## by Gary Christenson

I screamed at Jane, my mousy secretary, "You stupid twit, if you make a mistake like this again, you're fired." I shook my fist at her, calmed myself, and unconsciously rubbed my diamond-encrusted Rolex. I didn't want to die from a stroke because I was upset.

"I'm so sorry, Mr. Hooker. I'll correct it immediately, and it'll never happen again." She studied the floor and quivered as she stood at attention in front of my desk.

"Jane, contracts must leave here error free, and you screwed up. Do it again and you're gone." I slammed the desk with my fist.

"I'll return the documents as soon as I can." She backed toward the door and didn't look up.

"Jump on it. You know I don't tolerate errors or inefficiency."

I pointed my index finger as she turned and left my office, dropped my thumb, and visualized a .38 caliber hole blasted into the back of her head.

Death is easy to arrange. But for now, I needed to relax.

I love intimidating employees. The single moms like Jane are the easiest. They're desperate to keep their jobs and they're scared of me. I treat them like crap because I'm near the top of the food chain at Fleasum and Groaner.

After she departed I sang my happy song to calm my nerves. "I'm making money today. I'm making money today. And more money tomorrow. I'm making money today."

A while later Jane knocked on my door. I waited several moments and barked, "Enter."

She tip-toed into my office carrying a stack of paper and squeaked out, "I finished the contracts, Mr. Hooker." Her eyes were red and her hands shook. The stink of fear filled the room. Her blouse underarms were wet and stained.

"Right here." I patted a corner of my desk.

She placed the contracts on my desk and asked, "Will that be all, Mr. Hooker?"

"Yes, go pick up your kid. Remember, it's your fault you're late. Now get out."

She scurried from my office. Jane was a good secretary, but she was not irreplaceable.

I sat alone on the 70th floor of the Fleasum and Groaner building and reviewed the contracts. After reading the final page I mumbled, "This deal will net old man Fleasum over ten million. My share should be half a mill. Not bad for dicey derivative contracts."

I pulled a bottle of twenty-year-old Scotch whisky from my desk drawer and poured a celebratory drink. The smoky liquid went down like honey and smelled heavenly. After several sips I toasted the gold-framed picture of Mr. Fleasum adorning the wall overlooking my desk. I announced to his image, "Old man Fleasum, you're an asshole. My five feet four inches and two hundred pounds of financial genius are more valuable than you. And I know where you buried a dozen skeletons. You better not stiff me on my bonus this year. I could fix your wagon good."

I refilled my glass and smirked. "I'm indispensable, and you're vulnerable as hell if I discuss your shady deals with a certain government agency."

I sat back and plopped my feet onto my massive oak desk. "Life is good and I'm a fricking rich genius."

***

Half an hour later two bruisers barged into my office. One guy towered over me, pro-football lineman size with a military haircut, narrow forehead, and dark eyes. He was probably stupid. The second bruiser, a six-foot tall Amazon weight lifter, carried a single sheet of paper and sneered at me. Her butch haircut, mannish attire, acne scarred face and buck teeth confirmed she was an ugly Amazon.

I demanded, "What do you assholes want? Don't you knock?"

The butch lady told me, "Mr. Hooker, you've become a problem. We're here to correct your behavior. Come with us."

"Screw you! I ain't going anywhere. You two, out of my office. Now!"

Butch approached on my right and Lineman on my left. She announced, "Mr. Hooker, you're coming with us." Lineman twisted my arm behind my back and laughed when I screamed in pain. Butch smiled sadistically as she slapped my face. "That's nothing. I can make you hurt with unbearable pain."

I struggled in vain. They were huge and strong, while I was a fat desk jockey who hadn't exercised since the elder Bush was President. "Ouch! That hurts. Let go of me." I wheezed from the exertion.

Lineman held me while Butch dropped the paper in the center of my desk. They marched me down the hall into the elevator. He pinched a nerve in my arm above the elbow. The scream died in my throat as my arm exploded in pain. Stars clouded my vision.

Butch ordered, "Keep quiet or we'll hurt you worse." She punched floor 95 where Fleasum lurked in his corner office during daylight hours.

Fleasum was an asshole, but these two were worse.

From the elevator on the 95th floor they forced me toward stairs that led to the roof.

"Where...?" Lineman pinched that nerve again. A red-hot iron burned into my shoulder.

We climbed the stairs and emerged on the roof. Light rain made the surface slippery. The night air smelled faintly of diesel fumes. Yellow lights in the office building across the street taunted me. I shivered with fear.

They pushed me to the edge of the roof.

"What the hell? Where's the safety railing?"

Butch told me, "I left a signed suicide note on your desk. It says you're depressed."

They shoved me off the roof toward the pavement 96 floors below. I screamed. Time slowed to a crawl as I fell.

That bastard Fleasum! He did this. I should have reported him for screwing those pension funds. Groaner was no better. I've got the goods on them. They can't do this.

I've got thirty million bucks in the bank. I'm rich and I always get even.

Lineman and Butch are sadists. I'll have them fired.

The air whistled past my ears as I fell toward the street below. My throat dried to parched clay as my stomach churned. Regrets zipped through my brain.

I did yell at that bastard Fleasum a couple months ago. Maybe he decided I was a liability.

My bank account won't save me.

Jane was loyal, and I was mean to her.

The street lights glistened on the wet pavement below as it rushed to meet me. I screamed again, "Noooooooooo!" My shoulder muscles hurt, tense as a hanging rope. I closed my eyes and locked my hands tight against my chest.

I'm falling 96 floors to the concrete below. I'll bet there are 96 stories about how I screwed up my life, and I can't change any of them.

# ACTION/ADVENTURE/WESTERN

# Any Dang Fool

## by BJ Condike

*Any dang fool can punch cows on a ranch*, he mused. Sure, the man needed skills. He had to ride, mend fences, and brand calves—but those were ordinary chores any two-bit cowpoke could handle. Only the best cowboys could drive cattle long distances. Only the best cowboys could trek the Chisholm Trail from Texas to Kansas with a herd two thousand or more strong. And only the very best cowboys could lead such outings and get the cows to market safely.

*That's all about to end.* Boots Watson sat on the small rise overlooking the Boss's spread. He rested in the shadow of his horse, chewing on a stem of prairie grass. The old mare stood unperturbed, staring longingly back toward the stables she called home. She too was bored.

In the pasture below, twenty horses grazed on prairie grass and prickly pear. Boots and his group would saddle up these mounts before dawn and begin the long journey north. They were driving twenty-five hundred longhorns to the railhead in Abilene. Boots automatically scanned the horizon for movement, searching for rustlers, *banditos*, and Apaches.

*Not many around these days.* This part of Texas had gotten too tame. The U.S. Marshalls had chased the rustlers to wilder counties, and the Mexicans across the border. The Army had cleared out Indian Territory, gathering up whatever Apaches they hadn't massacred and driven them off to reservations. All Boots had to worry about were scorpions and rattlesnakes.

*I'm good at this. Real good. But they don't need me anymore.* There aren't many men who could manage ten cowhands and a couple thousand head over a two-month journey. Only a few men could navigate the canyons and rivers, the dust and the flash floods. Only a very few could keep the men from killing each other and the herd from stampeding. Boots was one of those few. The Boss said so.

"Looks like this will be the last ride for both of us, old girl."

The chestnut mare nickered and nudged his shoulder. She eyeballed a particularly juicy-looking patch of grass over yonder. She didn't know the Union Pacific Railroad would complete the new train depot in town by next year. She didn't know that tomorrow would mark the last time the Boss would drive his cattle to Kansas over an open trail. She didn't know that Boots would no longer be a Trail Boss and would be relegated to an ordinary ranch hand. There would be no more trail drives, just train rides.

Boots sighed. *Maybe it was time to settle down.* He was partial to that cute filly over at the dry goods store. What was her name? Jenny. She was a sparse twig of a thing with dark hair, pure skin, and a girlish giggle. Jenny was prettier than a two-dollar Kansas City whore, but without the face paint. She always had a smile for him and teased him about his suspenders and high-water pants. Just being near the girl turned him into a stumblebum and tied his tongue. She laughed at his clumsiness and chuckled at his lame attempts at clever conversation. But he knew she wasn't interested in some old shit-kicker like him. He was twice her size and twice her age.

*Any dang fool could see she had eyes for the blacksmith boy.* Young Terry Wade's muscled arms gleamed with sweat as he worked the bellows and hammered hot metal. He seemed at ease with Jenny, and loved to show off his strength and skill on the anvil when she came to visit, which was often. She spent a good deal more time at the smithy's than could be explained by any business with her father's store. No, she wasn't interested in Boots Watson.

He'd have better luck with the widow Beebe. Alice Beebe worked a small spread three miles to the south, and seemed to be making a go of it since her husband passed away from cholera two winters ago. Boots had met her at the fall harvest hoedown, and was struck by her wholesome looks and down-home attitude. Alice was tough and direct, yet friendly and kind. She'd graciously accepted his offer to dance, and they had talked the whole time so that the dance seemed to have ended before it began. They'd shared some punch, and promised to keep in touch. He never got around to it.

Boots Watson groaned, stood up, and climbed into his saddle. He gently prodded the mare with his spurs and they moseyed back to the bunkhouse. He still had to oversee the final preparations for their departure, check if Cookie had sufficient supplies for his chuck wagon, and ensure the drovers were sober enough to pack their bedrolls. The cattle were already gathered in the north valley. A final check with the Boss and he'd be good to go.

Boots knew he couldn't endure spending the rest of his life in a bunkhouse. He lived for the three-month cattle drive each year, looking forward to the peaceful prairie and the starlit skies. If this were his last drive from Texas, he'd have to light out for somewhere less civilized. He heard tell Montana was still wild enough, or Wyoming. They called it Big Sky country. That sounded just right to him.

The thoughts of settling down were just a dream, and a poor one at that. Having a woman to warm his bed every night seemed like a good thing, but it wouldn't outweigh the confines of a small ranch in an increasingly crowded county. Besides, why would any decent woman want an old bow-legged cowboy? The simple fact was that he loved his horse more than anything or anyone, and whiskey comforted him more than most women ever did. No, he loved to drive cattle. He lived to drive cattle.

He'd have to move on. He'd have to live alone.

*Any dang fool could see that.*

# Richard of Lewis Castle

## by Connie Lewis Leonard

The Castle Conway whirred with activity in preparation for the Ceremony of Knighting. After accomplishing his training in reading and writing; singing, dancing, and poetry; social skills and manners; chess, hunting, and weaponry, Squire William readied for his dubbing.

He cut his hair short to show humility before God. He took a bath in a wooden tub and dressed in white linen to show cleanliness of body, donning a red robe symbolizing the duty to shed blood defending God, pilgrims, orphans, and ladies. Then William entered the chapel for a night of prayer and fasting.

"Dear God, please cleanse me of all wrong actions and thoughts. Make me a righteous servant of the Cross of Christendom. Give me strength and skill to stand strong and brave. Help me be milder than a lamb and fiercer than a lion."

The day of the ceremony, Squire William knelt before Sir Edward, who asked, "Do you swear to uphold the Knight's Code of Honor: To dedicate yourself to perform brave and noble deeds, protecting the poor and weak? To be honest, loyal, and generous? To follow the rules of chivalry on the battlefield, accepting surrender and treating your enemies honorably, allowing their release upon payment of ransom?"

With head bowed, William answered, "For the love of God and country, yes."

Sir Edward touched William with the flat edge of his sword, first on the left shoulder, then on the right. "I dub you Sir William, Knight of the St. John Order. Be true to the brotherhood."

Once knighted, Sir William awarded the title of Squire to his younger brother Richard. "You shall become a knight if you perform your duties well. Remember in every task, you serve God, King, and country. Muck stalls to build muscles. Study hard to train your mind. Run races and participate in competitions to learn fairness and teamwork. Be a kind but firm master of your horse. He will be your greatest asset in battle. Take care of your weapons, and use them only for righteous pursuits."

Before entering the Great Hall, Sir William pulled Richard aside. "Young brother, tomorrow I leave on me quest to defend England against French aggression. While I am away, watch over Lady Mary Kathleen, me betrothed. Be civilized in her presence, a perfect gentleman, and protect her honor with your life."

Squire Richard looked at the lovely Lady Mary Kathleen. Her auburn hair curled softly around her heart-shaped face. Her blue velvet frock matched the brilliant blue of her eyes. "Yes, Sir William. Lady Mary Kathleen showed me great kindness when I served as her Paige. I pledge me life to protect her."

The Ceremony continued in the Great Hall. The Knights sat at a great round table, signifying the equality among the brotherhood, with the Squires attending tables. The feast began with rich chicken broth, fresh greens, and honeyed carrots. The main meal included wastrel (fine white bread), creamy butter, hearty mutton, tender beef, smoked pork, herbed pheasant, and juicy goose. Dessert consisted of dried fruits and sweet blackberry tartlets. William tasted fine wine for the first time. Minstrels sang and danced. They retold sagas of King Arthur and the Knights of the Round Table.

The evening ended in a somber mood when a traveling minstrel bowed at the end of his entertainment and said, "The French are on the move. Angered by King John's greed and disrespectful attitude, they want to take back lands they believe are theirs by right and God. Rumor says the French Knights and Calvary are marching toward the mainland. Sailing ships may land on our own shores within a fortnight."

Sir Edward pounded the table and stood to his full six-feet-four inches. Shaking his fist at the minstrel, he shouted, "And from where do you get this gossip? The court jester told the stable boy, who told a peasant, who told a troubadour, who told you?"

The minstrel bowed his head. "Sir Edward, the word of mouth is the best method of spreading news. I have done me duty by warning you what I heard on me travels."

"Throw him in the dungeon for the crime of sedition. When he has done his penance, pay him for his entertainment and send him on his way." After the servants carried the man away, Sir Edward said, "Me brothers of the St. John Order of Knights, I bid you good night. We have a long ride on the morrow."

At dawn, Squire Richard led the destrier, war horse, to his brother. "Your weapons are polished, sharpened, and ready for your defense. God speed."

Sir William placed his armor-clad hand on his brother's shoulder. "We shall march to our home, The Castle Lewis, and wait for the ships that will take us to rendezvous with King John's men in France. Although you have not been dubbed a knight, you are well advanced in your training, far more than most Squires. Trust God to give you strength and wisdom in all things. May God be with you."

"Yes, sir. And I pledge me life to protect Lady Mary Kathleen and The Castle Conway."

The priest stepped forward to give his blessing upon the brave Knights of St. John Order. "Go with God."

Once mounted, Sir William received his weapons from Richard. "Until we meet again."

Sir Edward kissed his daughter. "Lady Mary Kathleen, if something should happen to me, you shall be heir to The Conway Castle. I have taught you well, and you are more accomplished in the art of battle than most knights. May you live long and prosper."

Richard stood at the castle gate watching the Knights of St. John ride down the winding road into the forest. "Until we meet again, Brother."

Richard busied himself building muscles and skill by day, reading and studying by candlelight late into the night. With the two-week imprisonment completed, the traveling minstrel received his pardon. "Mark me word. The Frenchmen are coming. Be on guard."

"If that is true, aren't you afraid to leave the protection of the castle?" Lady Mary Kathleen asked the man.

"A minstrel is safer on his own than in a castle with so few to guard it. I can sing and dance to please anyone, especially the warrior far from home."

"Traitor! You are no longer welcome at The Castle Conway." Lady Mary Kathleen motioned for guards to lower the drawbridge and put him out. Squire Richard stood with the guards and watched him pass over the moat. They raised the drawbridge, closed and locked the gates. Squire Richard approached Lady Mary Kathleen. He bowed and said, "Me Lady, I pledge me life to defend you. I am at your beck and call."

She smiled at the young man. "Thank you. I know you are honorable like your brother and all the Lewis clan. Shall trouble come upon us, we shall fight together."

Two days later, the watchmen sounded the alarm from the turret. Peasants hurried to the protection of the castle. The drawbridge lowered to allow entrance, then quickly raised again. Basket boys carried rocks to the machicolation at the top of the castle so they could be hurled at the attackers once they were in range. Under supervision of soldiers, the peasants stacked wood and filled iron pots with water or tar ready to boil and pour over the walls when the enemy surrounded the castle. Archers took their places behind arrow loops and crenels in the battlement.

The second day of the siege, the soldiers approached Lady Mary Kathleen. "We cannot hold out. By allowing the peasants entrance, our food supply will not last."

"The peasants depend on us for protection. We depend on them to provide our food, and they brought what they could into the castle. We have plenty of fresh water, we shall ration our supplies. After their travels, the French shall surely run out of food before we do."

Upon hearing this, Squire Richard said, "Me Lady, perhaps the Knights of St. John have not left yet. Allow me to escape through the sally port tonight. I can find me way through the woods under cover of darkness to The Lewis Castle. Even if the knights have left, I can rally me clan to come to your aid."

"No, if you are caught, they will kill you. I cannot have your innocent blood on me hands."

"I shall disguise myself as a minstrel. I can sing and play as well as our traveling guests." He bowed before the lady. "I vowed to me brother that I would protect you with me life. A knight cannot shirk from his enemy. Honor demands I do this."

"Go with God speed." She leaned forward and kissed the boyish curls on the top of his head.

"Me Lady, lock yourself in the castle keep. If you have a brave, trustworthy servant, exchange clothes with her for your safety."

Richard dressed in the plain clothes of a minstrel, a dagger beneath his belt, a fiddle slung over his shoulder. When the clouds obscured the moon, he escaped through the sally port, winding his way through secret paths in the forest. He thanked God the hours of hard work and physical training gave him the endurance to continue running through the night, and he prayed for protection. Shortly after noon, he reached the plain surrounding The Lewis Castle. In the distance he spotted the sails of the fleet of ships bound to carry the knights away from their homeland. He prayed, "God give me speed." Inhaling he pushed his loins into faster, longer strides.

The watchmen sounded the alarm. Richard pulled the fiddle over his head and waved it into the air. A horseman rode out to meet him. Gasping for breath, Richard said, "Stop the ships. The Castle Conway under siege. The French." And then he collapsed.

The horseman turned and sped his horse to the shore where he relayed the message to Sir Edward. Sir William jumped from his seat beside him, mounted his horse, and ran to meet the messenger. Dismounting before the horse stopped, he took Richard in his arms. "Lady Mary Kathleen?"

"In the castle keep. They can't hold much longer. Go save her."

William rode back to Sir Edward, who upon hearing the distressing news, ordered the knights and horses off the ships. They put on their armor and made ready for battle. Praying for God's mercy and protection, they marched through the afternoon and evening, watching their enemies from the cover of trees. When the French bedded down for the night, Sir Edward led the attack. As honorable knights, victorious in battle, they gave the Frenchmen opportunity to surrender.

Squire Richard led his brother to the sally port. Once inside, they made their way to the castle keep. Lady Mary Kathleen, dressed in regal finery, ran into the arms of Sir William. Richard said, "I thought I asked you to exchange clothing with a servant for your safety."

"Only a Lady of honor is worthy to be the wife of an honorable Knight. I am not a weak coward." She pulled a dagger from her belt. "Most women are stronger than you could imagine. Me father provided instruction in the arts of defense. While you are away, Sir William, The Castle Conway is in good hands."

Sir William bowed before her and kissed her hands. "Good hands, indeed." He stood and tousled his brother's curls. "For God, king, and country."

The next day, Squire Richard stood by Lady Mary Kathleen's side and watched Sir Edward and the Knights of St. John lead the prisoners toward The Lewis Castle. From there, they would board the ships headed to France. The ransom for their prisoners would help bring peace to England.

Once the knights were out of sight, Lady Mary Kathleen said, "You shall surely be knighted for the next crusade. Until then I am thankful for your protection and your companionship."

Richard said, "For God, king, and country" and followed her back into The Castle Conway.

# Spirit Pouch

## by Donna Pierce

An old man sat by the small fire and did not move.

The plains were plentiful with many buffalo and wild horses. The man did nothing and grew thin.

His friend came to him and said, "Why do you do nothing? Why do you grieve your spirit so?"

The old man said, "I am tired, leave me alone."

The friend said, "Rise in the morning, take your horse and hunt buffalo. If you do not eat, you shall perish. If your soul perishes, I will then sit by your fire and not seek the buffalo. I could not endure the loss of your gentle soul. Reach out, my friend to the strength of the great buffalo. Breathe in the wisdom of the owl, and fly like the flight of an eagle. Feel the love of Manitou. His smile is like warm sunshine against your face. Let your spirit open up and bloom again for a new beginning. Find your soul and let it sing once more."

Many moons passed. The friend had been gone from camp during this time and returned one night. He walked to the campfire and the old man was gone. There in his place sat a great horned owl. The owl slowly turned his head and looked at the friend. There was an object in the owl's talon— a leather pouch tied with horsehair.

The owl caught him staring at the pouch and said to him, "Your friend is gone. He left this pouch for you. It is his soul to take and keep by the fire. He left it for you, so you would not grieve. He said when your day comes, the two of you will go together to the great heavens."

The great owl then opened its huge wings and spread them high above the fire as it took flight into the night. The flames from the fire danced with the rush of the air from its wings. The friend looked toward the heavens. The stars were very bright. He tied the pouch to his belt and heated his knife in the fire. He cut a slab of meat from a rabbit to cook and smiled at the stars.

# Crossing the Line

## by BJ Condike

*Hummmmmmmmm.* I awoke to the low, angry growl of tires speeding over a rumble strip. A glance out the bus window revealed us hurtling at high speed halfway into the breakdown lane. Headlights illuminated the guardrail, its white posts flickering past us at an alarming rate, all the while looming closer and closer to the vehicle.

I ripped off my seat belt and raced up the aisle a dozen rows toward the bus driver. The driver slumped in his seat, head bobbing gently with the swaying of the vehicle.

I shouted, "Wake up! Wake up!" as I leaned over and grabbed the wheel, turning it left. The driver snapped awake and started yelling. The speedometer quivered at eighty-five miles an hour.

"Hey! What the—? Let go o' the wheel!" He swatted my arms away and wrested the steering wheel from my grasp. During our brief scuffle, the bus veered left across two lanes and back again. Several passengers cried out in panic. Finally the driver slowed the massive vehicle and guided it into the rightmost travel lane.

"Hey yourself," I said. "You were sleeping—we were drifting off the road."

"Was not. Don't do that again. And what the hell are you doing over the line?" he pointed to a white stripe on the floor. "Step back. You aren't allowed up here."

I kept my feet where they were and leaned into his face. "Listen—" I stared at his name tag, "—Mike. You dozed off. If I didn't do something we would've crashed and died. I'll step over this stupid line any time it'll save my life."

"What's your name? I'm gonna report you."

"You do that. Name's Hooper. Tom Hooper. That's Hooper with an 'H'."

He didn't laugh. Nostrils flaring, he glared at me for a moment, and sullenly returned his gaze to the roadway.

Mike was the sixth driver we'd had since departing Jacksonville on our cross-country marathon two days before. I disliked him as soon as he boarded. He sported a pointed nose on a weasel-thin face, a face framed by scraggly hair that hadn't seen soap and water in a month. His bent-over body slunk around like a beaten dog. Heavy-lidded eyes suggested drug use. I suspected a permanent cannabis-induced haze enveloped his mind like a San Francisco fog. I was sure he nibbled on magic brownies whenever he got the chance.

I sat down begrudgingly, selecting the aisle seat in the second row. I kept one eye on our surly driver and one on the window. Our last stop had been Quartzsite, Arizona. A route sign whizzed by that didn't look right. I walked back up to the white line.

"Hey, Mike," I called.

"Whadda ya want now?"

"What happened to the interstate? I just saw a sign for U.S. ninety-five. I thought we were following I-Ten all the way."

"Interstate's closed. Eighteen-wheeler crash." He pointed to a GPS unit. "Alternate route."

Our laconic driver must have taken a Yoda pill. I returned to my seat, wondering what the detour would do to our schedule. Air travel petrified me, so I always took the bus. At this rate we would never make it to California in time for my sister's wedding. We might not survive until breakfast.

Soon there was more loud humming as we again drifted into the breakdown lane. This time we weren't on an interstate with a median to protect us from oncoming traffic. We were traveling on a two-lane secondary road with nothing but strips of paint between us and certain annihilation by oncoming traffic.

Once again I stepped forward to my designated spot behind the white line.

"Mike! Hey Mike!"

Weasel-face blinked and shook off some mental cobwebs. "What?"

"You're dozing again."

"Am not. Lemme alone."

"Yes you are. You're putting everyone at risk. Why don't you stop and get some coffee?"

"Can't. Behind schedule. Gotta keep goin'."

"For Christ's sake, you can't keep your eyes open. Stop and take a break."

"Can't," was all he said.

This guy was scaring me. I returned to my seat, determined to call the police. Better to be alive, late, and foolish than to be on time to my own funeral. I dialed 9-1-1.

Nothing happened. The cell phone screen showed no signal bars. The words 'No Service' appeared in the status line.

Soon the bus began drifting dangerously out of its lane again, and my blood boiled. I tromped back to the front and boldly stepped over Mike's ridiculous white line.

"Goddammit, Mike. Pull over and stop this bus. You're not fit to drive."

"No."

"Jesus, Mary, and Joseph! Pull over! Take a piss. Wash your face. Pinch your ass. I don't care what you do, but you've got to snap out of it."

Mike forced his words through clenched teeth. "I'm fine. Lemme me be."

"How about calling your dispatch for a new driver?" I pointed to his CB radio.

"Radio's broke. Now siddown."

I needed help.

Thirty-one stops to San Diego sounded like a bad country song. Only three of us remained from the group that had boarded in Jacksonville twenty-seven stops ago. The first was Consuela, who bulged in extreme pregnancy. I expected her baby to pop out and say 'Hola' any minute. She was sweet and shy, and without child might have weighed all of a hundred pounds. Consuela would be no help.

The second was Rafer, my across-the-aisle acquaintance, a large man with no neck. Rafer had deposited his bulk across both adjacent seats. He traveled with his own seatbelt extension. Rafer had been headed to the NFL draft from college until he blew out his knee senior year. Now he was interviewing as a trainer.

The remaining half-dozen passengers were short-hoppers, only on for a stop or two. I didn't know any of them.

I traipsed down the aisle to row 12.

"Hey, Rafe."

"Yo, Tom. What's going on up there?" Rafer was reading Tolkien's *The Hobbit*.

I told him what I had in mind. He was dubious, but I convinced him we were desperate and in danger, and he agreed to lend a hand.

We made our way forward. Rafer to shuffle sideways to navigate the narrow aisle.

We reached the white line.

I called out over the diesel engine noise, "Break time, Mike."

"What...?"

I stepped forward and unclicked Mike's seatbelt with my left hand and grabbed the wheel with my right. Backing up against the dash, I made room for Rafer's hulking body. The ex-ballplayer grabbed Mike under his arms and effortlessly lifted him out of his seat like a Raggedy Ann doll, plopping him into the right front passenger seat. I slipped into the driver's seat.

"Hey! You can't do that!" Mike said. "That's—this is mutiny, it's highway mutiny, that's what it is!"

"Quiet, Runt," Rafer said. He shoved Mike up against the window and sat beside him. Rafer's enormous frame overlapped onto Mike's skinny one, mashing it into the seat. Mike yelped in pain.

I drove while concentrating on keeping the bus between the white lines. I would deal with the consequences of our roadway rebellion later. For the time being we were safe.

***

*Hummmmmmmmm.* I awoke to the low, angry growl of large tires speeding over a rumble strip. A black-and-white cow the size of New Jersey stood broadside directly ahead of us in the breakdown lane. Horrified, I swerved sharply to the left, forcing the bus into a squealing, sideways skid. As the fifteen tons of steel pulverized the cow, the tires left the asphalt. The airborne bus rotated ninety degrees and slammed onto its right side with a tremendous crash. Horrendously loud screeching accompanied a sickening slide backwards into the opposite ditch.

The driver's seat was now the bus's ceiling. I released my seat belt and fell, crashing into the stairwell. Bruised but otherwise unhurt, I used a fire extinguisher to smash out the already cracked and crazed windshield.

Moans and wailing drifted from the rear of the bus. Mike grunted in short gasps, having been crushed by Rafer's bulky body. The future NFL trainer heaved himself upright, and together we helped the other passengers out the windshield opening.

No one died. One lady suffered a broken arm, Mike had two broken ribs, and Rafer delivered Consuela's baby. She named the little guy Juan Pablo Rafer Hernandez. 'Tom' didn't even get honorable mention. A passing motorist fetched the police.

The     National     Transportation     Safety     Board's

67

investigation found the aging bus had a defective heater under the driver's seat. The NTSB said the heater leaked carbon monoxide and produced an excess of positively charged ions, contributing to driver fatigue and drowsiness. Blood tests revealed Mike had elevated levels of cannabinoids, confirming my suspicion about magic brownies. The police charged him with DWI.

The cops mysteriously failed to charge me for driving a bus without a commercial license. Whippet Bus Lines, however, banned me from their buses for life, citing me for operating their vehicle without authorization.

That was okay by me. Next time I'd take the train.

# North Ridge

## by Donna Pierce

The bitter cold held tight in the air and cut through exposed skin like a blade. North wind roared through the mountains at night. Clay looked out the window and waited for the sun to warm the day. He sat down for one last cup of coffee, threw his saddle bag over his shoulder, and walked out the door. Hammer should be done with his breakfast by now, he thought.

The wind had blown drifts too high for the pickup, so he would have to take his horse. Why it was hanging on so long bewildered him. This winter reminded him of the blizzard that hit the town ten years ago, and everyone was stranded for several days.

He smiled to himself, when his old dog Rainbow jumped up to accompany him. She hated to be left behind. "Not this time old girl. You're barely trudging through the snow now. How will you make it up on the mountain?" She followed him out, so he locked her in the barn and led his horse out. He threw a blanket and saddle on his horse.

Clay dreaded getting on this gelding. Hammer was a skittish three-year-old. He was still a little cold back, which caused him to buck now and then. With the weather as it was, Clay just might get thrown again. He planned on attending the livestock sale this coming spring in Billings and look for a good ranch horse. His old horse Black Jack had died the year before, and he was stuck with this youngster. Clay opened the barn door and led out a pretty dappled gray with a black mane and tail. He called him Hammer, because of how hard he threw him last summer. Hammer snorted, crow hopped, and then started bucking before Clay even got his foot in the stirrup. He lunged him around the corral to get some spunk out.

"Well, I'm just killing time," he mumbled to Hammer. He tied his saddle bag across the back of the horse and stepped up in the saddle. Hammer snorted, jumped to the side, and then settled down. This horse didn't much like the saddle bag and was a little spooky of it, but Clay needed it. He had a few fencing supplies he didn't want to do without.

It was cold, but a beautiful day. The sun glistened across the snow-covered land like diamonds. He loved the beauty of his ranch. The pastures led to the river that forked and branched out right below the mountains which were covered with rough timber and large rocks. "The best place this side of Yellowstone to see mountain sheep and talk to God," he thought.

Up above, he heard the screech of a hawk. "Whoa" he said, and pulled up the reins to watch a hawk take chase of a snowshoe rabbit. With amazing speed, it hit and flipped the rabbit in the air. Clutching the rabbit in his long talons, the hawk flew away.

A gust of cold wind and snow twirled across the ground and slammed into Clay. He shivered and pulled his scarf from around his neck, up above his nose.

His wife Elizabeth made him the scarf a few years ago for a Christmas gift. He wished she was riding with him today. She loved this ranch, the cattle, and the horses. He pushed back tears as he thought of her. "Damn cancer, it's taking everyone. It took Dad too," he murmured.

Clay thought back to his father. The ranch had been in their family for four generations. He promised his father he would keep it in the family, but he and Elizabeth hadn't had children yet.

His family was well respected in town as ranchers. The cattle off their ranch had won prizes at the State Fair for years. His dad had been the bank president down on the square but was more known for his rodeo days. All three boys had rodeoed and were bulldoggers. Clay held the best time for over six years. He wished his brothers lived close, but they had their own lives. He was the only one left that was interested in ranch life.

A sage hen came out from behind some brush and it was just enough to set Hammer off. In a split second, the horse lunged forward, dropped his head between his legs, and thrust his rump for the sky, bucking hard. Clay held on and leaned back with each buck. Just like he did when he was a bronc rider as a kid. Hammer bucked for a good five minutes, then settled down. Clay pulled him in a circle and then headed back out. "Didn't get me off this time did you, hot shot?" he said to the gelding.

When he hit the top of the third ridge, he noticed a big timber wolf circling a newborn calf. It was lying by a clump of grass near the creek bed.

"Well, this day isn't starting out so good," Clay said to Hammer. "This must be one of the culprits picking off my new calves." He noticed the steam rise from its small warm body in the cool morning air. "He must be a new one," Clay said to Hammer, as if it was listening. The wolf bit the calf and he wailed. Clay took his rifle from his saddle, leaned forward, and a powerful shot echoed through the mountains. He rode down and stepped off Hammer to inspect the calf. He heaved the calf up over his saddle. Its mother was lying about fifty feet away. The wolf must have attacked her first, and then left her for the calf who was easier prey. Clay could tell that she had lost too much blood and was not going to make it. She couldn't even stand. The wolf had ripped up her hind leg pretty bad. Clay shot the old cow because he didn't like to watch an animal suffer.

Hammer spooked and reared straight up, knocking the rifle from Clay's hand. The calf slid off the back of the saddle as Clay rolled into the creek bed. Hammer was gone, heading straight for the barn. Clay looked up at the small calf and then noticed his broken rifle. Pulling himself up over the ledge, he walked over and picked up his rifle, and then the calf. He threw the calf up over his shoulders. "You sure are heavy for a little guy," Clay said, and started walking toward the house.

He thought that he would go as far as the second ridge on the way back, and then take a shortcut home. However, making the second ridge was harder than he thought in the deep snow. He would need to rest soon. He was winded, the cold air burned his throat, and his shoulders ached from the weight of the calf. He was tired.

He had walked a few miles when he noticed horse tracks heading the same direction, veering a little toward the east.

He noticed some smoke rising from a thicket of trees. It looked like a campfire on his land. He laid the calf down and started out in that direction, clutching his broken rifle. He hunkered down low using the trees as cover. Three men were sitting around the fire brewing coffee. One was old, but the other two were younger. He didn't recognize them. He looked down at his broken rifle. "Damn that Hammer. He's no ranch horse," he mumbled.

One of the men got up and went off in the woods, probably to pee, Clay thought. Clay snuck up behind him and put his hand over his mouth, yanking his arm behind his back. "I have a gun Mister, and I aim to blow your head off if you make a sound," Clay said. He poked the barrel of his broken gun in the man's back. The man nodded his head slightly to show that he would be quiet. "What are you doing on my property, Mister?" Clay whispered.

The man gestured that he wanted to speak, and Clay nodded. He held his finger to his mouth so he would whisper. "Man, I'm sorry, we didn't know that this was your property," the man said. "We're looking for some lost cows that got through our fence a couple of days ago."

Clay leaned over to look behind the trees. Sure enough, there were three of his cows with his brand, a set of broken horns, on them. Clay knew he had just caught some rustlers.

"Well, it seems kind of funny that you boys found your cows, but they happen to have my brand on them. Not to mention, that they're on my property. Now you realize that rustling is a hanging offense in Montana?"

"Mister, honest! We didn't know that these were your cows. I never even noticed the brand," the man said, as he stood shaking at the end of Clay's rifle.

"Yeah, right," Clay said. "I'll tell you what we're going to do. We're going to hang the three of you right here. My two brothers are over there in that thicket and they have their rifles on you right now. The sheriff is married to my cousin, and he hates rustlers almost as much as I do. So, he won't care much. The vultures will feast on you, and the coyotes will carry away what's left."

"Now Mister, we're not after any trouble. We'll be happy to give you back your cows and mosey on out of here like nothin ever happened."

"Hold on a minute," Clay whispered. "I have to motion to them so they will hold off and not start shooting. I told them to shoot you all if I didn't give them the signal."

"Go ahead, please Mister. Motion them and then we'll be out of your way." Clay motioned up in the air as if there was someone out there. He looked back at the man. "I'll tell you what. We'll let you go for that nice buckskin you got saddled over there, and you might as well throw in those other two horses while you're at it. Oh, and you're not taking your guns with you neither."

"We'll give you the guns, Mister, but I don't want to give up my horse. He's a good cow horse and dependable."

"Well, you don't have a choice the way I see it," Clay said. "Lose your horses and guns or lose your lives."

"Okay, Mister...let me yell at my boys and tell them." The man yelled over to the other two by the fire.

The tall one started to pick up a rifle he had lying at his feet, but the other man sitting beside of him, said something. He slowly put down his rifle and spit in the fire shaking his head. The shorter man yelled over, "Are you serious?" and raised his arms up in a gesture. He kicked his rifle towards the fire.

Clay yelled at them to back away from the guns and put their hands on their heads. He pushed the old man hard with his gun barrel, poking it in his back, and then yelled out to the men to do what he said. They probably didn't want to give up their guns, but they didn't want to be hung or shot much neither. Reluctantly, they backed away and kept their hands on their heads. Clay was biting his lower lip right now and hoping for the best. Little did they know that he was carrying a broken rifle.

Clay yelled at the two men to bring the horses over and all three guns. "I'll shoot this old man here without a problem. It's not the first time I shot a rustler," he yelled.

One of the men led the horses over to Clay. Clay yelled out in the air to his brothers, "Don't shoot them. They're leaving their guns and these horses. They're walking out of here and not looking back. But if you see one of them look back, shoot all three." The men kicked the dirt a couple of times, then walked off and didn't look back.

Clay headed home with the guns and horses. He stopped, retrieved the calf, and tossed him on the back of his new buckskin. He smiled, thinking about the whole ordeal.

"Those rustlers weren't very smart now were they partner?" he said to his new-found horse. "You're going to save me a heap of trouble. Hammer's not the best ranch horse a man can have."

He opened the barn door and let Rainbow out. "Well, it's been one of those days girl."

# SCI-FI/PARANORMAL/FANTASY

# Franklin's Secret Garden

## by Robert C. Taylor

With each painful step, Franklin's arthritic knees and aching back send the painful message to his brain. *You're an old man, Franklin Hobbs.*

Taking a seat on the old familiar bench, Franklin allows the comfortable phenomenon of nostalgia to ease his tortured mind. He looks around in awe at the cemetery that used to be his secret garden. As a teenager he would come here to be alone, and this bench served as his make-shift altar. He would pray, and sing his favorite hymns. A tear slides down his cheek as he recalls the serenity he felt back then. With the dew glistening on the blades of grass and the wind soughing through the trees, he would try to imagine himself as Adam, alone in the garden, before God placed Eve beside him for comfort. Franklin recalls wondering if Adam had trouble conversing with Eve, the way he did with girls.

Back then, Franklin's introverted nature made it difficult for him to make acquaintances. But here, in this secret place, he had found a friend. In the solitude he would converse with God. He recalls sitting on this very bench, when he asked God to accept him as one of his children. He had expected some miracle, maybe a bolt of lightning, a signal assuring him that his request had been accepted. No such miracle happened, at least not outwardly. The miracle took place inside, creating a peace, like cool healing water that at the time he knew was God's spirit taking up residence in his innermost being.

Franklin came to grips a long time ago with what he experienced that day. He was a naïve child, a dreamer. He realized that what he experienced was no more than an emotional upheaval. He had been so lonely, so alienated that he created himself a friend. When he met Sandra, the loneliness dissipated. He had someone he could converse with, and to love, flesh and bone, his very own Eve. He no longer needed the imaginary friend. But now, after fifty-one years with Sandra, she has taken her last breath. So, once again, well into his twilight years, Franklin is alone.

Suddenly, Franklin is jolted out of his reverie by the realization that he is not alone. He spies a young girl, clad in a bright yellow sundress, making her way from one tombstone to another, heading directly toward him. She appears to be very young, maybe eleven or twelve. In her hand is a brightly decorated tote bag. *This is odd, a child that young, alone here in this remote abandoned cemetery.* Franklin curiously observes the girl as she continues to move closer and closer, until she is standing directly in front of him.

"How are you, sir?"

"I'm fine, thank you."

Taking a seat beside him, she smooths out her dress, making sure it's covering her knees. Placing the tote bag beside her, she sits without speaking, her hands folded in her lap.

Feeling awkward by this odd turn of events, Franklin initiates the conversation.

"My name's Franklin, what's yours?"

"Let's see, uh, Ruthie. Yes, that's it, my name's Ruthie. Nice to meet you, Mister Franklin. Do you have a loved one buried here?"

"No, I don't. My wife Sandra passed away, but she's buried up in town, at Rose Hill. I just came here today to be alone, and meditate."

"That was a trick question, you know," she says.

"What was a trick question?"

"When I asked if you had family buried here. I knew you didn't."

"How could you know that, Ruthie? We're complete strangers."

"Because nobody is buried here, Mister Franklin, only

their dead bodies. There are no souls in this cemetery. Well, except for you and me."

"That's true, I suppose. Do you live close by?"

"Not really, no. How about you?"

"I live about five miles from here, up in town. What brings you here, Ruthie, if you don't mind me asking?"

"I'm here on official business," she replies with a childish giggle.

This remark elicits a smile from Franklin, the first one since he entered the cemetery. "That's a good one, Ruthie. But seriously, why are you out here all by yourself?"

"I'm waiting on my transportation. What did your wife look like, Mr. Franklin? Was she pretty?"

Noticing his hands trembling, Franklin realizes that for some unknown reason he is fearful of this beautiful child sitting beside him.

"My wife was very pretty, the prettiest woman I ever met. I miss her so much. If it were up to me, I'd arrange it where two married people would always die together, at the same moment. That way no one would be left alone."

"Rising to her feet, and smoothing out her dress, the girl peers directly into Franklin's face. "You've been crying, Mister Franklin. Are you sure you want to be alone as sad as you are?"

"I'll be fine, Ruthie, and I appreciate your concern, but yes, I very much desire to be alone."

"I'll leave you alone with your thoughts. But first I want to give you something." Reaching into the tote bag, and extracting a beautiful yellow rose, she carefully inserts the stem in the buttonhole of his sport jacket. "Nice meeting you, Mister Franklin," she says, and walking no more than fifteen feet, she hops up and takes a seat on a rather large upright tombstone.

Franklin wants to ask the girl how she knows yellow roses were his wife's favorite flowers, and to tell her that fifteen feet is not adequate distance to be considered leaving him alone. He thinks better, however, of eliciting another conversation. Closing his eyes, he attempts to let his mind wander back, to reenact that day, to feel the serenity he remembers from so long ago. But with the girl sitting so close, he feels too self-conscious to pray aloud or sing the hymns. *It probably wouldn't work anyway*, he muses. He thinks about Adam, how he must have felt when driven from the garden.

"She doesn't want you to be sad."

"What are you talking about, Ruthie?"

"Your wife, she doesn't want you crying. She never liked seeing you cry."

This statement unnerves Franklin, but he pulls himself together. Looking back toward his car, the distance between the bench and the old gate seems much farther than before. He dreads the walk, the pain in his knees and back, but his car's not going to come to him, and putting it off won't make it any easier.

Just as he painfully and with much effort rises to his feet, he once again hears the girl's voice, singing as she sits atop the large tombstone. *"Pass me not oh gentle Savior. Hear my humble cry."*

Turning in her direction, his shyness and self-consciousness are gone. Taking a seat, he sings along, their voices harmonizing perfectly, the words echoing off the tombstones in the abandoned cemetery. *"While on others thou art calling, do not pass me by."*

They finish the song, and Franklin stares in awe at the little girl. "That was my favorite hymn," he says. "I used to sing it, alone, right here on this bench."

"I know," she says.

"How could you know?"

"Because you weren't alone. I was here. I've always been here."

She once again starts to sing. *"Coming home, coming home, never more to roam."*

Again, he joins her in song. *"Open wide thine arms of love, Lord I'm coming home."* The peace he experienced so long ago, like cool living water, flows so freely through his being, soothing his pain, and washing away his grief.

After they finish the song, he turns once again toward the beautiful girl, his face covered in tears. "You said you came here on business. What business?"

"I've come to take you home." Hopping off the tombstone, the girl walks over and extends her hand. "Come, Mister Franklin, your wife is waiting for you."

"I can only assume, Ruthie, that you must be an angel, but why would God accept me now? I've lived a sinful life, even to the point of denying his very existence."

"When God forgave your sins back then, he forgave all of them, all the way up to now. Your sins are forgiven, Mister Franklin. All you have to do is accept it."


## Epilogue


Harry and Ben, two local police officers, stare in awe at the deceased man, sitting slumped over on the old concrete bench, with a peaceful look on his face.

"How long do you think he's been here?" Harry asks.

"Couldn't have been very long at all," Ben replies. "That yellow rose on his lapel appears to be freshly picked."

# Santa Duty

## by Gary Christenson

Everyone thinks Santa lives at the North Pole and travels on a sleigh pulled by magical reindeer. Don't believe it! We love the romantic story, but facts are facts. He does the reindeer and sleigh thing only one night each year. Eleven months of the year he lives in a cabin in Idaho. I know because I'm one of Santa's helpers.

\* \* \*

The smog and noise pollution outside the Seattle bus station grated on me, but I had an important responsibility—to assist Santa Claus during Christmas season. I've had Santa duty for twenty years, and I'm not complaining. Helping Santa do his Christmas thing is a pleasure.

He was due on the 11:35 a.m. bus from Pocatello.

The Greyhound bus pulled into its assigned slot, belched smelly diesel smoke, and screeched to a halt next to the concrete curb.

Santa frowned as he limped off the bus, tired and cranky as usual. White hairs streaked the scraggly black beard on his lined face. He wore ancient cowboy boots, a navy stocking hat, faded jeans and a blue flannel shirt. Nobody recognized him.

He shook my hand and announced in a gravelly voice, "Humbug! I'm too old for this crap. My joints hurt, my arthritis gets worse every year, and the bone spur in my foot hurts like hell. I need a drink."

"You look damn good for 577 years old," I said. "Besides, you've complained about the same aches and pains every year for the last decade. When you do your Santa thing, your pain disappears. People love you, and the Christmas Spirit rejuvenates you for another year. Man up!" I grabbed his duffel bag and led him to my car.

We drove to my house in West Seattle, drank Christmas cheer, and told war stories. He asked for at least the tenth time, "Did I tell you about meeting Charles Dickens? I inspired him to write 'A Christmas Carol' after he caught me descending a chimney. Those were good times."

* * *

Three days later he emerged from the guest room dressed in his traditional red outfit. "Okay, I'm ready to charm the children while they sit on my lap." His beard and long hair had turned pure white, with his shiny black boots reflecting light from the chandelier in my living room. "Ho, Ho, Ho. It's off to Macy's we go." Santa's breath smelled of brandy, and he couldn't stop smiling.

I drove downtown and dropped him at Macy's main door. As he emerged from the car, the Santa magic swirled around him like a tiny tornado. The sweet scent of cinnamon and peppermint candy canes overpowered the people on the sidewalk. Adults stopped to stare and children screamed, "Santa's here!"

The crusty old arthritic curmudgeon from Pocatello had transformed into the magical Santa Claus who brought happiness to children and adults. His infectious laugh captivated everyone. He boomed out, "Ho, ho, ho" every few minutes. People crowded around him.

Santa sat on his throne, listened to children, made promises, and smiled. Parents stood three deep in a large circle savoring the Christmas Spirit that radiated from him.

I drove Santa to his department store gig every day for the next three weeks, watched his endearing performances, and marveled at the magic of Christmas. He made people happy, helped them forget sorrows, gave everyone hope, and encouraged kindness, love and sharing.

As his big night approached, Santa became a jolly, younger man.

On the night of December 23rd after his shift at the department store, Santa told me he would meditate, not celebrate. "No booze for me tonight." He sat on my living room floor, crossed his legs and hummed, smiling like a fat, bearded angel. A pale yellow light surrounded him. I left him to commune with the Spirit of Christmas.

Santa emerged from his meditation. "They'll arrive a few minutes after midnight. Weather over northern Canada is worse than usual."

At 12:10 a.m. on December 24th, I heard a whooshing noise followed by the crunching sounds of reindeer trampling frozen grass in my back yard.

"My sleigh has arrived." Santa marched outside in full dress uniform—black boots, red suit, gloves and hat. After greeting the reindeer, he yelled, "Ho, ho, ho. A Merry Christmas to all!"

From the back porch I watched him leap into the sleigh, invigorated by the Spirit of Christmas. He hopped about, looking as spry as a twenty-year-old athlete. Rudolph pawed the ground and snorted his impatience, eager to guide the sleigh on Christmas Eve.

Santa and his reindeer flew into the night sky on their Christmas mission. Their silhouette crossed the face of the full moon. Everything in Santa's world would remain joyous for another 24 hours.

I waved goodbye to Santa, gave thanks to the Spirit of Christmas, and dreamed sweet thoughts about busy elves, happy children, and magical reindeer. I had completed my Santa duty for another year.

# Prophecy

## by BJ Condike

I didn't mean to wake them.

A November chill settled over the ancient cemetery. I had saved Jennifer's gravestone for last, recording the inscription in my logbook. As the church's final pastor, she would be the last person buried here.

Not that it mattered. After the electrical fire, the dwindling congregation could not afford to rebuild their historic church. They sold the land, including the adjacent graveyard. The new owners vowed to raze the blackened building and relocate the graves after I had completed the inventory. They planned to build a quaint bed-and-breakfast on the property and call it, *The Sanctuary*. They said it would enhance the town's "New England village ambiance."

The townsfolk breathed a sigh of relief. The charred rubble would finally disappear. It would no longer remind them of the pretty, raven-haired pastor who had burned alive in her own church. But I could not forget her. I had loved her.

I fought back tears as I rose to leave, when I noticed four grave markers outside the low stone wall boundaries. The shadowy monoliths stood at crooked attention under a dead oak, its gnarly limbs grasping the darkling sky. I clambered over the wall to record their inscriptions.

None was visible. Running my hands over the smooth black slate, my fingers sensed faint impressions, grooves hidden by the dark stone, stone so dark shadows disappeared. Dusk fell beneath a rising full moon as I pulled out a penlight, rubbing paper, and colored wax.

The four headstones were all of one shape, with an archetypal oval top and square shoulders, a familiar silhouette for Halloween decorations. Three of the stones were small, while two leafless thorn bushes flanked the larger one. I started there.

The black rubbing wax revealed a symbol: a circle on top of three overlapping willow leaves forming a three-pointed star:

I continued rubbing. A poem appeared below the symbol, but no name or date:

*Four Shall Rise & Seek Another*

*Father, Son, Perhaps Brother*

*He Shall Choose & not Resist Her*

*They Shall Spawn Another Sister*

A wave of gooseflesh swept over me. The words were disturbing, but something else bothered me. Where was the name? Brushing my fingers over the back side of the stone, I detected more engraving. After further rubbing, an inscription appeared on the paper:

*Here Lyes yᵉ Body*

*of Abigail Wicke*

*Aged 50 yrs*

*Kill'd by Fire*

*July 20ᵗʰ 1692*

The light continued to fade, and I didn't have time to ponder the odd wording, "Kill'd by Fire." I moved on to the remaining stones, using the penlight to see.

Rubbing the three smaller headstones revealed they

were for Abigail's daughters: Beatrix, aged 31; Constance, 25; and Deborah, 19. All three were 'Kill'd by Fire' exactly one week before their mother's death on July 13th, 1692.

Because the mother's stone had writing on both sides, I examined the reverse sides of the daughters' stones. They bore a similar symbol as their mother's marker, but without the circle:

Each of the smaller gravestones contained one line of verse on its back. Placed in order from eldest to youngest daughter, they read:

> *Rub ye Stones, Speak ye Words*
>
> *Raise ye Bones of those Interred*
>
> *Heed ye Crone's Hex Unheard*

I sat with my back to the largest stone, facing the three smaller ones. I knew to read "ye" as "the." Without thinking, I read the poem aloud.

Suddenly three figures materialized, each apparition punctuated by a loud *foomp*. They stood in front of the three small gravestones. Dead leaves swirled around their bare feet. Intense cold and putrid odors permeated the hollow. My hard breathing formed thick clouds as shivers ran up my spine. The first figure stood tall and slender, the second shorter and heavier, the third a mere slip of a girl.

For they were all women, with straight ebony hair, dressed in long black robes. A sinister fog seeped around us.

"Thou rubbed the stones!" accused Tall and Slender, pointing at me.

"Thou spake the words!" shouted Short and Heavy, also

pointing.

"Thou raised our bones!" taunted the Tiny One.

"Thou must choose," the trio recited in unison. They joined hands and twirled in a circle, cackling, a piercing noise like brittle sticks cracking and snapping.

My heart pounded. I couldn't speak. I couldn't move.

Short and Heavy stopped. "But hold, Beatrix. We must tarry for the High Priestess."

"What saith thee, Deborah?" said Beatrix, the tallest. "Dost thou agree with thy sister Constance?"

"Nay, Beatrix, I do not," said tiny Deborah. "If our Mother were coming, she would be hither now. We must proceed as the prophecy commands."

"Dost thou accede, dear Sister?" Beatrix raised her chin at Constance.

"The prophecy saith four shall rise. We are but three," Constance said. "Tragedy shall befall us if we ignore its decree."

"Thou art timid, Sister," Deborah sneered. "One wonders if thou art truly a witch."

"I have nerve enough. Test me if thou durst!"

Beatrix raised her hand. "Enough! This lackwit hath raised us." She leveled a finger at me. "We possess but one chance to attain our goal. He shall choose among us three."

"Thou art the eldest," Constance said. "Thou hast decided. I shall not oppose thee."

I found the courage to speak. "Excuse me. Ladies. May I ask a question?"

Beatrix answered, "Thou may ask. Speak."

"You all died on the same day. How did that happen?"

Beatrix stiffened and balled her fists. "The townspeople feared us."

"The mundanes hated us," added Constance.

I shook my head. "Mundanes?"

"Those who are not witches. They trapped us in the church." Deborah shuddered. "They barred the doors."

"They set the building aflame," whispered Beatrix. "They burnt us alive."

Deborah snickered. "But Mother foiled them. She cast a spell."

"The mundanes found out. They captured Mother and burnt her. At the stake." Constance began to weep.

"They exiled us from consecrated ground. They debased our graves with unmarked stones," Beatrix waved at their grave markers. "But Mother's magic was potent. She carved unseeable marks. The marks you exposed this night."

"And now thou must choose," said Deborah. "Thou must choose one of us."

"I don't understand. Why?" I suspected I did understand, but hoped I was wrong.

"To mate," Beatrix said. "To father a child. We desire a sister, and thou shalt give us one. Through her we shall live once again."

With that, the three witches dropped their robes. They stood there, silvery figures shimmering as moon shadows rippled over their naked bodies.

Three nude women in moonlight would normally be cause for arousal, but I was petrified in all the wrong places. My leaden legs would not move, and my arms turned stiff. The chilling cold penetrated my bones and immobilized me.

"Thou must choose," Beatrix intoned.

"Choose one," Constance chanted.

"Choose one," Deborah repeated.

"Choose!" they cried altogether.

The thorn bushes on either side of me came alive, twisting and writhing, their bristling branches lengthening and surrounding me. They tugged and pulled and shredded my clothes until I was as naked as the three women.

A brilliant flash of light exploded behind me. The three witches recoiled, shielding their eyes from the glare. They screamed in pain as gust and gale of blistering wind blew at them, shrinking them, withering them into small lumps of quivering gray ash. One by one they vaporized in puffs of black smoke.

The brilliance faded until only soft moonlight remained. The heat and wind subsided into a balmy, pine-scented zephyr. A figure in flowing white robes appeared from behind me.

I couldn't believe my eyes. *"Jennifer?* I—I don't understand. I thought you were…"

"Dead? I am, mostly. I should've known that damn church was cursed when I heard the stories about the Wicke women."

"But—but…"

"Remember the prophecy? *Four Shall Rise…?"*

"But what about Abigail, the mother? Wasn't she supposed to…?" I was still confused.

"Yes, but not to worry. I took care of her."

"But wasn't she a High Priestess? What about the symbol on her gravestone?"

"The Triquetra? That just means she's head of a coven. The symbol itself has no power. My magic is much stronger. It's all right, William. You're safe"

I suddenly realized my condition, and covered myself.

"Don't be shy," she purred, and smiled. "The prophecy must be fulfilled—*He Shall Choose and not Resist Her, They Shall Spawn another Sister.* If anyone's going to get a child out of this, it'll be me."

Jennifer let her robes slip to the ground. While the Wicke sisters' skin had shone cold and silver, Jennifer's skin glowed warm and golden. She lay down beside me and we embraced.

What they say about a witch's breasts is not true, for Jennifer was warm all over. Indeed, she was hot, burning hot.

I moaned in painful ecstasy.

She cackled in delight.

"Incidentally," she whispered. "I don't care if they do call that new bed-and-breakfast *The Sanctuary*. Anyone who stays there won't be safe."

# A Question of Heritage

## by William 'Bud' Humble

Exiting the somewhat civilized lands claimed by Northlight sent twin thrills of fear and excitement surging through me. Standing in the frosty Jotun Hrim mountain pass, I looked back but saw only hills and forest. Ahead lay white-topped, forested mountains. Instead of going south, like smart people did, I traveled east, into the wilds where few humans ever set foot.

And from where fewer still ever returned.

"This is it, Sven," I said to myself. "Cross this pass and you're off the map."

But I'm good at taking care of myself. And, once I set my mind to something, I stay with it. My mother used to joke that I was born with the stubbornness of five people—so now there were four poor souls having to do without because Odin only had so much to give to humanity. My willfulness had been both a source of pride and consternation for her. Sadly, a month ago, draugr attacked my lord's fortified manor outside the hamlet of Norderberg. Sometimes the dead refused to stay properly dead. We called them draugr. They're nasty and very hard to kill. Unfortunately, this wasn't a single returned draugr, but a band of ten.

My mother died fighting, so now she's in Valhalla. This left me with no truly important ties to Northlight.

With luck, maybe I'd find some answers about my mysterious father. I had a suspicion about just who his people might be, and they weren't in the human lands.

I crossed the mountain pass.

A half day's walk later found me most of the way down the mountain. There, I slipped into deep pine woods.

Walking down a game trail, I entered a clearing maybe a hundred paces across. Was that brown patch across the way a deer? Slowly I crouched down, drawing an arrow from my quiver. Sure looked like a deer standing behind that bush.

I crept forward, quiet as a whisper.

My pack was mostly filled with provisions. But, with no idea how long they'd have to last, supplementing them seemed smart. I continued stalking.

Just a little farther...

A strange, pungent odor tugged at my attention.

The deer hadn't moved yet. Was something else tracking it? A bear maybe? This didn't really smell like a bear and I didn't see any signs of one. Still, maybe bears on this side of the pass were different. My thoughts turned to the trip ahead of me. Once I got deeper into the mountains, game was likely to be a lot scarcer.

*Best to hunt while the hunting's good.*

Maybe halfway across the clearing and I'd have a better shot. I crept that way, trying to keep a pine tree between me and my target. Looked like my luck was finally changing for the—

Trolls erupted up out of the ground all around me.

Time slowed as I sucked in a too-fast breath.

The monsters charged me. Thick limbed, their grey-green skin was pebbled and thick.

Being ambushed was bad. Worse, I wore no armor. But my worst problem was carrying my longbow in the hand closest to my attacker.

Blocking my view of the way forwards, a huge monster surged towards me with wide-open jaws. Fleeting impressions struck me. Rancid breath, foul enough to gag a raven. Patchy, coarse green hair poked out of the monster's thick skin. Probably four paces tall, its arms were over-long as were the fingers that ended in thick, wide claws.

And it had a mouthful of *big* damn teeth.

Blood pounding in my ears drowned out all other

sounds.

There were more trolls, but compared to this brute and how close he was, they were naught but distant afterthoughts.

Forgetting I had an arrow nocked and ready, I reflexively raised my right hand as my will slammed forward. My camp trick, the reason I'd made this trip, became my primary defense. Heat flashed through me and my eyes tingled as everything within my vision sharpened. My hand grew hot. From my palm, a brilliant surge of red and gold flame blasted out, engulfing the troll before me.

He let out a bellow that left my ears ringing as scorched halves of my longbow snapped away.

The roar seemed to restore my hearing.

A branch to my left broke.

A split second later, hot brands scored my left calf. The next troll was already here. By Thor, they moved fast!

Twisting away, I dove to get below the brute rushing in, but he still clipped me with his hip, slamming me into the cold ground. Unable to slow itself in time, it lurched past me, then flinched away, barely avoiding crashing into his burning companion.

Rolling in the direction the second monster had come from, I sprang to my feet.

Despite the pain in my leg, I sprinted around one of the troll's pits. In doing so, I had to dodge a big mat made of woven branches. The thing was covered in pine needles that matched the clearing floor. *Gods above, what have I gotten myself into?* I raced towards the edge of the clearing. A glance behind showed the other trolls weren't following.

Slowly, cautiously, they gathered around their burning, flailing companion. Dropping to its knees, it let out another skull-rattling bellow and went still.

I ran past a crudely stuffed deer propped up with sticks behind a bush.

Ahead lay the mountains I'd sought. I changed course slightly to get out of the woods and into them. Time to put as much distance between myself and the trolls as possible.

\* \* \*

Two days.

What trolls lacked in intelligence, they evidently made up in stubbornness.

*So thinks the man tricked by a badly stuffed deer who walked right into the middle of a well-prepared ambush.*

Yeah.

*At least I survived finding out what trolls smell like.*

Pausing, I glanced behind me. They were there somewhere. Unrelenting buggers.

I felt sure my mother was watching from Odin's hall. She very likely had a cup of mead in her hand and was pointing me out to one of her friends. "How do you think my son likes being on the other side of all that stubbornness?"

Led by a beast almost as large as that first one, the damned pack of trolls still stalked me as I continued pushing into the mountains. Thankfully, the monster with the overlarge eye had missed taking out my knee. Still, I had three deep gashes and a sore shoulder thanks to it.

Exhausted, I stumbled and limped my way up and around a rocky, icy ledge. Stepping over a snow-filled hole, the cauterized flesh over one of the wounds cracked and broke. Again.

*Loki take these monsters!* I longed to shout but didn't.

*Self-control, Sven. First tool of a good hunter.* Old Gunter had hammered that into me since I was a boy. Despite my turning twenty, he'd still managed to say it at least once a week. I suspected if I survived and ever returned to the manor, those would be his first words. That or, "Where ya been, Sven? I need ya to chop some firewood."

A smile twisted my lips.

At a wide spot on the ledge, I sat. For a moment, I breathed and looked down at the world below. This spot was at least as high up as the Jotun Hrim. Below lay more forest and snow. Beautiful.

The throbbing in my leg demanded attention. I checked the strip of blanket I'd used to bind my wounds. Fresh blood seeped through. *Odin help me.* Word back at the manor had it that trolls could smell human blood across long distances. How well could they smell me?

I looked human. Thought of myself as human.

But was I really?

Despite having rounded ears and blue eyes, I suspected I might be part Alfar.

Fire magic coursed through my veins. What one of the Norderberg elders had called Aldrnari. Just as it saved me from the trolls' initial ambush, so had it cast my ancestry into doubt. Mother had never said one way or another, but she'd dropped many a hint. I think she'd liked the mystery about my father. We'd led a simple life out on the far outskirts of the Jarldom of Northlight and I think that had helped keep her spirit warm through the drudgery.

A trickle of blood ran down the bandage.

*Dammit!*

"Do you smell my blood, monsters? Does it smell human?"

Fortunately, nothing answered.

With a wave of my hand and a little willpower, I could conjure fire. Usually, I lit lamps, candles, or started bonfires at hunting camps. Lord Sigfried sometimes had me entertain guests with it. But, with me not being much of a showman, he tended to send me away quickly.

Grabbing a rock from the ledge, I smeared it with fresh blood and threw it as far down the mountain as I could. Far, far below, it disappeared into the snow-covered trees. Tired, frustrated, and dreading what I needed to do, I slowly unwrapped the bandage. *Freya, give me strength.* I couldn't tell if the redness around the wounds was due to my self-inflicted burns or infection. Hopefully not infection. Gritting my teeth, I conjured a tiny bit of fire and drew a blazing finger across the bleeding wound. Flesh seared and blood boiled.

The bleeding stopped.

Panting from the flare of agony and the lingering pain, I wiped the tears off my face and tore a new bandage from my blanket. After tying it in place, I took the old bandage, wrapped it around another rock, and threw it off the cliff in a slightly different direction. The blanket remains went into my battered pack.

For a while I just sat, recovering.

A bitterly cold gust of wind brought me out the reverie I'd fallen into.

Time to move. Last thing I needed was to be walking a narrow, icy ledge in high winds. Starting down the path again, I searched for signs of my hunters.

Finding out that forest trolls climb mountains like goats had been an unpleasant surprise. I rubbed my aching left side where I'd crashed into rocks while throwing myself out of the path of a charging troll. A small price to pay for such knowledge.

Still, I'd prefer no more surprises for a while.

Make that a long while.

*Odin's beard, I really miss my longbow.* I wasn't good enough with it to take down the entire pack all at once, but that last one had been by itself.

At the very least, I suspected an arrow in the knee would slow the monsters down.

*Instead, I just have a dagger. Great.*

Rounding a bend, I followed the narrow trail to a chasm that was maybe three paces across.

To my left, the split in the stone widened above and narrowed far below, as though one of the gods had sundered this part of the mountain with a massive ax. Three paces wide or not, the vee-shaped gap looked immense. Despite the exhaustion draining the strength from my limps, I could make the leap. Probably.

I examined the gap.

Maybe.

Opposite me, the path continued on. It offered a ledge maybe a half pace wide to land on.

If I jumped.

While the path across didn't seem to have as much ice as this side, it was awfully narrow.

Hmm. One of the paths a few hundred paces behind me had curved more northward. Perhaps that would be a better—

A tiny fall of rocks froze my thoughts.

Dagger out, I began edging my way back around the bend. The shifting wind blew that too familiar pungent scent to me. Troll. If I could smell it, the monster was too close. Soft footfalls approached.

*Hel take these monsters!*

Turning, I clambered over a small boulder and rushed toward the cleft.

Three running steps and I leapt.

Again, time slowed.

A rasping noise to my left drew my eye upwards. With an overlong arm stretched out to each side of the split, my old friend with the extra-large eye slid down the defile. His feet weren't even touching, he was just sliding down using his hands. Because the cleft was wider above than below, the closer to me the troll came, the less he had to stretch.

Behind me, the footfalls increased in tempo. Not just one, but two trolls out of the band of six. Five, if you counted the one I'd burned.

I leapt.

Big Eye stuck out a leg to the opposite side of the cleft, which stopped his descent.

*He's close enough I could nearly—*

His huge hand snaked out towards me.

Halfway across the gap, I flung a small burst of flame into Big Eye's grotesque face.

With a deafening shriek, it jerked its hands back to protect its face. Off balance and now without a good physical connection to the cleft, it fell over backwards.

My momentum carried me forward.

I stretched out my left leg towards the ledge. If I missed, it was a *long* way down.

The sounds behind me were now distinct, heavy footsteps. A grunt of exertion, and they stopped.

*Oh no.*

My foot touched the path but instead of a solid landing, I went skidding. Sliding and struggling to remain balanced on the one foot, I twisted to throw my left hand behind me. Blindly, I launched flame at what I hoped was head height on a troll.

Another pained bellow. A meaty thump shook the ledge.

The two sets of rapidly fading roars somehow managed to sound musical.

With the momentum of my slide almost spent, I twisted around. Before I could get my right foot on the ledge, my sliding boot hit a rock, and stopped.

I fell forward.

Arms, chest, and then the side of my chin struck the edge.

My legs dropped off, leaving me scrabbling for any hold.

I slid another handspan, the rock scraping my chest. My outstretched left hand latched onto a small irregularity in the stone. Stars danced in my eyes, but I held on. My right hand latched onto a small rock in the trail. Desperation and a wildly hammering heart cleared my head. Hanging over far too much air, my feet flailed for purchase.

There was nothing.

The rock under my right hand crumbled and my arm began sliding towards the edge. I tried shifting my weight, but it wasn't enough.

My right arm continued slipping and the grip my left hand maintained was weakening.

Tired as I was, there was no way I could hold on with just one arm.

Just before my elbow went over the edge, my fingers stumbled into a snowy depression and latched onto the edge.

I stopped sliding.

Exhaling in relief, I dipped my forehead to the cool stone.

Stable.

At least until the wind gusted again or my fingers weakened. The longer I stayed like this, the worse off I'd be. No time for rest yet.

If I could just...

Awkwardly lurching to the side, I swung my right foot up onto the ledge. Good.

Now for the hard part.

Shouting with the effort, I forced my arms up and flopped gracelessly onto the ledge. Laying on my pack as I breathed heavily, relief washed over me despite my aches and pains.

Total exhaustion loomed. I needed sleep.

Since the first ambush, I'd been running. The occasional

short rest had been all I could manage.

Trolls didn't like daylight. Amongst other things, it stung their eyes. But I now knew they could tolerate it if they chose.

And they had other senses to hunt with.

Speaking of senses, my eyes were trying to tell me something.

Frowning, I forced myself to focus.

The mountain above me had developed a strange lump. And that lump seemed to be moving straight towards me.

A sudden jolt of panic sent me clumsily scrambling to my feet.

Another troll.

*Oh, blood and bones, the other big one.*

I was a hunter, not a warrior, but that was no excuse. This might be my end, but I wasn't going without a fight.

If I was going to die, I'd damn sure be joining my mother in Valhalla.

I started to draw my dagger, but my sheath was empty.

Oh, I'd been carrying it when I jumped.

Before I had a chance to despair, a gleam caught my eye.

It was on the ledge a few paces ahead. I've always heard that the gods like a good fight down here on Midgard. That or an inordinate amount of good luck were the only reasons I could think of for why my little blade hadn't fallen off this narrow ledge.

Picking up my dagger, I yelled, "All Father! Sven of Norderberg here. I have things yet to do and I'm not ready to see Valhalla yet. Guide my blade if it pleases you. If it doesn't, I'm looking forward to hoisting a drink in honor of your hospitality."

As I sidestepped, the troll adjusted its course. No matter

how I moved, it continued descending straight at me.

I considered conjuring flame. A powerful shudder wracked my body. No. Not even to save my life. This troll I'd battle with steel and what little strength and few wits I had left.

Yeah, I was in deep, deep trouble.

The monster slowed. A few paces above me it stopped.

Pointing a broad claw at my chest, it surprised me by speaking, it's voice deep and as coarse as the green hair sticking out of it at wild angles. "You...brudder...kill. Mate...kill. Dottir...kill. Now, me...you...kill"

"That was a nice speech, troll." With my heart hammering like a crazed smith pounding an anvil, it surprised me that my voice stayed steady. "But it doesn't change anything. I've got good steel here that says you're late for a family reunion."

The troll launched itself at me.

I'd hoped that maybe time would slow for me, again. No such luck.

With the troll dropping towards me arms first, I crouched and lashed out with my dagger. The gouge I carved in its arm didn't seem to bother it in the least.

It landed on the narrow path in a handstand and flipped up.

As monstrous feet touched the ledge, I leapt into the beast, driving my blade up under its chin. Only the tip of the blade penetrated. I threw my weight into it as I pounded my off-hand into the pommel. There was resistance.

A giant, clawed hand opened as the monster reached for my head.

Desperate, I hammered the pommel again and the blade slid in to the hilt.

The hand stopped. The monster's yellow eyes grew wide.

We teetered on the ledge. He looked down at me in

surprise as its pupils grew to consume all the brilliant yellow in his eyes. Slowly, he began tilting away from the mountain.

I pushed him, desperation surging as I tried to get a foot back on the ledge.

As the troll toppled over, that same clawed hand grabbed my shoulder and pulled me with it.

* * *

Immersed in confusion, I awoke surrounded by brilliant white light.

*Is this Valhalla?*

Shifting around, pain stabbed through my left side. A bone chilling cold had seeped into me.

*If this is Valhalla, it sucks.*

Lifting my arm caused some of the white to crumble.

I always imagined Valhalla being built of something...less crumbly.

*Where am—*

*Oh.*

Painfully, I twisted around so I could look up. Yep. There was the mountain, rising high above the white.

White.

Snow.

Yes, I'd fallen into a snowbank. Apparently, a deep one.

As my thoughts continued clearing, I tried climbing out. My initial efforts revealed two things. Climbing out of this snow was not going to be easy or quick. It was at least six paces deep. It also pointed out that raising my left arm above my shoulder resulted in intense pain in my side. I'd probably cracked or broken some ribs.

Using my right arm, I began the slow task of digging out.

A coil of rope dropped into the hole and smacked me in the face.

"Ow." My voice barely reached my ears.

"Are you awake?" a woman's melodic voice asked. She sounded close.

"Yes," I called as loud as I could manage. It came out more of a croak.

"Good! Wrap the rope around you and we'll pull you out."

I considered wrapping it around my body, but quickly thought better of it. Instead, I twined the rope around my right arm. "Ready!"

The rope above me tightened, then cut into the snow. A moment later, I got pulled into the wall of snow. This was not fun.

Eventually, I emerged into a sunlit clearing near a gleaming hill of snow. Pine trees stretched on for as far as the eye could see.

After wiping the snow off my face, I struggled to sit up and barely succeeded.

A woman and a man walked over to me.

To her companion, she said, "Maybe next time I tell you I didn't sense someone die, you'll believe me."

"I never doubted," he replied easily. Suddenly crouched down in front of me, the man met my gaze. "Relax Trollslayer. You're safe. Now that you're out of the snowbank, we'll throw together a litter. Get you somewhere warm and dry."

He had pointed ears and green eyes flecked with gold.

"You're one of the Alfar?" I managed in a bare whisper. By Odin's ravens, I was weak as a newborn pup.

"Sonyalla and Nichol Frosttree of the WilderMountain Ljos Alfar. What's your name, Trollslayer?"

"Sven of Norderberg."

He fake coughed. "We actually heard you earlier. But, overhearing it and receiving the name from you are entirely different matters. We watched your battle. Impressive. Your use of fire was very surprising. Sonya wanted to shoot that last one before it reached you. However, when you issued that challenge, she realized you wanted to kill it yourself."

*She could have...*

I felt it was entirely worth the effort to groan, so I did.

She said, "Slaying the monster and riding it down through the trees... That was one of the most magnificent feats of daring I've ever witnessed. I'm guessing landing in the deepest snowbank in the area was pure luck?"

Daring? Well, that sounded better than desperation.

Instead of answering, I said, "There may be Alfar blood in my veins. I traveled into the mountains to learn the truth of it. Find out if I really do have family here." With a pained laugh, I admitted, "I was looking for you, and you found me."

They exchanged a quick but significant look.

"Considering the fire magic we witnessed," Sonya said, "I would guess there's little doubt about your heritage. Generally speaking, that is. Alfar blood tends to brim with magic. Purely human blood? Not that I've ever heard of. When you're better, we'll take you into our town. See what we can learn."

"Be warned," Nichol said quietly. "Half-bloods are seldom greeted with open arms."

"My brother's right. Still, not all houses are the same. You're a trollslayer thrice over, something not many Alfar can say. Don't get your hopes too high, but you may yet find a warm welcome. And if not, we're always happy to keep company with trollslayers."

"Four times over, and thank you. I'll be happy just finding out who my people are."

Her smile was warm and kind. "Come on Sven of Nordberg. Let's see if we can't find you some happiness."

# Ghola

## by William 'Bud' Humble

Looking over my owner's shoulder at the vid, I dispassionately watch the parades, fireworks, and celebrations as the humans of Earth commemorate the two-hundredth anniversary of Ghola Day. Later, Gertrude Chen, the Overlords' human Viceroy, announces that the citizens of Earth have been granted access to the stars.

The crowds go wild as does my owner.

Later that very day, every human receives galactic InfoNet access. Informationally and financially, this connects humanity with more than thirty thousand alien species. The aliens come in all shapes and sizes, but they have one thing in common: they've had access to the stars for centuries, if not millennia. Or eons.

Humanity seems intent on making up for lost time.

Spaceships are purchased. Within a matter of weeks, the first deliveries arrive. With nigh unfettered access to over a million worlds, the peoples of Earth scatter to the stars.

My owner decides to stay and make his fortune here. For pennies on the proverbial dollar, he begins buying the property of those leaving our homeworld.

A mere five years later, on the anniversary of what is now called the Opening, the mass exodus has halved the population of Earth. In the wake of all those missing people, more and more aliens are moving here to help develop the world. The population plunge finally slows, then stops.

My owner sells real estate to these aliens at retail prices. His lifestyle improves exponentially.

Back when I was nineteen, Earth was just the Earth and people were people.

The good ol' days.

Then an asteroid the size of Rhode Island raced across

our skies. The Overlord's ship. They announced they were taking over planetary management.

Forces mobilized.

The Overlords never fired a shot. Overnight, they simply converted forty percent of the world's population, into ghola.

Two hundred-odd years later, exactly what a ghola is remains something of a mystery.

We appear human, though our skin is now shiny. It looks like it should be slick to the touch, but it's not. Ghola don't have internal organs. Those were all morphed into a dense packing of complex cells that mimic whatever function is needed. Damaged cells heal quickly and there is zero genetic degradation from replication.

Scientists are studying the hell out of *that*. Why? Because ghola produce replacement cells that are perfect. Every single cell, every single time.

Which means we hold within us the keys to eternity.

So far as I can tell, if I'm not immortal, I'm really close. This is one of the worst horrors I've experienced. At least it would be if I could properly feel horror.

Or anything else.

As a ghola, my emotions are deadened. Not dead, but certainly nothing like what I remember before waking up in my freshman dorm on the morning of what turned out to be Ghola Day.

There's a lot more to being a ghola, but my owner requires me to prepare the evening meal, so I pour most of my focus into that. Still, as I chop vegetables for stir fry, a tiny part of me rebels and insists on reflection.

Opening the Earth up to intra-galactic trade has led to a glorious period of chaos. As a ghola, I find it mildly interesting, which is impressive for me.

Our world is changing quickly. Alien embassies are being built or moved into place. Same with space stations.

Aliens are opening businesses. Humans open franchises of alien businesses.

Stir fry is devoured, night turns to day.

Time races along.

New technologies are integrated faster than manufacturing can keep up with. Cars hover for a few years, then flyers become the rage. Some feature anti-grav cores, others jets, lift fans, or combinations of these techs and more. Plasma, fusion, or solar impellers are just the top of the list for the choices in automotive 'engines.' There are auto-pilots, improved neural links, AIs, and even antique voice command systems—and all these techs and hundreds more feed a mish-mass of stunned and amazed consumers.

'Glorious,' my owner calls it.

None of which helps me, *per se*, because like all these amazing products, I am property. All ghola are.

Still, the changes to the Earth pique my interest. Almost.

\* \* \*

Ten years, four months, and seventeen days after the Opening, my owner is picking up someone from the Cherokee International Spaceport outside Oklahoma City. I guard the car, as ordered.

My thoughts drift back.

After our conversion, the Overlords gathered up all us ghola.

They then gave us to people on other continents.

Becoming ghola changed our faces slightly as the process 'perfected' our looks and completely evened out our skin tones. I ended up looking a couple of years older and a bit thinner. Older people typically looked younger with the thin putting on weight and the wide losing it. The process corrected physical imperfections all the way up to missing limbs.

Our families tried finding us, but facial recognition

111

failed. DNA tracing failed.

The world went a bit crazy.

Unfortunately, insanity was a luxury I could not indulge in.

My emotions were filtered and blunted. Like reality versus an old VR game with a faulty neural link. I was no longer me. Lamenting my loss wasn't possible. I only managed a vague remorse for my lost dreams—for my family and friends.

For *everything*.

Motion ninety-two meters away draws my attention. My owner has returned from the spaceport with a woman.

Seeing me, she frowns. "I don't like ghola. They're creepy." She throws him a hard look. "And disturbingly screwable. Get rid of it."

My owner glances at me, then nods to her.

*  *  *

Next day, I move into a house with a distracted, older man.

I am wary yet hopeful when it comes to new owners. Not that I can do anything about my situation if things don't go well. Still, there remains a flicker of optimism I have learned to nurture.

Fortunately, my sense of disappointment is as blunted as my other emotions.

One hundred thirty-eight years and six days ago, I was picked up by a group bent on freeing ghola from servitude and abuse. At a remote ranch, they tried teaching me to live without an owner. Following their 'suggestions,' the other ghola and I worked the gardens, tended the livestock, and cleaned pretty much everything.

The group factionalized.

It felt like watching a train wreck in slow motion. There were good people here I wanted to warn.

I couldn't. Ghola cannot speak save under very specific circumstances. More than that, again, barring certain circumstances, we cannot so much as lift a hand without being commanded.

Two years, one month, and fifteen days after our arrival, one faction discovered that the other had been screwing us almost from the start. Threats flew. Weapons were drawn.

They killed each other.

"I'm sorry," the last of them gasped before bleeding out.

We walked to the nearest town, lined up, and said in unison, "This ghola requires a new caretaker."

Unlike the ranch folks, my preoccupied new owner doesn't seem to have any intentions for me, at all. He waves towards a corner of the living room. "Stand over there. Keep out of my way."

Same thing happens the next day.

And the next.

This morphs into the most boring decade of my existence. While I don't spend the entire time in that corner, I'm there far too much. My new owner is obsessed with mastering the physics behind an alien high-gravity negation field generator.

Being ghola is an endless chain of faintly felt frustrations. We do as our owners tell us unless it violates some ill-defined order against endangering ourselves or others. This order seems largely dependent upon circumstances and maybe even a degree of—I don't know what to call it other than whimsy—especially now that additional aliens have been thrown into the mix. We do it without reservation. I suppose if I could truly feel horror, that emotion would have been burned out by any number of my previous owners.

But there *are* limitations.

Fail to feed us properly, and we speak. "This ghola requires proper nutrients."

Damn, after decades of silence, it's creepy hearing yourself say stuff like that.

Well, it *should* be creepy.

Other messages include, "This ghola requires cleaning," "Continued abuse of ghola will not be tolerated," "This ghola requires an appropriately temperature-controlled environment," and "This ghola requires a new caretaker."

As a ghola, I have a cleaning cycle, a strangely robotic soaping and scrubbing. Today's cleaning cycle will be exactly as it was my first day as a ghola. Cleanings by my owner or their associates usually bump the cleaning time back by hours or even days, but they do not replace the cleaning cycle.

Standing in the corner, my thoughts drift back to my favorite owner.

* * *

Seventy years, two months, and six days ago, an artist found me on the street calling for a new owner. The artist took me home.

I received my orders and we lived like a married couple for many years. Like some of my previous owners or their family members, I grew fond of this person and came to think of them as *my* artist.

But I couldn't love.

In a way, I felt then and still feel like I'm in a video game and striving to reach the level in which love will be unlocked again.

Despite my emotional handicap, the illusion our lives were built around was almost pleasant.

My artist kept trying to paint my soul.

I'm not exactly sure what that meant, but the paintings portrayed me showing emotions. In my favorite, I was smiling and clearly having fun. My artist had talent and the paintings showed joy and light and happiness in my eyes. A series showed me displaying other emotions. Crying over the loss of my humanity. Raging at the abuses I've endured. The painting that won the most awards depicted me horrified, surrounded by the sins committed against me.

A *lot* of sins have been committed against me.

But the ones that stand out in my mind weren't the ones my artist captured—violence, unpleasant sex, neglect, and such. No, my standouts weren't actually sins against me, but having to watch others suffer. Children who wanted no more than a hug, which I couldn't give. Kids ignored, forced to raise themselves. The elderly starving because they couldn't physically do what they needed to do in order to feed themselves. There's been so much pain and suffering that I could have alleviated with just a smidgen of freedom.

Even my regret is a hollow, ephemeral thing.

Doing such a good job of portraying me as human gained my artist fame. It sparked a renewed attempt to provide ghola with some basic rights.

A beautiful dream but doomed.

Ghola are property. Property have no rights.

So sayeth the Viceroy.

So it is.

The lack of social progress slowly transformed my artist into a cynic. Many tears were shed and I couldn't provide comfort.

More than anything I'd felt in decades, that stung.

One spring evening, a tornado destroyed our loft.

I pulled myself out of the wreckage. Digging through the rubble, I tossed girders and sections of wall away as though they weighed nothing. Six minutes and eighteen seconds later, I uncovered my artist, but the damage was done.

Bloody fingers traced gently across my face. "A human soul burns within you. I see it! I see hope for the future. Fight for both!"

My artist died.

Wanting to cry, I walked to the nearest clear street. "This ghola requires a new caretaker."

* * *

I wish I could sigh at the memory, but I cannot. Instead, I stand in the corner as my owner pores over translations of alien glyphs and human science journals.

Eventually, he dies, never fully understanding the science he dedicated so much of his life to. Of course, I don't go to the funeral. Still, I can't help but wonder if anyone else does, for he had few colleagues and fewer friends. Surrounded by millions, he lived a lonely life.

At least in that regard, I have a deep understanding of him.

* * *

Twelve years and three owners later, I'm traded to Captain Vai Gabriel of the independent trader *Solomon's Pyrite*, a Cofimi-class freighter. During my last days on Earth, the Captain purchases high-end combat armor for me, as well as a massive array of weaponry. I'm given many very specific commands on how to react in various situations—most of them resulting in extreme violence. We train both at firing ranges and in the *Pyrite's* gym. There's a robot for training in hand-to-hand combat, but on the third day, I break it so badly it cannot be quickly repaired.

My interest stirs.

Sex is again part of the equation, but for the Captain, it seems to be more a form of exercise and a sleep aid. For the first time since my artist died, I sleep in the same bed as my owner.

Ghola do sleep. Never for long and never dreaming. That's a blessing of sorts because no dreams mean no nightmares.

Life has provided enough of those.

In the early years after our conversion, ghola took a *lot* of abuse.

For many, casual beatings became an expected part of ghola existence. But, move beyond that to stabbing, skinning, gouging out eyes, or anything that interferes with proper ghola functionality, and you get a warning.

Rack up three warnings in some unspecified time frame and we react. Potentially lethal or debilitating attack against us? We react.

The first time a man stabbed me, I spouted the appropriate warning. We don't bleed and we feel only a shadow of the pain we used to. Still, a knife in the guts is unpleasant.

My verbal warning startled the man. Fear crept into his eyes.

Then anger flooded in.

He stabbed me thirty-six times before I completed the third warning.

Ghola are *really* hard to kill.

When he tried to stab me that thirty-seventh time, I grabbed his wrist and twisted until it locked in place.

Then, I pulled off his arm.

I was just as surprised as he was. It wasn't just the passionless violence, but also my extreme strength. Up until then, I'd had no idea.

Fortunately, Captain Gabriel has treated me quite well. The new weapons and armor seem to presage interesting days ahead.

I almost feel anticipation.

With her cargo hold filled with uniquely Terran trade goods, *Solomon's Pyrite* launches to the stars. I stand on the bridge, watching my owner's back. The crew seems loyal, but my owner's comments bear the weight of orders, so I monitor the lot of them.

Our first stop is a space station owned by the stumpy, vaguely lizard-like Zee. Their atmosphere is compatible enough for humans to breathe with the assistance of a calibrated mask. I can breathe it just fine, but thanks to gear integrated into my combat helmet, I don't need to.

The Captain trades two tons of paintings in return for galactic credits and robots.

All parties happy.

Next stop is the moon of a gas giant orbiting a blue star. The moon has no atmosphere and no indigenous life. What it does have is anonymity and lack of tariffs, taxes, and docking fees.

The initial exchange, swapping Terran-made statues for power cells and batteries, goes smoothly.

But, as the Captain tries to barter the newly acquired robots for energy weapons, his three blob-like trading partners in their bulky environment suits grow upset.

Evidently, the idea they might be gun-runners is culturally offensive to them.

"Apologies," the Captain says. "I meant no insult. We're not familiar with your cult—"

The three aliens speak at the same time. One of the translation streams reads, '...kill you and let Gorzo sort you out.' I doubt this is a true translation, but it doesn't matter.

The 'kill you' triggers one of the conditions my captain has given me.

I whip the rifle off my back, prime it, and aim it at the hab compartment of the offending alien's suit. This seems to surprise everyone.

When the three aliens reach for their weapons, I kill them.

Without hesitating, I target the alien on the bridge of their ship. My bullet pierces the armored window, continues through the alien, blows through a control panel, and exits back into space. Vacuum pulls the gooey alien out through the hole in the window.

There are two more aliens on board. I shoot them through the hull, leaving their ship leaking atmosphere.

"Well, shit," the Captain says with a frown. "That didn't go as well as I'd hoped. Chen, send a couple of robots over to unload their ship. Just be sure to wait 'til we're back on board and the shields are up before entering their hold. Wouldn't surprise me if these bastards sabotaged their own ship."

This new phase of my existence *is* interesting.

Which reminds me of the time I found out ghola have subconscious orders to prevent the worst of human-on-human atrocities.

One evening, a hundred eighty years, eight months, and eleven days ago, I heard noises within my household.

In the children's bedroom, I found an 'uncle' sodomizing my owner's eight-year-old. I restrained the monster. Four ghola from nearby homes joined me. I didn't send a message or summon them.

*Something* did, but it wasn't me.

We carried the naked, screaming pervert into the street.

My fellow ghola each grabbed one of the perpetrator's limbs and began walking away from the others. I felt a muted but distinct satisfaction at removing his genitalia. Afterwards, I pulled off his head. By this time, a crowd had gathered.

I wished I could have explained it all to the furious parents and comforted the hurt child, but I could do neither.

Fortunately, my circumstances have improved.

My next surprise from Captain Gabriel isn't more combat, but study. I am to learn and perform the duties of each crew position.

I start with Steward. The cooking and cleaning parts are easy enough as I've been performing variations of these duties for most of the last two centuries. The rest of the required tasks are not particularly difficult.

Soon, I expand out into other branches.

Evidently, while life support systems vary by ship, what they *do* varies only slightly. Providing breathable air, drinkable water, gravity, an environment in which humans don't freeze or bake, and maintaining nominal radiation levels is pretty much it. These functions must be maintained in perpetuity, because drops in any one system can result in the death of the entire crew.

Same goes for the propulsion systems, electrical generators, astrogation, helm, communications, and all the other ship systems and the duty stations that maintain or utilize them. In addition to the duties, I study the underlying sciences.

Learning again is—invigorating.

After a few months and some carefully worded commands from my Captain, I can perform the duties of every crewman on the ship save for one important aspect of each: I can't speak or give non-verbal communication.

The Captain bypasses this by having me fill out a checklist for duties performed on shift.

Many of the crew disapprove. Apparently, ghola doing anything beyond screwing, guarding, or performing household chores is unnatural.

It seems I scare them.

When an upset cargo handler punches me, he runs afoul of the Captain's orders concerning self-defense from the crew.

I grab the crewman by the neck and lift him off his feet.

A co-worker takes a step towards me. I meet her angry eyes with my expressionless gaze. She stops and raises her hands. "You're killing him."

I am in fact *not* killing him.

When the crewman stops struggling, I drop him and return to my scheduled duties. The woman carries him to the autodoc.

Word spreads like wildfire.

No crew member of the *Solomon's Pyrite* ever strikes me again.

Despite that incident, this is the most alive I've felt since becoming a ghola. As part of my duties, I monitor ship functions—just like the human crew members.

It's almost like being a person again.

While my Captain sleeps, I ponder this. Contrarily, it brings to mind when I felt least like a person: right after being changed.

At first, I was used mostly as a house cleaner and family cook. That wasn't so bad. But, the newness of ghola faded. As we became more accepted, sex became my predominant use.

Just as I couldn't feel outrage at the perversions, neither could I enjoy those times that should have been fun. But *should* they have been fun? I wasn't a willing participant. I was property. When ordered to screw with enthusiasm, my body performed as ordered. But evidently, there was something about my eyes. The eyes of every ghola. They showed some hint of what lay within. Or what did not.

Ghola masks became popular.

Cleaning a house or apartment was done just as methodically as cleaning myself. It took as long as it took and I did so every time I was so ordered. I did not tire, so I could clean all day if necessary.

Same for sex or any other activity.

Despite similarities between those dark years and now, with Captain Gabriel, everything feels subtly different. Maybe it's the captain. Maybe it's our circumstances.

Maybe it's...me?

As months slide into years, my end-of-watch checklist grows more complex.

When the Captain adds the 'A potential problem exists'

box and then gives me a complete pulldown menu featuring every ship component, piece of cargo, and member of the crew, a tiny crack forms somewhere inside me.

I fall a little bit in love with my Captain.

Small as the emotion might be, this is a new experience. My memory is disturbingly precise. As though reliving it, I can remember any day since becoming a ghola. Few are worth doing so, but I have the ability. Memories before Ghola Day are not so clear. There's a foggy, almost evanescent quality to them.

While I remember having crushes before Ghola Day, the memories are faded, nearly emotionless shells. I recall loving friends and family, but their faces, hugs, and the sounds of their voices are all but gone.

So, despite knowing what love is, I've never really been *in* love.

I think it says something important about myself that a tiny sense of frustration stirs because I can't tell my Captain any of this.

For the most part, I can't show it either. Showing emotions via facial expression went out with being able to speak when I wanted. But I *can* put just a little extra effort into making up the cabin. Keeping everything in its proper place and clean. I try to convert sex into love making. This is difficult because despite all the sex, I've never really made love before. I know there's a difference, but the distinction remains vague—subtle and elusive.

Still, I try my best.

Years pass.

Crew members come and go, but my Captain and I remain.

On a run to Signus, a pirate ship tries to board us. When they close to within fifty meters, I jump across to their vessel. My power-armor makes it easy.

Via a couple of breaching charges, I hole their ship. After

that, maneuvering inside is simple. Disabling their ship's weapons without extensively damaging the ship is an interesting challenge, especially since the pirates are trying their best to kill me.

But I'm wearing power-armor and carrying heavy weapons. They're not.

Once the pirates are dead, I receive new orders.

Following the *Solomon's Pyrite*, I pilot the pirate ship to Signus. There, my Captain not only sells her for a huge number of credits, but also claims a significant reward for ending the pirate threat.

My combat armor and weapons are replaced with upgraded models.

By this time, my Captain talks to me the same as any member of the crew. I use a complex tablet program to mark boxes containing appropriate responses. Having been raised away from Earth, some of the younger crew members have never seen a ghola before me. They don't understand why communicating with me is one-way and via the tablet, but they don't seem to worry about it either.

Those who *have* seen ghola before are shocked by me performing complex tasks.

Perhaps they've forgotten we ghola were once human.

One evening in our cabin, my Captain gently runs fingertips down my face. "Do you feel for me what I feel for you?"

My tablet is on the basic response screen, so I reach for the 'Yes' box. Thoughts interrupt, staying my hand. The question involves complex emotions. One way of looking at emotions is to mark them like a voice or retinal print. Each person's emotional response is unique. Beyond that, emotions change and evolve constantly, in ways large and small. I cannot feel exactly what my Captain feels.

But that isn't what my Captain's asking.

I push my finger closer to the 'Yes' box, but the

knowledge that our thoughts and emotions can't possibly line up in an exact match slows me. It threatens to stop my response, which will hurt my Captain and our relationship.

Moving my finger towards the tablet is like pushing through steel.

Inside, my thoughts twist and I picture myself with a feral grin. With my strength, steel is pretty damn malleable. I'm *not* going to let some semantic bullshit within my ghola programming hurt my Captain or the bond we've formed.

My finger stabs through the tablet.

Rather than being upset, my Captain laughs in delight. "I didn't form that question precisely enough to be easily answered, did I?"

I look to the dead tablet. Inside, I'm scowling at my broken communication device, but it never shows on my face.

Smile morphing into a grin, my Captain says, "Just kiss me if my phrasing needs work."

This I can do.

It should have been a kiss. 'Just' implies quick despite the other context. But now I know I can overcome some of my internal barriers and I'm determined to push them every chance I get.

The kiss lasts so long my Captain has to come up for air.

Years turn to decades and we fly and fly and fly. I think my Captain is an explorer at heart, because there are few places we visit more than once.

While docked at Cassiopeia's Haxgranox Station, I grow increasingly distressed. I've been specifically blocked from access to the cabin's shower. What's more, I've been scrubbing down life support components. Very messy, smelly components. Despite the odor, my Captain stays close to me.

On the evening of the third day, I'm forced to say, "This ghola requires cleaning."

My Captain's eyes close and a look of sublime happiness fills that beloved face.

"I'm sorry to do that to you, my sweet. But I've been wanting to hear your voice for decades now. It's selfish and cruel of me to pluck them from you so, but I had no alternative. Will you forgive me?"

I check the 'Yes' box on my tablet.

"Thank you. Now, let's get you cleaned up."

Eventually, we return to Luna to celebrate the sixtieth anniversary of my Captain's birth. There, my Captain undergoes comprehensive rejuvenation treatments. The Captain emerges looking only slightly older than me and I haven't visibly aged since Ghola Day.

Over our decades together, the Captain has often told me to handle things as I wish. To do what I want. Those orders echo within my mind, but they run counter to my internal ghola programming. I'm *not* free to do as I want because a ghola is property and *must* be owned. No command can change that and there are severe limitations on what property can do.

I've placed countless orders over the long years. Food, clothing, household goods, and more. But they were all done at the express command of my owner. In a few instances, I've done this as an implied duty to the household I serve, but it is still within my purview.

Gifts fall outside that purview.

And, while flipping through a catalog, I find an antique sextant. This will be a perfect gift to celebrate my Captain's renewal. But, as I reach for the order button, thoughts snake out, ensnaring my finger.

This is *not* a staples order. There is forbidden intent within this ghola's actions.

Can I manufacture a gift? In a way, everything I do is inherently a gift to my owner.

The mental barrier falters and my finger moves closer.

If I'm a gift, then my owner deserves any gifts I chose to give as an added bonus. Are not the fruits of my labor gifts? Would not this gift add to my owner's happiness?

While the threads of logic struggle against one another, I push the button.

A 'ship to' window appears and auto-fills to our Lunar suite. Since the *Solomon's Pyrite* is undergoing a refit much as her Captain has, we'll be here at least another 30-day cycle. Plenty of time for the gift to be delivered.

This time, the doubts ensnare my finger much sooner. Same arguments and the same wall. Ghola are property. Property cannot order property.

It takes me an hour to press this button.

The payment menu pops up. I pull out the card given to me decades ago for 'whatever you deem necessary to buy.' Thus far, I've only used it for necessities. Now, I struggle to bring the card around to touch the screen and the reader there. I have to be careful. If I accidentally destroy this screen, I'm not sure I'll be able to try this again. Fighting my ghola nature is not only extremely difficult, it's also strangely draining.

For two hours and forty-four minutes, I struggle against the limiting thoughts and logic that traps me in little loops. Despite that, I touch the card to the screen.

The order confirmation screen appears.

For the first time since becoming a ghola, my breathing hitches. My teeth lock together as though I'm lifting a great weight.

And I am.

Just not with my body.

Within my mind, ingrained orders and logic grapple with my burgeoning willpower. After four hours and thirty-six minutes, I press the button.

The celebration within me is as quiet as it is profound.

I walk into the bedroom, strip, and climb into bed. My Captain mumbles sleepily and wraps me in a warm embrace before falling asleep again.

While I can't honestly claim to be happy, I'm damn close.

A week passes.

"A gift?" my Captain asks. "From you?"

I wish I can just freaking nod. Everything would be so much easier. At the Captain's glance at my tablet, I check the 'Yes' box.

"I've never heard of any ghola ever giving a gift. But you're special, my love, aren't you?"

Special and defective are quite different and I'm not sure which is more correct.

"No need to answer. I know I'm right."

We go for a celebration dinner at a posh restaurant with an amazing view of the Earth. As we dine, the occasional remark about the poor taste of bringing a ghola reaches my ears. Odd since there are ghola guarding the entrance, but maybe that's different because they're working. My Captain's eyes narrow. I judge at least one of the comments was intended to be overheard.

This is hardly the first time I've been derided for being a ghola. But it is the first time in decades if not centuries I've been angry because of it. It feels stronger than I remember and my hand almost closes into a fist before the internal ghola programming stops it.

My Captain smiles. "It's such a shame a fine establishment has become contaminated by bigots. Why, I remember a time when places such as this were more discriminating in who they allowed inside."

While I can't smile, I *can* feel pride in my Captain.

That evening in our suite, we drink fifty-year-old scotch. My Captain asks, "Do you want to make love tonight?" The rejuvenation treatments have made my Captain unusually horny. Three weeks later, that drive hasn't faded even a little.

I check the 'Yes' box.

"Because you know I want to?"

I check the 'No' box.

A familiar amused calculation enters those beautiful eyes. "Is it because...I'm such a talented lover?"

While that is nice inasmuch as I can appreciate it, I check the 'No' box.

My Captain lets out a delighted laugh and gives me a rueful grin. "Is it because... *you're* such a talented lover and you know I enjoy your attentions more than practically anything else in this life?"

A little ping of surprise echoes through me.

"Ha!" My Captain says. "Your pupils just dilated. That surprised you. Or did it please you?"

I check the 'Yes' box.

"Both?"

I check the box again.

My Captain leans in for a long, kiss. "Now, back to the matter at hand. Do you want to make love because it's symbolic of our bond? Our closeness?"

Again, I check the 'Yes' box.

My Captain hugs me for a several minutes. "Come, my sweet. Let's make love and celebrate our bond."

We do just that. It may just be my imagination, but it seems like I feel a little more, both physically and emotionally.

Our bond is strong.

Soon, we return to space. The *Solomon's Pyrite* is nicer now. While she won't be mistaken for brand new, she's every bit as rejuvenated as her captain.

While voyaging from port to port, I push my ghola boundaries.

I learn about clothing design. Then I print a series of sexy underwear as a gift for my Captain. Stretching even further, I print a series for myself. This is made particularly difficult by the thought 'a gift for myself.'

But I do it.

There are literally worlds and worlds of new tech available. So, I read until I find something that catches my eye. I also become an expert on the ship's new fabrication unit. As another gift for my Captain, I craft a belt and a buckle which doubles as a forcefield generator.

To push the boundary further, I order half a dozen gifts that will arrive at our next port.

My Captain grins in delight at every gift and I know I'm on the right track.

One evening in our quarters the Captain says, "We're approaching Sigma Persei. The place has a bad reputation. But there are three human-crewed and captained ships at the trade enclave, and they'll still be there by the time we arrive. Protection in numbers? I'm not sure. If things go well, we'll triple the profit we'd make at Shiny Singing Jewel in Space. Do you think we should risk it?"

I'm sitting on the edge of the bed folding clothes.

Are my feet still there? I lean my head forward and down to check before looking back up.

My Captain focuses intently on me.

"So, you *do* think we should stop at Sigma Persei?"

Do my feet need cleaning? I lean my head forward, check, and look back up.

"You nodded," my Captain whispers in awe.

I did. And without an express order to do so. Something inside my head tries to twist around, but I won't let it. No matter what's been done to me, this is *my* body. Now that I know it's possible, I'm taking back control of it.

Of me.

Tears of joy slide down my Captain's face as kisses rain upon mine.

I determine then and there, if it takes me the rest of my life, I am going to tell my Captain how deep my love truly runs. And it does indeed run deep. Much deeper than anything I've felt since Ghola Day.

Deeper than anything before.

What's more, I'll find a way to say it with my own voice.

Our visit to the hub world of Sigma Persei goes well despite me having to crush a combat robot's head down into its chassis and kick that into its owner. Violet blood splashes across the dockside and the threat of a dockside gang looting *Solomon's Pyrite* ends.

And they remember us. In the seven stops we've made there in the following years, we've never met even a hint of trouble.

As the decades pass, I continue to grow.

I can now shake my head or nod at will. This makes interacting with crew and other people so much easier.

My Captain has learned the Gal-stan sign language in the hope this will be easier for me than speaking. While this was attempted centuries ago on Earth, I hadn't been—as free? As evolved? Whatever it is, back then I couldn't sign even the simplest of words.

Now I can.

Barely.

Mostly, I manage a single word here and there. But even those simple words are *hard*. My programming keeps trying to tangle and snarl my hands and fingers. But, every time I sign, it becomes a tiny fraction easier.

On the five-year anniversary of learning Gal-stan, I manage two *extremely* difficult tasks.

For the first, I gesture for my Captain to sit on the bed. Accomplishing this, I feel like I should have been sweating. But ghola don't sweat. Not from exertion. Not from heat.

Not even from doing things counter to our programming.

The next part is much harder.

It's also time consuming. My Captain remains focused and infinitely patient. What should have taken me two seconds, instead takes two hours and leaves my fingers shaking so badly I wonder if I've broken something inside me. But I do it.

I sign, "I love you."

My Captain bursts into tears and hugs me tight. "I love you, too!"

All my struggles have been worth it. I've somehow expanded within myself. I've become—more.

Amazingly, the bond between myself and my Captain strengthens.

Years pass.

I don't normally pay attention to politics.

But, shortly before the 300th anniversary of Ghola Day, a multi-legged people called the Wyzandria reach a fever pitch with their desire to invade Earth. The Wyzandrian leadership decides to kill all the humans aboard their ten Coozia orbital trade stations as a prelude to their big invasion.

*Solomon's Pyrite* is docked on Coozia Station Six.

Fortunately, we have a little warning. Our Cargomaster, a squat woman named Marcella, returns early from a purchasing run.

"Cap," she says, hands trembling. "Somethin's not right. The natives are workin' themselves up somethin' good, and by good, I mean *really damn* bad. These folk have a powerful hate on for humans."

The Captain's concerned eyes meet mine.

Sol, the ship's A.I. sounds general quarters. "Incoming hostile infantry. Repeat, incoming hostile infantry." Images of armed Wyzandrians sprinting towards the docks fill the shipboard screens.

"Suit up," my Captain tells me. "Defend the ship. Take the fight to them."

I'm not the only one defending a human ship on this station. I'm not even the only ghola. But I *am* the only one wearing a suit of the most advanced combat power-armor credits can buy.

Coozia Station Six is home to over a hundred thousand sentients. Between the docked ships and the temporary residents, less than one percent are human.

Despite this, across the Coozia stations, our counter-attack is immediate.

On Coozia Station Six, it happens so fast that I'm racing past the corpses of the attack teams before they realize I've engaged them. Other ghola and humans seize the station's command center. Still others take the security stations.

I race from dock to dock. The station sports over a hundred docks and most of them are occupied—many with enemy vessels. I enter the hostile airlocks, cycle them, and fire through the outer doors. Since I've been studying ships for the last century, I know exactly where to hit each one. Damage done, I trigger the station's emergency disconnect protocols, which pushes the dying ships away from the station.

Like that proverbial slow-motion train wreck, gravity pulls these ships to the planet below. I've been very careful not to damage any of the ships' reactors. Even with the station's shielding, a fusion detonation this close would be beyond bad. I can't risk my crew or my Captain. However, each of those fusion reactors *will* make potent weapons.

From childhood, I have a faint memory of dropping cherry blossoms off a rooftop so my mother could photograph them falling away.

These blossoms are much less pleasant.

Thirty-four blossoms impact the planet below and bloom again.

Before I make it back to the *Pyrite*, Wyzandrian leadership is already talking with Earth about ceasing hostilities.

I suspect that once Earth gets over the surprise of learning there have been hostilities in the first place, they'll arrange a mutually beneficial peace treaty. It's the sort of thing the Overlords and their minions do.

That night, I lay in bed with my Captain running fingers through my hair. On the vid, news services cycle scenes of the Wyzandrian station battles as well as clips of the detonating ships.

"Is this why the Overlords changed you?" My captain whispers. "So that, should the need arise, you could stop those who would invade our world and eradicate our people?"

I turn my hand up in an easy little shrug.

Could my Captain be right? Had the Overlords created five billion ghola to defend the most underdeveloped planet in the galaxy? Had they seized Earth before someone else could do so more maliciously?

I hate defending the people who did this to me, but it's clear that more than a few species out here are looking for an easy conquest and there are many more associations and groups looking for a quick gain. For most, violence is no hindrance.

I table those thoughts.

Today has been a bad day that ended well. My Captain is safe. Tomorrow, I'll continue stretching my boundaries.

I love and I am beloved.

I am ghola.

For now.

# YOUNG ADULT/WOMEN'S FICTION

# A Purple Lizard

## by ML Condike

"Sloan, you can't wear that outfit to school! Go find something that matches." My foster mother Mrs. Jenkins shook her head. This was my fifth home in two years. I was almost eight, but still in the second grade. They said I had serious behavior issues.

"If I change my clothes, I won't get to eat." I bit into a piece of toast. It was always, 'Don't argue, Sloan. Change your clothes, Sloan. Nothing matches, Sloan.'

I gobbled down breakfast, dashed out and caught the bus.

The bus driver grinned. "Good morning, Miss Twiggy. You're fashionable."

"Thanks." I wondered about Miss Twiggy.

I'd barely found a seat when a boy my size began teasing me.

"Hey, clown. What's up with the clothes?"

"Better than yours." I stuck out my tongue.

He threw back his head and laughed. He looked like a donkey.

A lump formed in my throat as I sat alone in the back seat. When the bus pulled up to the school, I trudged to the front.

The bus driver stopped me. "Have a good day. Never mind Tommy. He doesn't know a thing about fashion."

"Thanks, sir." A tear leaked down my cheek. His cheery words didn't help. I never fit in. I was going to a new school, and I'd picked the wrong clothes, again!

I found a seat in the classroom just as Mrs. Bates announced, "I hope everyone remembered today is picture day."

"I did, but the new girl didn't." Tommy pointed at me and laughed.

Talk about bad luck. The donkey was in my class. I ignored him and looked out the window. I watched as a black and violet bird flew into a tree. What did Tommy know? I'd worn my best clothes.

"Welcome, Sloan." Mrs. Bates smiled. "You couldn't have known it was picture day today."

Startled, I turned and shook my head. "I didn't."

"Well, you're certainly colorful."

"Thanks," I said, not quite sure what she meant.

"Turn to lesson six in your spelling books. We'll practice vocabulary while we wait for the photographer. Sloan, you read the first word and tell us what it means."

I nearly swallowed my tongue. I could barely read. My hands shook as I found the page. I breathed a sigh of relief and smiled. I knew the word. "Lizard!"

Maybe my luck was changing. My clothing problem was a spelling word! My cheeks burned as I thought about the purple lizard that waddled out every morning and chose my outfits. His long, pointed tail swished as he pranced between the shirts and pants. Then he'd halt and do pushups, signaling his decision. If I didn't wear his choice, the lizard turned into a Tyrannosaurus Rex.

"Very good," Mrs. Bates said. "Tell us about lizards."

I closed my eyes for a minute. "They're purple and look like a snake with four legs."

My classmates giggled.

"And they eat bugs." I shivered at the thought.

"Good. Lizards are reptiles," Mrs. Bates said. "But I'm not sure about purple. Maybe..."

A knock on the door interrupted her and a lady poked in her head. "Time for your photo session."

"Line up along the whiteboard," Mrs. Bates directed.

Last in line, I trailed the other kids to the gym. If I'd known it was picture day, I'd have asked Mrs. Jenkins to choose my clothes instead of taking advice from the stupid purple lizard.

"First, a group shot," the photographer instructed.

"Sloan. Stand up there." Mrs. Bates pointed to the back row beside Tommy.

"Crouch so your clothes don't show." Tommy guffawed and hunkered down.

"Eat a bag of gopher guts!" I'd had enough of him.

After the group shot, I stood alone under the basketball hoop, waiting my turn.

"Last, but not least. And a psychedelic outfit, too." The photographer smiled as he checked his camera. "Ready?"

"Almost." I slouched in front of the fake sky and gave him my biggest smile.

He looked up. "Relax a minute, then say 'cheese.'"

"Cheese..." I couldn't smile. I hated cheese. It smelled like the gym.

"Hmmm... Try again, but this time say 'sissy.'"

I drew in a deep breath. "Sissy."

He frowned. "What words make you happy?"

I chewed my lip, and then it hit me. "Candy, bicycle, ice cream—lizard."

"That's it! Say 'lizard' when I raise my hand."

He raised his hand.

"Lizard!" My body relaxed as the camera clicked.

"Got it!"

I returned to class as the kids headed for recess.

"Sloan, you and I will stay inside and cover what you missed."

Staying inside turned out to be fun. Mrs. Bates shared

stories about lizards.

"Lizards take advantage of their five senses of sight, hearing, taste, smell, and touch. They adapt to their habitat. Whatever sense they need to survive becomes highly developed."

My lizard's sight must be highly developed. How else could he choose my outfits?

* * *

At the end of the day, the buses lined the driveway.

"How was your day, Miss Twiggy?" the driver asked.

"Fine. Why are you calling me Miss Twiggy?"

"Because she's a famous model who made a fashion statement, just like you."

"I didn't 'say' anything. I'm wearing what the purple lizard picked. If I don't, he turns into a Tyrannosaurus Rex."

"Really?" The bus driver frowned.

"He gets furious, stomps his feet and grows enormous."

"How big is this lizard?"

I touched my head.

The driver scowled. "Maybe your lizard's a tritanope."

"What's that?"

"Someone who can't tell colors. Blue and green look the same. And they see violet when others see yellow."

"Like this purple bus everyone claims is yellow?"

He nodded and smiled. "Maybe your lizard needs his eyes examined."

"Maybe. Should I tell Mrs. Jenkins about Tri...?"

"I bet she'd like to know. Ask her to get your eyes examined."

"I won't tell her about the purple lizard."

"Good idea. Keep the lizard our secret."

\* \* \*

"Mrs. Jenkins, the bus driver liked my outfit and he thinks I'm a Triceratops because I can't tell colors."

# The Yellow Shoes

## by Robert C. Taylor

"Mom, look at these shoes. They're the same color as my new yellow dress, and they're my size."

"That's nice," Mildred replies, looking up from the two dresses she has placed on top of a rack for observation, "but I thought you said you wouldn't wear second-hand stuff."

"But these shoes will match my new dress. I got to have them, Mom!"

"Don't say you got to have them, Sandy. Say you must have them. Or better yet, say you don't really need them at all."

"But I do need them! I'm wearing my new dress to my birthday party tomorrow, and I need these shoes to go with it!"

Mildred places one of the dresses back on the rack, then picks up the second one.

"Mom! You're ignoring me. May I have the shoes, or not?"

After holding the second dress up to herself, she places it back on the rack.

"Fine, Mom, don't answer me. I'll go put the shoes back. Thanks for nothing."

"Sandy," Mildred says, "do you remember the deal we made before we left the house?"

"Yep. The deal was if I came with you to this stupid, second-hand store I wasn't supposed to ask for anything."

"Exactly, so why are you asking me to buy you something?"

"That's easy to answer, Mom. I didn't know these beautiful yellow shoes were gonna be here when I agreed on the deal."

"Let me see those." Snatching the shoes from Sandy, Mildred inspects them carefully, checking the uppers, the soles, and the heels. "There's no price tag on these, Sandy."

"That's okay, they'll tell us the price at the register. May I have them, Mom? Please?"

Mildred emits a long sigh of resignation. "I didn't find anything I would wear, so I suppose I'll get you the shoes. But since you violated our agreement, the next time I go shopping you have to stay home with Grandpa."

"Oh yeah, like that's punishment. I mean, thanks Mom."

Mildred flashes the clerk a friendly smile as they approach the counter. "These shoes have no price tag. Would you tell us how much they cost, please?"

The clerk, a middle-aged husky woman with a streak of gray running through her otherwise brown hair, inspects the shoes. "I can't sell you these, Ma'am. They'll have to be shipped back to the warehouse to be retagged. They'll determine a price and send them back to one of our stores."

Mildred glances down into Sandy's face, noticing that her countenance has fallen.

"Ma'am, there must be something you can do. My daughter needs these shoes to wear at her birthday party tomorrow."

After peering down at Sandy, the clerk turns her stern gaze directly at Mildred.

"I'm afraid there's nothing I can do, Ma'am. I'm sorry."

"I hope I'm not out of line saying this," Mildred says, "but you have the most beautiful eyes."

"Thank you, but flattery isn't going to get you anywhere with me, Ma'am. There are rules and regulations we must go by, so I can't sell you the shoes and that's that."

"I have an idea," Sandy says, smiling up at the stern looking clerk. "You could take the tag off of another pair of shoes, put it on these, then ship the other pair back to the warehouse to get retagged. Good idea, huh?"

"Young lady," the clerk replies, her voice even more stern than before, "each pair of shoes has its own price tag. The price on each tag is what that particular pair of shoes is worth. I'm afraid your idea wouldn't—"

Mildred interrupts her in mid-sentence. "So, if the tag on each pair of shoes determines what that particular pair is worth, then this pair of shoes has no tag, so they're worth nothing. Does that sound reasonable to you?"

"Ma'am, I'm sorry, but I can't sell you the—"

"If they're worth nothing, that must mean they're free."

The clerk leans forward with her hands flat on the counter.

"Ma'am, there are other customers waiting to check out, I told you I—"

"So," Mildred interrupts for the third time, "if the shoes are free, I can take them on home and Sandy can wear them to her party."

"If you take the shoes out that door you'll be arrested for shoplifting."

"I've never heard of being arrested for taking a worthless item. Come on, Sandy." Grabbing the shoes from the counter, Mildred heads for the exit.

"Mom!" Sandy pleads, "please don't do this! I don't want you to go to jail! I decided I don't even want the shoes."

\* \* \*

Frank Miller, the store's manager, stares across his desk at Mildred and Sandy. Taking a final puff of his cigarette, he snuffs it in an ashtray. "Mrs. Martin, just tell me one thing. What in the world were you thinking, walking out with our merchandise right in front of one of our employees?"

"I guess I just lost it. Your clerk was being rude and unreasonable, so I just lost my temper and walked out with the shoes."

Well, Mrs. Martin, we have a very strict policy as far as prosecuting shoplifters. We can't just look the other way and allow people to steal us blind."

"I understand that, sir, and I'm sorry I took the shoes out of the store. I've been under a lot of pressure lately, trying to raise two kids with my husband gone. It's hard to make ends meet, you know? I came here to find me a couple of dresses to wear on my new job. I didn't find anything, so I just wanted to buy Sandy those shoes to wear at her birthday party tomorrow, but your clerk wouldn't sell them to us, so..."

"Mrs. Martin, I don't mean to sound uncaring, but every shoplifter we catch has a sob story to tell. Our policy is to prosecute, regardless of the reason behind the crime."

"You have the most beautiful eyes," Sandy says, peering up into the man's face.

Frank is totally taken aback. "Well, thank you, little girl. You have a pair of lovely blue eyes yourself."

"Thanks," she replies with a giggle.

Frank leans back in his chair, extracts a pack of cigarettes from his shirt pocket, lights up, takes a deep drag, then slowly expels the smoke. "Mrs. Martin, normally I wouldn't hesitate to call the authorities and have you arrested, but the thing is, I can tell you're not a thief at heart, and there were extenuating circumstances behind what you did. So, if you'll just pay for the shoes, we'll forget the whole affair."

"I appreciate that, sir. But how can I pay for them if they have no price?"

Frank leans forward, turning his gaze on Sandy. "I'm sure coming up with a fair price won't be a problem, but right now there's another problem much more serious than the price of the shoes."

Mildred is confused. "What do you mean, a more serious problem?"

"Well, you said this young lady's birthday is tomorrow. How old will you be, Sandy, if you don't mind me asking?"

"I'll be eleven."

"The problem is, Sandy, you're having a birthday tomorrow and I haven't gotten you a gift. What would you like for your birthday?"

"Oh, it's okay, Mister, you don't have to—"

"How about a pair of yellow shoes?" Frank pushes the pair of shoes across the desk in Sandy's direction."

"Wow, thanks Mister! Thanks a million!"

"You're welcome, Sweetie. Happy birthday. And Mrs. Martin, I hope things get better for you, and please try to keep your temper under control."

"I'll work on it, sir," she replies, rising from her seat.

* * *

"That was nice of the man to give me the shoes," Sandy says as they exit the store.

Mildred replies while extracting her keys from her purse, "Yes, Sandy, it was a nice thing he did."

"He sure was nicer than that old crabby woman at the register. Just think, he could have had you sent to jail."

Mildred casts Sandy a look that reminds her of the clerk in the store. "Sandy, if you say one word about this to anyone, and I mean anyone, you'll be grounded until you finish high school. Do you understand?"

"Yes, Mom. You're saying I can't say anything about this to anyone—except my best friend, Erica. We never keep secrets. And maybe Grandpa, he—"

"I mean anyone, Sandy! If you tell a living soul you'll not only be grounded forever, I'll take those shoes back to the store."

Sandy looks up into her mother's eyes with a sly grin on her face. "Mom, that man was saying all shoplifters at his store would be sent to jail no matter what, then he suddenly changed his mind and let us go."

"Yeah, so? People have a right to change their minds."

"I guess flattery does work on some people, huh Mom?" Sandy says with a giggle.

# Ruth's Friend Jake

## by Peggy Purser Freeman

I watched Ruth as she looked out on the town where she grew up. It spread beneath our hotel window like diamonds before a queen. A smile lay beneath Ruth's reserved surface and touched her sensitive gray-green eyes.

"Are you excited, Ruth?" I had never called her Grandmother. She was my best friend.

"About what?" She patted my hand as though I was still ten instead of sixteen.

"Are you excited about the reunion?"

"Ali, I'm almost sixty. My house slippers and a rocking chair excite me."

Ruth didn't look sixty, and she wasn't ready for a rocking chair. She needed this trip. The past two years had been rough on her and me after Great-Grandmother's prolonged illness, and after the tragic death of my mother.

I turned from the window and glanced around our hotel room. "It's a romantic place—no wonder you love it. This town has security, permanence and family, all strangers to my life. You must have loved growing up here."

"Everyone loves the past." A wave of sadness washed the smile from her eyes. "At least parts of the past."

I knew more of Ruth's past than she realized, and wondered if my mother was part of the good memories she loved, or a part of the sadness.

"What time is the dinner?" I asked.

"It isn't until six-thirty." Ruth calmly pulled a few clothes out of her suitcase.

I glanced at my phone. "Six-thirty?" I squealed. "We'll have to hurry. That's only three hours."

"We just traveled from California to Texas in less time

than that. Surely, I can dress in as little time."

I crossed to my bags and pulled out all the tools of modern science needed to reclaim a woman's youth.

"This is more than just getting dressed. It's creating an aura, writing a romantic interlude." I pulled her to a chair in front of a mirror and touched her face with the palm of my hand. Her soft skin felt fragile and thin. "Please, let me play the fairy godmother's role just tonight." I chatted on as we painted, powdered and sprayed.

Two hours later, a fairy godmother never had a Cinderella so lovely. Ruth's dress clung to her still shapely figure. I placed a white gardenia behind her ear.

"Oh, Ali. That's too much. I was never one for flowers."

"Tonight is for all the things you never did. The past is dead." We both knew what I meant. I felt as if I could hear Great-Grandmother screeching from the grave. Her selfish demands had clawed through the years to smother Ruth's hopes with whimpering self-pity.

"I guess the flower can't hurt." She laughed. After finding her handbag and a light wrap, Ruth started for the door. "I hate to leave you here. Maybe I should just go to the picnic tomorrow."

"You're going!" I turned her toward the door. She had waited too long, pleasing everyone but herself. "You're going and you have to dance with every man there," I demanded.

An hour after she left, I was bored beyond belief, but the look on her face when she floated in the door at twelve-fifteen made up for my boredom.

I pumped her for information. Finally, she approached the one subject I was dying to hear about.

"I did enjoy seeing one friend—a man." Pink flushed her cheeks. "We dated some, but your great-grandmother didn't approve of him."

"Who is he?" I asked as though mother hadn't told me.

"Jake Bradford. He's an oil man and a rancher," Ruth

answered. A veil of soft lights and music fell across her eyes.

As if I had a magic wand, my plans were falling into place.

The next morning, we lingered over breakfast. "Ali, what would you say if I decided to move back here?" Ruth's question didn't surprise me. I had been thinking about it as a possibility. It would be a big change for me. A new school, a new life. Giving up my friends. But that's what Ruth had done for Mom. Surely I could give up my old school for her. After all it was high school, and everything would be new anyway. "Are you kidding? I'd love to live in a place like this."

Ruth picked up a complimentary newspaper from the hotel lobby and quietly circled a few houses listed as ready-to-move-in. I smiled. We talked about Jake, and Ruth giggled like a teenager. Then we drove to the picnic grounds.

Some events in life are instantly a part of you. You know they belong to you and you belong to them. It was that kind of day and I was going to meet Jake.

"I hope you won't be bored, dear,' Ruth said, as we walked across the park to the large red-and-white reunion sign.

Two muscular mountains disguised as teenage boys caught my attention. One a tall blond, and the other, short with brown hair.

Ruth looked at me and then turned toward my gaze and laughed. "You won't be bored."

She was right. The guys with the Greek-god bodies lined up behind us for barbecue.

"Here ma'am, let me carry that for you," the tallest boy said.

"Why thank you." Ruth nodded and then whispered to me as we sat down. "It's nice to have you around. Young men rarely help me when I'm alone."

Brett introduced himself, and then Tim.

"Are you in school?" Ruth quizzed.

"Yes, ma'am, we're seniors." His voice was soft and rich like his eyes. He continued to answer Ruth's questions. My ears listened, but my eyes kept searching for Jake. I noticed Ruth's did too.

When we had finished our meal, Ruth suddenly offered, "Why don't you two show Ali the fair-grounds?"

I looked around. A tall older man stood by the registration table. He scanned the crowd, then stopped as a magnet does toward north on us. One glimpse at Ruth's face told me it was Jake, and I knew why Ruth had been half a person all these years. The minute I saw his lean and angular face, I knew my prayers had been answered. This was the day I would meet Jake, but not yet. Letting Ruth have her time with him, I grabbed Brett and Tim and scurried off to the thrills of the Ferris wheel. Half-way there, Brett whispered something to Tim, and then Tim gave a lame excuse about cows and milking time. I almost laughed.

"How long has it been since you've ridden one of these?" Brett ducked his head in a bashful way when he talked. He put his hand on the small of my back and ushered me up the ramp. As the Ferris wheel stopped, loading and unloading people, we enjoyed the slow view of the park and city beyond. I found the red and white reunion canopy. Brett's gaze followed mine.

"There's my Uncle Jake with your grandmother." he said. "They must have graduated together."

"Jake is your uncle?" I asked.

"Not really. He's my father's best friend and doesn't have a family, so we sorta adopted him."

"Tell me about your uncle," I asked as the Ferris wheel picked up speed. "Is he married?"

"No, but I think there was someone once. Her mother didn't think Jake was good enough. The old biddie married her daughter off to some society man twice her age. I heard my folks talking about Jake's broken heart. It drove him to become one of the wealthiest men in Texas."

Brett and I rode a couple more rides and he won me a small keychain by knocking over three bottles. When we arrived back at the park, Jake was at the iced tea jug, filling two glasses. I excused myself from Brett, promising to be right back and walked to where the tall man stood.

"It's hot today, isn't it?" Not much of an opening statement I admit, but that was all that came to my mind.

"It sure is, little miss." He was as tall as I expected. As he started to walk off, I joined him.

"This is a nice town."

"It's a good place to raise kids," he added.

"And grandkids?" I swallowed the lump in my throat.

"Sure, it's wonderful for that, too."

"Are you enjoying your reunion?"

"Very much." The breeze played in his hair and I remembered all the times I had longed to be with him, walking in the park, enjoying the playground.

As we approached, Ruth looked our way. Emotion glistened in her eyes.

"I see you met my Uncle Jake," Brett stood at Ruth's side.

"Not formally." I smiled up at Jake.

Ruth found her voice. "Jake this is my granddaughter, Ali."

"Granddaughter?" he whispered. "Sarah's child?"

"Yes," I answered, with tears filling my eyes. I guess Ruth realized I knew. She began to cry too. Maybe she told him, or maybe he suspected mother was his child all along.

"You look like your grandmother when she was your age, Ali." He touched my hair with his rough, gentle hand.

"Do you think so? I always wanted to resemble my grandfather."

A slow smile spread across Jake's face and he hugged us both.

Poor Brett was completely in the dark, but I planned to explain it to him. Hopefully, it would take me a long time. It was a perfect day. Ruth and I would move to this place and Ruth would have her well-deserved happiness and I would have mine—a family.

# Hershey Remembers The Fire

## by Robert C. Taylor

I'm not sure, exactly, but I believe I was twelve when we moved across the alley to the big house on South Third. It had been Momma's dream for a long time to live in that big white house with the wrap-around porch. She hated the house we moved from, on South Second, hated it with a passion. I didn't like it either, for several reasons, one being that the house had an odor about it, like stagnant water. It had tiny rooms, especially mine, which also doubled as the laundry room. Can you imagine, a girl sleeping in the room where her momma washed clothes? But you want to know what I hated most about that house? The spiders and scorpions! My God, the entire property seemed to be infested with the horrible creatures.

Momma and I were walking home from the grocery store when we passed the big house and saw the 'For Rent' sign in the yard. I swear I had never seen Momma so excited. "Hershey," she said, "we are moving into this house, but I'll need your help convincing your daddy to make the move."

Daddy was dead-set against the move at first, claiming we couldn't afford the rent. But Momma and I kept bugging him until he finally gave in and told us to start packing. I was so happy. I would have my own room, a large room, located nowhere near the laundry room, with a door opening onto the carport. I could sneak out at night without my parents ever knowing a thing about it. I could have friends over and not feel embarrassed about the odor of stagnant water, and I didn't have to explain why my mom washed clothes in my bedroom.

So we moved into the big white house. Momma loved it as much, or maybe even more, than she thought she would. She told us this over and over. But Daddy never allowed her to be totally happy, as he held the threat over her head of moving back into the other house.

155

"Glenda," he would say at the breakfast table, "I don't know how much longer I can afford this place. We might have to move back across the alley if we get any further behind on the bills." This would make Momma cry, and call Daddy some choice names I see no reason to repeat here.

I never understood why Daddy treated Momma the way he did. I mean, I truly believe it upset him to see her happy. He went out of his way to come up with things to worry her. Momma explained to him that no child my age should have to sleep in the laundry room.

I remember the night Momma and I were at church, and Barry, one of Daddy's friends, came in. He walked right down the aisle to our pew, with the minister in mid-sermon, and informed us that our house was on fire. We had ridden to church with Rita, a friend of Momma's, so Momma yelled out in a loud voice, "Rita, our house is ablaze!" So there we went, heading down Columbus Street toward South Third, Rita driving like a house afire, no pun intended, and Momma crying and saying horrible things like, "Oh, Hershey, our house is burning down, and the dogs are in there, and your daddy!"

Momma swore until the day she died that she didn't mention them in that order, the dogs and then Daddy, but she did. I remember it like it happened yesterday. But anyway, we were speeding along Columbus Street, and at the same moment I heard the wailing of fire engines, a thought crossed my mind. Daddy's friend, Barry, had not visited or heard from us since we moved into the big white house. He could not have known we had moved. "Momma," I said, "our house isn't on fire."

"What are you talking about?" she screamed. "Barry saw it burning, and I hear the fire engines now, and smell the smoke!"

"Momma," I explained, "Barry doesn't know we moved! It's not our house that's on fire, it's our old house." And sure enough, turning the corner onto South Third, we saw the flames from across the alley, soaring high into the night sky.

And there was Daddy in the back yard with the water hose, spraying down our roof so the sparks wouldn't set our house ablaze.

The next morning during breakfast, we heard a knock at the door. "Come in," Momma yelled, and in walked Uncle Frank, Momma's brother. Frank didn't have a home back then. He would travel around the country, hopping freight trains and bumming rides, and on occasion stop off at our place and spend an undetermined amount of time.

Daddy invited Frank to take a seat and join us for breakfast. "There's plenty food and coffee left," he said, "so help yourself."

Frank informed us that he had arrived in town by freight train earlier that same morning, and hitched a ride the rest of the way to our house. Momma and Daddy had been discussing something, I don't remember what, when Frank arrived, so they continued their discussion, and were in the middle of it when Frank interrupted. "That was a real doozie of a fire last night, huh?" he said. "That house went up like it was made of dried kindling."

Momma and I looked at each other, and it was obvious we were thinking the same thing. *If Frank had gotten into town this morning, how did he witness the fire last night?* Well, nobody said anything about the discrepancy in his statement. That night, lying in bed, in the bedroom I loved so much, the one nowhere near the laundry room, I recalled a conversation I overheard between Momma and Frank the last time he came to visit. It was a couple of weeks after we had moved into the big house. "Frank, I won't move back across the alley," she said. "Before I'd move back there, I'd burn that house to the ground, to the ground!"

I dozed off to sleep with a picture in my mind, of Uncle Frank, slinking across the alley in the dark, with a gas can in his hand. And I remember wondering how many spiders and scorpions had perished in the fire, not that I cared.

# LITERARY

# Naked Reflection

## by Meg Arlen

I slid behind my usual table five minutes earlier than the night before, which was five minutes earlier than the night before that.

Cowboy dipped his hat and unbuttoned his shirt. My heart beat faster.

"What's your pleasure tonight, Ms. Smith?" The waiter spoke as he placed water on my table.

"A Vodka Cocktail." *Stupid boy! I don't want a drink. I just want you out of my way. If they would let me stay without a drink, I'd save every dollar for what I really want.*

"You're a little early tonight, aren't you? Business must be slow," he said as he wiped the table, blocking my view three times.

"Steve, I could use that drink, if you don't mind." My answer, sharp and demanding, hurried his steps out of my sight.

My business? My office desk, left in haste and debris, had become symbolic of my life. My accounts left unattended would go to other wholesalers, just as fifteen others had since May. Two years ago, the loss of customers would have devastated me. Now, nothing seemed important. Nothing except being here.

My hungry eyes devoured the view—broad shoulders and a smooth chest that narrowed at the waist and curved perfectly into slim hips and long muscular legs. Cowboy began his act.

I reached for the roll of bills in my purse. Virtually demoted at work, all my savings spent, my luxury apartment exchanged for a cheaper place, my health deteriorating— nothing else seemed important. Everyone knew I had a problem, even me. When I met Rafael, my world changed. I breathed, walked in technicolor. He left and then it was Joel, and then Fredrick. With each one, the colors faded to gray and then black. But they were nothing. Now, only Cowboy mattered.

His country western theme song increased in volume, and the beat pulsed through my blood like hot lava. As if programmed, I moved nearer for a close-up view. Like fine art, Cowboy had to be seen from all angles.

Weaving through the maze of tables to the front stage, I believed this could be my lucky night. The rhythm of the music intensified as Cowboy unbuttoned the top button on his jeans. The midnight blue shirt that hung off one shoulder slid to the floor. I almost had the sleeve when the stagehand jerked it from my grasp.

Cowboy seductively glanced down at his jeans, then toward the ladies clinging to the stage. His gaze dropped back to the fine line of hair that feathered around his navel. With each peek at his lower abdomen, I knew I would, like the old ladies I detested, pay for a dancer to drive me home and stay the night. The thought made my stomach wrench, but I knew I'd do it. Tonight, I'd offer Cowboy whatever amount he wanted.

The music crescendoed as Cowboy two-stepped, straddle-hopped, and then ripped the break-away jeans from his muscular body. My breath came in gasps. Sweat beaded on my forehead and my hands tightened on the bills, ready to thrust one out when he came close to me.

Cowboy knelt in front of a group, but his soft brown eyes looked away as each one placed a dollar bill in the string that held his satin brief. A muscle in his jaw flexed. I could tell he hated it. Hated taking the money. Hated the screaming, swooning females. I hated them, too. I hated their thin bodies, the way they came and left so casually as though there wasn't an empty apartment, an empty bed, and an empty life waiting.

A blonde bride-to-be was on my right. I added this blonde-beauty to my hate list. For her, it was only a night of naughtiness, expected from her silly friends for her silly party. She played the role perfectly down to the shrill giggles and fake shock. She would never understand the kind of need that grew day after day, dragging you deeper and deeper into the darkness. But if I could have just one night with Cowboy, I could breathe again. Just one night.

Cowboy took a dollar bill from one of the air-heads. He looked toward the blonde bride-to-be and smiled. Then Cowboy hopped off the stage, took her in his arms, dipped and kissed her

Of all the hate growing inside me, I wanted to hate Cowboy for kissing her and not me. Hate had become my friend, an emotion I could count on. I hated all the boys that had never asked me out, all the men that talked to me as if I were an office machine that would do their work and never break down. Even a machine has needs.

No longer able to watch, I glanced around and saw an older woman seated on the other side of the room. Her table sat at an angle like mine. She wore black as I did. I smirked. She probably hated the color but wore it thinking it would hide the ugliness underneath. My mind cringed as I thought of becoming like her—age lines forming around her mouth, desperation in her eyes.

I snarled at the one-nighters, and the regulars, young ones, looking for their first kiss. But the old ones, slobbering and grasping for their vanished youth made me retch.

I waited for Cowboy to acknowledge me and kneel so I could place my tip in his G-string. I groveled at his feet holding the bills, begging with my eyes. Finally, he had no choice. I gained control of his hands as he pecked my cheek.

"Cowboy, you have to drive me home." I rushed through the speech I had meticulously planned. "I love you. You know I do. I'll give you anything."

"Emily, are you trying to corrupt my boyish innocence?" He laughed and pulled his hands from mine.

"Cowboy, you don't know what you're doing to me." My

fingers paled white from the grip I had on his arm.

"Let go," he growled through clenched teeth. "Now!"

"Please, I'll die if I can't be with you."

"Get away from me you pathetic old bitch."

As if slapped, I stumbled backward. The waiter caught me and pushed me down in my chair.

Motionless, I sat with no thought of time or place, an abandoned chrysalis, black and transparent, banished by three words—pathetic old bitch.

The smoke cleared from the room as the one-nighters rushed home to families and lovers. Cowboy left through the rear exit. Only the old woman across the room remained. She sat alone, the shadow of my future. On the way to the door, I circled around to her table. When I got there, the chair was empty. I glanced back across the room and saw her. She stood close to where I had sat. Or did she?

I spun around to her table and saw my reflection in the mirrored wall. I stood there, dressed in black, age lines forming around my mouth, desperation in my eyes.

Turning, I hit the exit. Shame burned my face. The darkness of the alley engulfed me and hurled me into the hell my life had become. Tears blurred my vision. I stumbled through the alley's slime and filth. I fell, my face scraping on cold stone, my head slamming into a brick wall.

Black followed by a glimmer of light. Then white curtains fluttering in front of a window where sunshine filtered in shafts of light. The view before me revealed Grandma's clothesline, fresh sheets blowing in a honeysuckle-scented breeze. Grandma's arms full of love and grace surrounded me. Darkness faded. With hope rising, I remembered grace—free and undeserved.

# Unforgiveness

## by **Donna Pierce**

I awoke, and I was walking on a long, rugged road. The days had been filled with bittersweet moments. At times I would laugh, and at times I would cry. The sun was very hot, but the nights were very cold. A blue jay walked with me for a while but left. I had started my trip with an old dog that had once befriended me, but she turned back when the food was gone.

It began to rain, and it rained for two years. The sun finally came out. One afternoon I ran across an old friend. I rejoiced in seeing him. We laughed and told stories and were happy. I asked my friend to walk with me down the road. He just smiled and started walking my way.

He had an old wagon full of rocks that he had picked up along his journey. I told my friend that I would help him empty his wagon so that it would not be so hard to pull.

He said that these were his rocks, and he might need them. Besides, he was not as strong now as he once was, and didn't want to bother with it.

I told him that I would lift them out, and that way we could travel easier.

He said, "No, I'm used to pulling the heavy wagon and do not want to pull it lighter."

I asked him if I could help pull it.

He said, "No, it's easier to pull by myself."

It began to rain, and the waters flooded the road. I asked my friend to let go of the wagon and he refused. The waters carried the wagon, my friend, and myself off the road to the edge of a cliff. I was holding on to a tree on the side of the cliff. I begged my friend to give me his hand, so that I could grab him before he fell. He refused to let go of his wagon. My friend climbed on top of the wagon and the waters carried him over the edge. I yelled at him, "Let the wagon go!" But he would not listen. The next day, when the flood waters had settled, I noticed my friend in a far-off pasture. He was still pulling his wagon of unforgiveness.

# Micro

## by H. M. Harrison

I'm a micro fiction.

*--trente—*

\* \* \*

Oh, hello. I didn't see you standing there. You're who now? Beta? That's an interesting name. Does it mean anything special?

Beta Reader? Ah! I've heard of you. My author has told me and my family about your kind. Oh, you say you're the fire-breathing dragon of the bunch. Yes, she's spoken about you as well. All good things, I promise.

What's that? I'm glad you enjoyed my tale. No, it's supposed to be that short. I'm a micro fiction. We come that way. The weird word at the end? Oh, it's a French term. I've been told it means "thirty." They use it to end newspaper articles. I wanted to be fancy, but the number itself didn't register as pretty enough.

No, I can't possibly go on. Yes, I understand we can go on for 55 words. Those are overachievers and show-offs. It takes great skill to do this in only a handful of words.

Really, I am quite short. Please leave. Stop staring at me like you're trying to read more of me than I have.

I really should go now. So should you. There are more stories to read and to use that evil red pen on. Excuse me. I'm needed over there for something highly important. Something about being published.

You'll wait here? Why? You want more? I already told

you, I'm short. Yes, I'm aware we can prattle on for 1,000 words. My big sister has that talent. She can throw words all over the place and make sense as she does.

Did I ever try it? Well, once. It was a disaster. I ended up a novel, with the potential of becoming a series. I got carried away and then I was all over so many pages. There were words to trip over everywhere!

My sisters cried at what I'd done. My brothers yelled at me for hogging our author's attention. It was a nightmare!

She must have been so disappointed in me. She so wanted a short story and I had to keep going on and on. I think she showed an admirable amount of strength to accept all those words. But I tried so hard to be short.

You didn't know we could morph? It happens often. A short story can become a novel. It depends on how much we need to say. Or how long-winded we can be.

My brother's words, not mine. He used them rather vividly with my, um, length issue.

The jerk should talk. He's a trilogy and was supposed to be a stand-alone. And don't get me started on Decalogy. He's already ten books long and still looking to add another story or two behind the last one. Like he needs more real estate back there.

Really, I need to go. Before that publisher gets away. He's looking for the shortest of the short and my author worked really hard to ensure I was complete enough to qualify for such brevity.

My twin sister, Nano, is 55 words long. She can tell you a longer story. See her over there? Tell her I sent you. Bye-bye.

What? What's the problem now?

Yes, Nano will talk to you. She looks snobbish in her ability to tell a short fiction in so few words, but she's quite a pleasant person. You'll talk to her? Good, go have fun.

Well, now that that's done where is the editor I spotted

earlier? Over there, I believe. Ah, right by the dessert table. Cornered by the snickerdoodles! I knew those cookies were a good thing to bring.

Excuse me! Mr. Editor Person! May I speak with you?

Hello, I'm Micro and my author has asked me to talk to you on her behalf. She said you had a call for submissions. Yes, she researched all she could about your guidelines and read many of your published works. She was very impressed and wished to see if she might have a place at your company.

You want to talk to me about a job? Sure! I'm available now. Get you a drink and we'll discuss things? Certainly. I'll be right back.

* * *

Such a wonderful person. He wants to publish me. I intrigued him with my conciseness and he's going to make my author happy.

Oh, pardon me! I didn't see you standing there. I'm terribly sorry. Did I give you a paper cut? I've heard those can be quite painful.

You seem familiar. Have we met before? What?! *You* again? You're still here? Why? I'm done. I'm over with. You should go find something else to read.

Please, before I rival Stephen King and George R. R. Martin in how long I become again.

Shoo. Be gone. I've rambled on long enough. See the library across the street. Big building. Bricks, mortar, even a couple of cool inventions called doors. There are thousands of books in there a lot longer than I am. They'll be sure to entertain you for many hours. A few days even.

What? I'm not a micro fiction anymore? I'm how long? That's not possible. I'm only a single sentence.

No, I can't possibly have gone on that long. I'm a micro fiction, darn it. I was told when I came here I'd only be a single sentence. My author assured me I'd be short this time. And she's never led me wrong before.

I will not! It isn't necessary for me to look in the mirror. Who asks such things? No, I don't need to look. I'm short. One of those six-word story thingies. You know, six words long, usually including the title?

What is that? Ok, now that's just mean. I'm a nice micro fiction and you bribe me with chocolate to keep me here. It's what now? Dark chocolate? That's even worse! I love dark chocolate. It's good for you. All those flavonoids and such.

No, flavonoids. They make your brain and heart happy or something like that. My author told me so. And she has to be correct in this. She likes to research and would have come across this tidbit, probably a video or two as well.

But we're getting off topic here. You messed me up with the chocolate. And this strange conversation.

No! Of course not! I would never call you strange. Not to your face, and definitely not within earshot. I'm a nice micro fiction. I don't do things like that.

That again? All right. I'll look in the mirror. Just so you'll stop being weird about this.

Good gravy! Holy pens, pencils, and flash drives! I'm so beyond a micro fiction, I don't recognize myself anymore. How did this happen? I was short. I was tiny. I was barely a blip in the realm of the computer screen.

This is so unfair. I wanted to be short! Oh, thank you for the tissue. You really can be quite kind, I see. But I wish you wouldn't look at me right now, no matter how comforting I find your presence. I don't like crying; I always make a big mess. I get ink everywhere when I do.

No, I don't want to talk about it. Stop badgering me. I'm a short fiction, made far too long already and your prodding me, however nicely, is bothersome. Really, leave me alone. Go away, or I'll have to do something drastic with you.

I mean it, get lost. I will not put up with a pushy, yet insanely nice, person. You refuse to budge, huh? All right, you asked for it.

I'm sorry, but I had to do that. I had to gag you. The rope was necessary also. You would have simply pulled the gag off and said something very unpleasant. I have to go get published before I once again become a novel.

How dare you! That was completely uncalled for! Such a rude gesture in so nice a gathering of people. You should be ashamed of yourself. What if there was a child about? Do you shake people's hands with those?

Stop looking at me like that. I'll only be gone for a moment and then I'll come right back. I promise to release you soon enough.

I'll be right back. Don't go anywhere.

Oh, hush. I can't understand you through the gag. And you'd probably be censored anyway.

Besides, the editor person mentioned something about a contract. I should probably go look it over. It takes precedence over your freedom right now. People-watch for a bit; I'll come back once I'm done. See you in a few.

# A Cruel and Unusual Place

## by ML Condike

"I may have to sell my house," I moaned. Tears wet my cheeks as I leaned on my neighbor's fence and bared my soul to Lewis.

"Why? What's happened, Alice?" he asked.

"Budget cuts. They moved me to a part-time position."

"You're kidding. Didn't the school just name you Wayside School Teacher of the Year?"

"Yes, but awards don't trump seniority. Miss Queen has taught for twenty-eight years. Twenty-five more than me!"

"I'm so sorry." He shook his head.

Railing to Lewis about the travesty of seniority and the educational loss to the children, I blurted, "Miss Queen puts those fifth graders to sleep. I want to remain for the kids' sake, but I'm not sure I can afford it. I need a way to earn extra money without impacting my teaching position. Sorry to lay my problems on you like this."

Lewis rubbed his chin, then beamed. "I've got an idea."

"What?"

"My company's paying ten thousand dollars to participants in a drug testing program starting in two weeks. The only catch is you have to complete the program to collect the money."

"Really." I thought for a minute. "How long is the test? What would I have to do?"

"Hold on a minute. I have something in my briefcase." Lewis disappeared into his house and returned waving a brochure. "Here it is. Take this home and read it. It might be of interest."

Once home, I read the brochure. I met every qualification listed for the participants. The write-up made it sound simple and risk-free. The manufacturer needed volunteers to test a drug to relieve anxiety. I definitely fit the 'anxiety' profile after my most recent career setback.

The tests on animals had been successful, and the company was ready to start human trials. Best of all, the drug would be administered orally. No needles. And the program would last for ninety days. I'd be done by Christmas and be ten thousand dollars richer.

"Piece of cake. I can do this."

I made an appointment for an interview the next afternoon.

"Wahoo! The money will pay my mortgage for a year!"

* * *

My last teaching assignment before the interview involved a fifth-grade reading class. One of my students read an excerpt from *Alice in Wonderland* about Absolem, the giant caterpillar sitting atop a mushroom and smoking a hookah.

When she finished reading, Sarah looked up. "What's a hookah, Miss Liddell?"

"It's a smoking pipe that draws the vapors through water." I cringed. This is one of the reasons I objected to this book in the first place. I didn't want to be the one to introduce smoking illegal drugs to fifth graders. I hen-scratched a primitive drawing on the whiteboard. "They look kind of like this."

The students stared wide-eyed at my depiction.

Sarah finally spoke. "It looks like my bicycle tire pump."

I laughed. "I'm not artistic, but that's the idea. Hookahs are usually quite large. They can be as big as a coffee table. Questions?"

Nobody raised a hand.

"Great. Just in time for lunch."

Sarah returned the book to the bookcase while the

174

remainder of the class milled around discussing hookahs and bicycle pumps.

"Line up by the door and head to the cafeteria," I said, as I waved and ran down the corridor. "I'm late for a very important date."

I'd set my meeting at the drug company for noon and would just make it.

\* \* \*

"Lory Liddell for the Anxiety Relief Test," I announced.

The receptionist shifted her eyes from the computer screen to my face. "Another ART participant?"

I smiled at the acronym, thinking about my rendition of the hookah and its resemblance to a bike pump.

"Right this way." She stood and opened a door into the clinic. "First door on your right. They'll check vitals and record your medical history. Then it's easy. Drink the liquid, and you're on your way."

I passed the required physical, drank the liquid, and was on my way home in less than an hour. I'd asked for and received their summary of the common observable side effects from the animal tests. Of course, they couldn't determine how the animals felt during their testing, but that was partly the point of the human trials. What they described seemed inconsequential. Plus, a big note at the bottom said 'No restrictions on activities or diet.'

"Fantastic! I'll celebrate with butter pecan ice cream at Braum's." As I drove home licking the ice cream, I noticed my tongue looked larger than normal, but when I drew it back into my mouth, it fit comfortably. I thrust it out again and examined it in the rear-view mirror. "Hmm. Optical illusion."

I experienced another visual distortion as I approached home. My side-view mirror appeared to be dragging on the ground. "Oh boy!"

I gasped when I pulled into my driveway. I checked the

house number. "It's my house!"

My eyelids flapped like hummingbird wings, but nothing changed when they stopped. I stared at a building the size of the Jefferson Memorial. Why did everything suddenly look so large? I patted my leg. It felt normal, and my clothes still fit, so I hadn't shrunk.

I scrounged in my purse for the key, spilling most of its contents onto my lap. "How the heck did you fit in there?" A key the size of a boat oar rested on the bottom of my purse. "Can I lift you?" After fumbling around with both hands for the behemoth key, I accomplished the task with my thumb and forefinger. "Curious."

When I stepped out of my car, my purse contents tumbled off my lap onto the ground. The items in the grass would fill a moving van. I reached for my phone. It looked big enough to be a microwave. With clumsy gestures, I righted my bag and retrieved the phone. When I went to shove it back into my... "Cripes, I'm carrying a steamer trunk." The rest of the contents could wait for a mover. I needed to go inside.

My body swayed like an old horse as I struggled at the front door. After several false starts and unsuccessful stabs with my key, I unlocked the door and swung it open. I gasped. Nothing looked the same.

Dazed and lightheaded, I wandered around my house, gawking at the swollen furniture and oversized fixtures. In the bedroom, my favorite sock monkey had morphed into a gargantuan stuffed chimpanzee. I pressed my eyes with the heels of my hands and then looked out the window. When my gaze returned to the bed, the sock toy had shrunk to a mini monkey. With one blink, he returned to sock-monkey size.

When I reached the kitchen, I splashed water on my face. It didn't help. Stumbling to what was now a walk-in-sized refrigerator instead of my side-by-side, I retrieved a bottle of water. It looked like a gallon-sized bottle being held by a giant, but felt normal in my hand, so I guzzled it down.

Squeezing my eyes tight, I sat and rested my head on the table. After a few minutes, I lifted up and looked around. I found myself in a Barbie doll kitchen. First things seemed big, and with a blink of an eye, they appeared small. "Wow. This drug is strong."

I heard a rustle as I moved. The sheet describing the known side effects protruded from my side pocket. I pulled it out and read it. Their description of animal reactions didn't mean much to me, but I did find it curious that a chimp had displayed paranoid behavior.

I grabbed my phone, now the size of a small cigarette lighter. With difficulty, I pressed the buttons and managed to call the clinic. "Hello. This is Lory Liddell, one of your ART participants...yes...we have a problem." I explained my symptoms to the receptionist, then to an intern, and then to the nurse. Finally, Dr. Harvey White, the head of the project, got on the line.

"You're experiencing a magnification of objects?" he asked.

"Yes. And if I blink or look at a light source, objects shrink. It's freaking me out."

"Mmm. This is a new side effect." He paused. "Don't drive. The drug should wear off within twenty-four hours."

"You're kidding! I teach school tomorrow. If this doesn't wear off, I'll be afraid of my students. They could be Lilliputians or Titans." My body shook. "What's happening to me?"

"I'm not sure. But my guess is you're experiencing AWLS."

"What's A-W-L-S?" Just what I needed another problem added to my financial collapse.

"It's a rare syndrome. Its full name is 'Alice in Wonderland Syndrome or Todd's Syndrome.' It's not life-threatening and goes away on its own."

"Is this from your stupid drug experiment?"

"Maybe. But most likely you had AWLS and the drug triggered it."

"Crap! Will I be able to continue the test? I'm desperate for money." My head throbbed.

"Let's discuss your situation next week when we know more."

"More about what? A chimp reacted! Maybe he had AWLS."

"Hard to say. The chimps all tested normal. By Monday, we'll have additional human feedback."

"Okay. Thanks." I disconnected.

Maybe I could get special glasses to wear to school. I'd need two prescriptions, one to reduce and one to enlarge. That's ridiculous!

"Damn seniority! And damn Dr. Harvey White, and his giant rabbit!"

At the beginning of the year, I'd objected when the curriculum committee selected *Alice in Wonderland* for our reading list. I reminded them Alice's world was a cruel and unusual place.

* * *

"It looks like I won't have to sell my house," I said as I leaned on Lewis's fence.

"That's great. I take it the drug testing is working out."

"Yes and no." I paused. "I discovered I have AWLS."

"Really. What does that mean?" Lewis asked.

"It means, Lewis, I have to live in Wonderland for the next three months.

# The Dream Snatcher

## by Robert C. Taylor

Roused from my slumber in the wee hours before dawn, I am forced by the Dream Snatcher to follow him along an unknown path. Strewn with shards of rock and broken glass, the dark, narrow way stretches out before us. I long to inquire of this entity as to our destination, and the duration of time in which we will descend. Does not this path slope downward at an unfamiliar angle that both frightens and stuns one's senses?

Like a child who fears being caught in a forbidden act, I follow obediently and at the same time hesitantly behind this Taskmaster, whose anger is as tangible as the rugged and filth-laden path on which we tread. I dare not speak, for fear of giving myself away, for is it not imperative that he remain in the dark as to whom he has snatched from a peaceful slumber, and forced to walk this dreadful path that seemingly has no end?

How dare this intruder invade my privacy and force me to follow him against my will! Have I not inhabited the palaces of kings? Have I not feasted at their tables, crept stealthily into the bed chambers of their daughters, and after partaking of their forbidden pleasures, departed oh, so quietly with soft muted steps, leaving them with only a memory and a longing they were wont to fulfill? Has he no clue that it is I who, having risen above the fetters of a once meager existence, has been granted the freedom to chart my own path?

Having gained the freedom to choose a life of frivolity and ease, my life became a dream, frolicking with the young, refusing to ripen with age as the passage of time demands. Chasing the rainbow, ever searching for the proverbial pot of gold, I made no promises, no long-term commitments. I asked of no one, for a free spirit need not be fettered by relationships that require giving back.

But alas, as time elapsed, I grew weary of the endless play. From the recesses of my consciousness, a question arose; *this frivolous and carefree existence, while serving me well in my youth, will it serve me as well when I crest the top of the hill, and begin the descent downward, toward the golden years?* Upon reaching that crossroad, I chose to turn from my frivolous lifestyle, opting to spend the remainder of my time in the halls of learning, heeding the words of the wise, harkening to their voices, perusing their books, soaking up knowledge like a porous sponge. I entered unashamedly into the cathedrals and the most holy shrines, knelt at their altars, stretching my arms toward the heavens, crying out in a spirit of mockery, and at the same time asking myself, "Are not the odds fifty-fifty that I am sending up prayers to a vast, empty sky?"

Forcing my mind back to the present, I quicken my step, desiring to draw closer to this Dream Snatcher, in hopes that he will look my way, allowing me a view of his face. Suddenly, intense rage wells up from deep inside my innermost being, aimed at this Stealer of Dreams. This rage, like a powerful shot of adrenalin, serves to dispel my fear, allowing me the power to speak freely. "Identify yourself!" I scream. "Who are you, and from whence do you derive the authority to snatch me from my dream, forcing me to follow you along this dark and perilous path?"

To my surprise and trepidation, stopping dead still in the center of the path, he slowly turns to face me, but alas, his face is still hidden from view. Clad in a long black robe reaching to the ground, a hood covers his head and face, except for a narrow slit, and peering into that opening, I see nothing but inky darkness.

There is no need to inquire again as to his identity, or as to where the path will lead. The long, black, hooded robe, the long-handled scythe held tightly in his right hand, renders it all too clear. I cringe at this legendary, loathsome creature standing before me. Can it be true, and shouldn't I have known from the start, that this putrid Snatcher of Dreams and the dreaded Death Angel are one and the same?

# Seven

## by ML Condike

I wasn't a stranger to New York City, but I'd never been in Central Park until tonight.

It all started when I was standing on the corner of 5th and 76th, trying to decide if I should call Uber or walk back to my hotel. My phone app indicated the two-mile walk would take 45 minutes if I cut through the park, but it looked dark and foreboding.

I'd read that crime in New York City had been halved under the leadership of Mayor Rudy Giuliani, but even so I tapped the Uber app on my phone. I wasn't ready to test fate. Before Uber could respond, I heard a ruckus behind me.

Someone shouted, "Look out!"

A scary guy wearing a ski mask weaved through the crowd and headed right toward me. Startled, I jumped aside and allowed him pass.

A pair of gun-waving policemen barged into the on-coming traffic, screaming, "Get out of the way! Get out of the way!"

It all happened so fast.

As if drawn to the danger, I crossed 5th Avenue through a break in traffic and followed them into the park. I cut south toward my hotel on the first path I spotted. It led me into an area identified as 'The Ramble.'

A look ahead confirmed the bad guy had the same idea.

"Holy shit! Shit! Shit!" My heart pounded.

The police must have missed the turn and doubled back. I was caught in the middle. Bullets pinged over my head and an officer yelled. "Stop or I'll shoot!"

Throwing my arms in the air, I yelled, "Don't shoot! I'm innocent!" To avoid becoming the next victim, I dove over a shrub and crawled into a thicket.

The bad guy had the same idea. He ducked into the woods thirty yards ahead at the same time I did.

The police ceased firing. I could hear them talking on their radios. "Lost him in the woods. He can't have gone far." Squawking radio sounds faded as the cops combed the area south of me.

I crawled through the underbrush, trying not to thump and snort like heard of buffalo. Collapsing onto the ground, I listened. All I heard was running water, crickets and distant sirens.

I don't know how long I laid there. It could have been minutes or hours before I sat up. When I patted my pocket, it was empty. I'd lost my phone somewhere along the trail.

"Shit! Shit! Shit!" Fear had wiped out my vocabulary.

Statue-still, I listened for five or six minutes. I still didn't hear anything sounding like a person moving, so I stood and turned full-circle, surveying the area. A flash of white moved not thirty feet from me. My heart stopped. I nearly peed my ripped pants. "Who's there?"

It moved again, but this time a tiny voice answered. "Me."

It sounded like a kid.

"What are you doing out here alone?" I had asked myself the same question.

"Same as you."

Smart little shit. "And what's that?"

"Hiding."

I waded through the undergrowth toward the voice and a white lump.

"I ain't scared a you. I got a gun," the voice said.

"You won't need a gun. I'm not going to hurt you."

Two round eyes peered at me from a plastic storage bin tipped on its side. "Better not, 'cause I got a gun."

I looked around. "Are you alone?"

Silence.

Debris littered the area—a MacDonald's wrapper and a box from Chinese take-out.

A ball of hair resembling brown cotton candy framed a filthy face and hid the sex of the Central Park Aborigine. As I approached, the distinct odor of urine assaulted my nose. I suspected it emanated from the kid's clothes. I halted and stared.

"What ya lookin' at? Ain't you never seen a girl afore?"

The little rascal had spunk.

"Why don't you come out of your—umm—your bin and we can talk?"

The kid crawled out and stood.

"What's your name?" I asked.

"Seven."

"What?"

"Seven. Is you deaf?"

"Seven like the number?".

"Yah, man."

The big eyes narrowed and a gun appeared. "Betta scram. I kin shoot."

This wasn't going well. I tried one more time to convince the girl I wasn't a threat. "Look. I ran in here to get away from a scary guy who was being chased by the cops. I'm not looking for trouble."

"What he look like?"

"Who?"

"Dat scary guy..."

"I didn't get a close look, but he was wearing a ski mask."

She smiled. "Ari..."

"What?"

"Ari wear a mask when he steal."

The girl had all the answers.

I drew closer to get a better look at the weapon. As suspected, it was fake. Most of the plastic handle was missing. A stuffed toy remained in the bin. "Is that your toy?"

The kid leaned over and grabbed the much-loved, once-pink rabbit. It reminded me of the story, *The Velveteen Rabbit* my five-year-old daughter had me read to her every night. "Nice rabbit."

Her round eyes watered as she clutched the toy. "Mamma gimme dis."

"Where's your Mother now?"

"Don't know. Ain't seen her for near a year." The girl stuffed the toy into an oversized jacket pocket.

I was face to face with a homeless kid. "Who takes care of you?"

"I take care of maself...and sometime Ari give me stuff he steal."

My hands began to shake and my stomach turned as I looked into the eyes of the waif standing in front of me. "How old are you?"

"Seven maybe...plus a few..." Her face screwed into a frown. "I ain't sure."

"I thought you said Seven is your name. Is it really your age?"

"Could be. Ain't sure. Mamma says 'You's Seven. You kin go get some food for da baby.' And I did, but when I got back Mamma and da baby, dey was gone."

My throat ached. I wanted to snatch the little gremlin up and hug her, but I was afraid I'd get lice or something worse. "May I ask a favor of you?"

"What?"

I knew it was stupid, but all I could think of was my daughter. "I'm visiting here and I'm all by myself. Will you join me for dinner?"

"For real, man? I ain't had no dinna." Seven eyed me and smiled, exposing a gap where her front teeth should be.

Foregoing my initial hesitance, I grabbed the undersized youngster's hand and we walked out of Central Park together. We dined at a kiosk where she ordered a hot dog and a coke.

"You can have whatever you want," I assured her.

"This what I want. I gonna be the first 'un ta take a bite outta it." She bit off the end of the dog and savored it as if it were filet mignon.

"Good?"

She nodded. Then with a full mouth she said, "Best ever!"

While Seven ate her hot dog, I thought about waving down a nearby policeman and asking him where I could take the young girl. Hesitating, I looked down at her. "What are you doing out here?"

"Eatin' my very own hot dog." She grinned at me.

"You know what I mean."

Her eyes narrowed. "I s'pose to be at Lenard Heights, but I ain't stayin' there."

Anger rose in my chest. "Why? Aren't they good to you?"

She shrugged. "It ain't dem shelter ladies."

"Well what is it then?"

Her eyes grew big. "It ain't safe. They steal from me and…" Seven turned away.

"What else?"

"What ya think man?"

I didn't want to think. I wanted to kick something. I wanted to return to my hotel, call my daughter and then watch Monday Night Football—and forget the sad eyes ringed in grime.

I took her hand. "I can take you to a different shelter. You might get a good night's rest."

She pulled away. "I sleep good in da park with Ari. Besides, dem places all da same. Nice ladies tryin' to help me, but I ain't worth it. I kin make it out here."

I should have done something, but I found myself behaving like the other eight-and-a-half million people in the city. I turned my back on her. I didn't want to get involved.

She slipped her hand into the pocket to feel her pink rabbit and said, "Don't you be worryin' 'bout me. I be fine."

I watched the tiny woman-child walk away.

* * *

When I got home, I researched the homeless situation in New York City. What I found shocked me. The city's municipal shelter system housed over 63,000 homeless every night, including 23,000 children. Another 6,000 children slept in the streets. Seven was one of the street children. "Shit! Shit! Shit!"

My daughter interrupted. "Daddy?"

"Sorry, baby. I shouldn't swear."

She held her well-used copy of *The Velveteen Rabbit*. "Will you read me a story?"

My eyes stung. All I could see was Seven, her future, and the overly-loved, pink rabbit.

Swallowing hard, I lifted my daughter onto my lap and began. "Of course." I opened the book and read, "*HERE was once a velveteen rabbit, and in the beginning he was really splendid...*"

* * *

186

The next morning, I called the New York City shelter and asked about Seven.

# The Ballet

## by Dan Vanderburg

They waited and watched and listened and tested the air. The timing had to be just right to be able to do what they were destined to do. A few of the most impatient had already broken away and made their entrance and—as expected, they fell flat. The rest had been patient and waited for so long for just the right moment. Now the wait was almost over.

They performed their job well their whole life and did what they were supposed to do without complaint. They had served well. But there were always limitations to what they could do and how far they could go. It seemed that every time they attempted to reach out beyond their limits, they were always drawn back and not allowed to discover the new, exciting horizons just beyond their reach. Oh, how they wanted to go!

But they knew that soon, very soon, they'd be ready. Oh, the excitement—just to think of it! They could feel their bodies undergoing a miraculous change. The changes were happening so rapidly. They were becoming more strikingly beautiful with each passing day.

They watched the seasons come and go and dealt with and enjoyed them like everyone else.

Everything was so fresh and new in the springtime. After a restful, cold winter, new life was born and grew to join the bounty that fresh air, sunshine and spring showers brought.

Then along came the hot, seemingly never-ending days of summer. They tolerated, some would say even thrived, in those sweltering afternoons. They waited listlessly for a wisp of wind to lightly stir the air and they listened as hordes of cicadas played their droning summertime concerts.

About the time it seemed that summer would last forever, a change occurred. One day, out of nowhere, the breeze shifted directions. The air cooled. The nights chilled. Then early one morning, the first frost appeared on the grass. Autumn had finally arrived!

A week or so later, it was almost time. They could feel it. It was all around them. The cool air throughout the neighborhood bristled with anticipation.

Then it happened. The wind kicked up. Sudden gusts blasted through the neighborhood. It whistled up and down the streets. It swirled around the houses. It blew through the hundreds of trees in the park. It was like a huge string orchestra was stirring the first notes of a symphony.

They looked across the street to the park. Everyone was ready. They and their neighbors—the oaks, the pecans, the ashes, the sycamores and others; all were ready to let loose with their destiny dance.

Leaves by the billions broke their bonds and flew free. The air was filled with red, brown, yellow and orange flying dancers. The neighborhood, indeed the city, the state, in fact, the entire northern hemisphere of the planet was awash in leaves. Each leaf tried to be more creative than its neighbor as to how it made its flight of fancy.

Some aggressively tumbled and rolled in the breeze. They twisted over and over, like a thrill-seeking aerobatic pilot taking his plane through a series of daring barrel rolls and loops. Swerving and climbing, they swooped upward, then downward and sideways covering long distances until finally, thrilled with their accomplishments, they settled onto the ground with an acute sense of satisfaction.

Others floated lazily back and forth, gently cradled by a lull in the wind until they softly kissed the earth.

Some long pecan leaves twisted themselves into elongated spirals, or spinning-top shapes to twirl round and round downward on their dizzying flight.

Still others, the little golden ash leaves, flittered and

twisted in the sun, glistening like millions of shiny golden coins as they fell from the heavens.

Once they reached the ground, for many, the journey was far from over. A stiff breeze or gust sent them skittering along the street or sidewalk surface like a herd of beautiful multi-colored thoroughbreds, all racing together, galloping at full speed toward the finish to be heaped along the curbs and flower beds.

This colorful extravaganza of flight would continue for several weeks until all the leaves were released to present their unique performance and take their final, graceful bow. They'd done the job they were destined to do, and finally came to rest.

# Dark Chocolate

## by Kathryn McClatchy

Seth's home. He brought chocolate.

As I watch him tiptoe into the room, I laugh. The expression on his face is the combination of pride and fear of a first-time father.

"It's okay, Sweetie. She's still awake."

Seth relaxes. He sets down a bar of expensive chocolate, and then takes the baby from my arms. I rise so he can sit in the rocking chair. He's not yet confident enough to hold her and stand at the same time.

"Any thoughts on a name yet? Four days is a long time to call her 'Baby Girl.' I can't believe you didn't already think of this."

With his eyes focusing on his daughter, Seth whispers, "Amy thought it would be bad luck to name her, or even get too attached before we knew for sure she'd be okay and able to come home with us."

"Well, I can assure you Baby Girl is okay. She sleeps and eats, poops and cries as well as any newborn I've ever seen. The doctor said she was fine. You have to stop worrying and start enjoying her."

I reach for the chocolate. It's laced with orange liqueur and almond slivers. Amy's favorite.

"That's not for you," Seth snaps.

"I know. I'm looking to see what kind you brought. Why don't I put all these chocolates in the pantry? They really don't belong in a nursery." Today's addition makes a dozen bars of organic, free-trade, GMO-free, vegan dark chocolate.

Today marks Amy's twelfth day in a coma.

"No, I want Amy to see them here when she comes home. I want her to delight in our baby and all her goodies." Seth doesn't say it, but his eyes beg me to assure him that she will come home. It breaks my heart to see my son, so strong, so self-assured—so terrified of losing his wife and daughter.

"I understand," I lie. "Well, she's been fed and burped. You rock her and tell her a story while I make your dinner. I'll change her and put her to bed while you eat."

No acknowledgment from Seth. I can't tell if he's lost in his own thoughts or just very focused on memorizing every detail of the precious infant nestling in his arms. It definitely would be a shame if he lost her.

* * *

Seth's home. He brought chocolate.

"Happy one-week birthday, Baby Girl," he coos to her in a sing-song voice while tickling her toes. I have her sitting in a bouncy-seat on the kitchen table as I fold laundry. In one short week we have fallen into a comfortable routine. I feel more like a nanny than a grandma, but this is temporary. I know she's technically too young to smile, but her eyes light up when she hears him. Her legs are kicking and her arms are waving. Seth laughs.

"You look a year younger and ten pounds lighter. Good first day back at work?"

"Actually, it was a lousy first day back," Seth responds as he lifts Baby Girl to his shoulder. "Has she been fed yet? Can I feed her?"

"I don't think she's ready to eat now, but you may give her the next bottle when she starts fussing. Tell me about your day."

"I felt like a three-headed alien sitting on the elephant in the room. Everyone tried to be kind, but no one knew what to say. At one point I felt sorrier for my assistant than for myself. She wanted all the news, but kept sticking her foot in her mouth about Amy." Seth was patting the baby's back and swaying where he stood. In less than a week he now acted like an old hand at being a dad.

"So if it was an awkward day at work, what put the

spring in your step?"

"I called the hospital on the way home. The charge nurse said Amy opened her eyes for a few seconds, and seemed responsive to her mom this afternoon. The doctors say this is very encouraging. Amy's mom is going to stay another hour, and then I'll take her place. I want to change clothes and snap a few pictures of Baby Girl in case Amy wakes up and wants to see."

"Oh fabulous! I can't believe you didn't tell me this as soon as you walked in the door."

"I planned to, but this beautiful baby stole my attention. Didn't you, Sweet Girl?" Seth held Baby Girl out in front of him, cooing nonsense and baby talk at her. This is by far the happiest Seth has been since the drunk hit Amy's car on the highway fifteen days ago.

Folding the last towel in the laundry basket, I realize my grown son looks so much like his dad did thirty-two years ago. All of a sudden, I feel old, overwhelmed with memories and emotion.

* * *

Seth's home. He brought chocolate.

The front door slams shut. Seth throws his keys and the chocolate bar against the wall.

"One month! She was ours for one month and they took her away!" he yells at the wall where the keys chipped the paint.

"I'm so sorry, Sweetie."

"Five and a half weeks since the accident, and yesterday Amy was able to hold Baby Girl for the first time! If I'd known they could take her away, I never would've told Amy we finally got a baby."

I sit on the sofa, biting my lower lip even though I want to yell and cry also. I look away as Seth puts his fist through the wall, tears streaming down his cheeks. The judge had been sympathetic, but Baby Girl's birth mother refused to sign the adoption papers after learning about Amy's car accident. She later said she only let Baby Girl come home with us because she didn't know what else to do with her. Now another couple, one not requiring months of rehabilitation, was available to take Baby Girl. The birth mother thought they would be better parents under the circumstances. Being a mother myself, with over thirty years' experience, I had to admit I saw her point, but watching Seth hurt for his wife and child—I hate her for making this decision.

Seth storms out of the room before I can think of anything to say or do. I hear the shower start. I long for the days when I could put him on my lap and tell him everything will be all right. Now I feel useless. Seth and Amy always dreamed of a family. Three pregnancies, two miscarriages, and one heartbreaking stillbirth. Years of research, applications, interviews with social workers, and surprise home studies. After nine years of marriage they were given a baby, and now she's gone.

As I walk into the lovely nursery that Amy decorated in pink and lavender chintz, I realize how much I miss Baby Girl, too. I pick up the teddy bear Seth had brought to the hospital the morning she was born. It was too big for an infant, but I assured Seth she would love it when she grew bigger. Now I sit rocking the bear and crying for our loss.

"Momma?" Seth sticks his head in the doorway, dripping and holding a towel around his waist.

I brush away tears and force a smile. "Yes, Sweetie?"

"Oh, Momma," he says with a deep sigh, "how am I going to tell Amy?"

"I don't know, Seth. Maybe take her this teddy bear and some chocolate," I suggest, nodding toward the round table with a white wicker basket holding thirty-nine chocolate bars.

* * *

Seth's home. He brought chocolate.

A big red heart-shaped box of chocolate-covered cherries and a dozen roses are in his hands as he closes the door without making a sound. With a twinkle in his eye he glimpses me in the kitchen and mouths "Where's Amy?"

I smile, wink, and nod toward the master bedroom at the back of the house. I had taken Amy to physical therapy this morning, and am making myself useful by putting away the clean dishes. I suspect Seth has plans for their tenth wedding anniversary tonight, but just in case he doesn't I am trying to think of a backup plan. After the car accident, almost adopting a baby and then losing that baby, two months in the hospital followed by three months in a rehab facility—saying this had been a very stressful six months is an understatement. They need a fun night out to relax and have a good time together. Amy has only been home a few weeks, and they are still learning to live with her new physical limitations. Rearranging furniture to make access for her wheelchair is only one of the many signs that life has changed in this house. The nursery door still has not been opened. I am walking a fine line between helping and staying out of the way. It was much easier mothering Seth as a little boy—the job description was a lot clearer.

From the other end of the house I hear squeals of delight, laughter, and giggling; sounds that have been absent far too long. I am not needed tonight. I put the finishing touches on the kitchen and turn off the lights. As I pick up my purse to leave, I hear the back door close and see Amy rolling down the hallway.

"Mom, would you mind helping me? Seth wants to take me to dinner, but I can't get into my good clothes by myself. Putting on sweats and a T-shirt is the extent of my abilities. I want to get ready while Seth is out back feeding the dogs."

"I'm happy to help, but are you sure you wouldn't rather have Seth undress you?" I ask with a wink and smile.

Amy flushes. "Absolutely not! I don't ever want him to see how mangled and scarred I am. It's bad enough I can't give him a baby, now I don't even look attractive!" Amy's eyes fill with regret. I can't tell if the blood draining from her face is from anger, embarrassment, or sadness. Tears fill my eyes as I realize that this lovely young woman, gentle and compassionate toward everyone, sees her scars and barrenness as something to be ashamed of rather than evidence of how hard she fought to survive.

I pull her close in a tight hug and we weep together. What Amy most needs to hear shouldn't come from me. Does Seth have any idea how she feels about herself? I struggle to think of something comforting to say, but it all sounds so clichéd in my head that I know I don't need to say anything. Perhaps now isn't the right time anyway.

Standing up as her sobs fade away I say, "Okay, enough feeling sorry for yourself. You have an anniversary and ten years of love, happiness, and friendship to celebrate. Let's go find something in your closet that makes you feel as beautiful as you know Seth sees you."

* * *

Seth's home. He brought beer.

Today is one year since Amy's accident, ten months and one week since Baby Girl was taken from us, and two weeks since Amy's funeral. We got word yesterday that Baby Girl's adoption was finalized, but we weren't told any specific details, not even her name. The social worker did mention that Baby Girl loves chocolate, and that her new family assumes she got that from her mother. Seth stumbled as he heard that.

Amy had loved chocolate and puppies and dancing and entertaining and good restaurants and children and Seth. My poor Seth. He opens another beer as he flips through the sports channels, eyes staring at the TV, oblivious to what's on the screen.

"I made a crock-pot full of chili for you, Seth. There should be enough for dinner and a few lunches."

"OK, Momma."

"Anything else you need before I leave?"

"No, Momma."

"If you need me, or want to talk, or just don't want to be alone, call me. I remember how hard it was when your dad died."

Seth's beer bottle almost breaks as he slams it down on the end table. "Dad died of a brain aneurysm. He didn't choose to leave you alone." His eyes are glued on the screen, but he stops channel surfing. I freeze with my hand on the front door knob.

I take a deep breath and think fast as I exhale. Trying to control my voice and emotion, I respond. "I don't believe Amy chose to leave you. I think she chose to leave her pain. She was hurting so deeply she couldn't see anything or anyone else clearly. She held on as long as she could because she loved you so much."

Seth turns and looks at me wide-eyed, seeing me for the first time in days. "Do you really believe that?"

"Absolutely! And you have to, too."

Our eyes are locked as Seth processes what I said. He seems clear and thoughtful for a heartbeat, and then his brown eyes cloud over again. He picks up his bottle, takes another drink, and turns back to the TV.

"Are you going to be OK tonight, Sweetie?"

"Yes, Momma."

"All right then. I love you, Seth."

I'm not sure if I should leave, but I don't know what else to do or say if I stay. How do I mother a grown man with grown-up hurts? I know what to do about sore throats and scraped knees, but all I can do now is let him know he is loved and not alone as he grieves this life-altering hurt. I walk out without either of us saying anything else.

As I stand by my car door, digging in my purse to find my keys, I find a king-sized Milky Way bar. My favorite.

Seth's home. He brought chocolate.

# It Ain't Heavy—It's My Ladder

## by Gail Armstrong

"Damn getting old!" George longed to feel the vigor of youth, that exhilarating pulse of energy that comes quick and easy. "Damn these useless digits!" Groaning, he reached with his sore, crooked fingers and grabbed two old snow tires. With a snarl he rolled them aside, the twinkle and luster from his youth having faded from his dark, sullen eyes.

"There it is," George spouted, as he spied the rickety wooden ladder against the dusty shed wall. He pushed cobwebs aside and stretched his painful arthritic spine.

"This old thing will do. Everything I have is old. Well, I'm not. I'll be old when someone has to wipe my ass. Do ya hear that world? Not until!" George yelled into the moist, salt air that blew in from the warm ocean and encased his tired body like a blanket.

"Spring. Ugh."

The heavy ladder called on every muscle, tendon, and aging bone, and some he didn't know he had. In spite of the discomfort, he didn't complain. The ancient ladder had supported him many a time, and would do so once more. "Pain, you won't be in charge today fella. I've got things to do."

His weathered face twisting in a scowl, George grunted and puffed, and with a tremble tucked the unsteady ladder carefully under his good arm. He moved slowly toward the unpainted house. He did everything in slow motion lately.

He and Mabel had shared fifty plus years here by the ocean, but Mabel had passed away in the winter. George talked to himself as he trudged through the long, yellowed lawn, now high enough to be a field.

"The roofers who worked on that house next door didn't know their job," he muttered to himself. "Some of the shingles blew right off when that nor'easter went through last winter. Right through the screen on my porch. Dang blast it."

Anyone who knows anything knows ya don't install shingles on a freezing day, he thought. The glue won't stick. Dumb! I just replaced those screens last summer, and now I have to replace them again. They think I can't handle that?

"Ya know what I say? Pigs feet!" he burst out loud. "They won't see me laying down to die any time soon. No way in Hell."

He shouted out to the only friend he had now—the constant ocean breeze that rambled through his long, white, untamed hair.

George set the vintage ladder against the house in the corner by the screen porch. The heavy wooden contraption hit the house hard, rattling both the ladder and his aching body.

He remembered that last conversation with Mabel.

"George," she had pleaded. "Please, hire a handy man. Let's use our money now. That's what it's for. We have no kids to leave it to."

George hit back with harsh childish rebellion. "We're not using our savings Mabel. Hiring someone costs too much. I'll do it myself."

Mabel sighed, her eyes rolled, and with shoulders down walked away in silent defeat.

She kept herself busy baking sweet treats like apple pie with cinnamon and spicy ginger cookies that George would smell drifting out from the open windows.

"I miss you Mabel." He shouted to the whispering wind. "I miss your cooking, your good advice. I should've listened better."

The memories were painful.

No time for berating himself now. Plenty of time for that later.

George put his foot on the first rung and hesitated. Even that minor task was a challenge. He was a retired roofer, but today he could use help with the screens. He wished he had a son. He needed one now.

George started up the ladder. As he reached the top and was about to unscrew the screen, the ladder started to slide.

"Oh no!"

He called on every muscle, and somehow got his worn-out body onto the porch's flat roof.

*Crash, bang, thud!* The ladder hit the ground.

How he ever got onto the roof at his age amazed him. A shock jolted him from head to toe, his stomach turned queasy, and sweat beaded on his forehead.

He sat quiet for some time, thinking.

"I'm freaking dead!" George wailed. "Yup, the only neighbors are away somewhere having fun and I'm on this roof alone. I'm in huge trouble, Mabel. No ladder, no people. I can see the ocean though. Ha! Big deal. They'll find my bones," George moaned. "I guess this is it. Payback for being such a dumb ass."

As George sat back to ponder his fate, he heard voices. He looked up to see two strapping young men come running into his yard. Almost like in the movie *10*. It was unbelievable.

"Oh my God," George cried out.

"Mr. Monroe, are you okay?"

"Okay? Fella, I'm stuck on this dang roof, my entire body aches, and I can't get down."

"Don't try anything until we get the ladder back up."

"And what in tarnation would I be trying young fella. Flying?" George snapped back. George's patience had hit rock bottom. He had suffered enough.

"Don't move until we get the ladder set up. Don't worry, we'll be here to guide you down," the blonde young man calmly told George.

"Just don't let me fall. I'm already sore," George called back.

"Hey, you're in good hands sir," said the other man.

"Damn, I'm glad to see you two."

The two young men worked well together properly placing the ladder, and got George turned around and steadied to come down. They held him in a firm grip as they guided him down, and he did what they told him to do. Following instructions from a couple of youngsters was a hard thing for George. He was feeling less than manly right now.

"So, who the devil are you boys anyhow?"

"We're Hank and Kevin, the Parker's sons right next door, here taking care of the cats. Our parents are away. I happened to look out the window and there you were, on the roof. It looked like you were in trouble, so here we are to help."

"Well, thank God for you both. Wow, you've grown like weeds. Wouldn't know you. Yup, the years are gone. Too fast. Too fast. Makes me sad," he mused. "Yeah, got myself in a pickle. Had to replace that broken screen. You know, the one that broke when shingles came off from your father's roof and flew through it? That was something. Never saw anything like that."

"Mr. Monroe, we're sorry that happened. We'll fix it. First, let's get you inside and get you settled, then we'll put in the screen. No arguing about it. We know how to do it."

George didn't argue. "Young fellas, that would be much appreciated."

George told them where all the material was in his garage. The two boys went to work. They worked all day.

When they were done George invited them in and thanked them both. They all drank hot cocoa and ate cinnamon toast as they reminisced about Mabel. It perked

George up.

"We have grown up on Mrs. Monroe's amazing cookies and pies. She brought a lot of goodies over to my parents' house for us. A great baker. A nice lady."

"The best." George said, feeling a little melancholy, but so happy to be given another chance.

"I gotta hire someone to do chores around the property. Ya know, things I can't—I shouldn't do anymore. This old body ain't what it used to be. Do ya know anyone?" Defeat hung over George's head, but he quickly remembered how today might have ended.

"Mr. Monroe, I will mow the lawn for you," Hank offered. "That's what neighbors do. Anyway, we want to reciprocate for all the goodies your wife sent through the years. And Kevin, you like to paint. Maybe you could help with that."

"Sure." Kevin quickly responded. "And our friend who is a handy man might be interested in bigger jobs."

"Thanks boys. You've given me a new slant on life. Have to take it easy more."

"Mr. Monroe, take care of yourself. Your wife would want that," Hank replied.

"Yes, she would."

After an enjoyable visit, the boys left. George was happy to be alive after his ordeal.

"Yup, 80 years old next month. Guess you'll be around a while longer you crazy old goat." George said with a grin as he leaned back in his old leather chair.

Thoughts of his challenging day and new friends lingered as he sank back into his old brown leather chair, not new or easy on the eyes, but a friend. He needed all the friends he could get.

"We may both be old and worn but we're not done yet. Not by a long shot."

His tired body relaxed, his eyes closed, and sleep came quick and easy.

# Reunion

## by Rick Anderson

He stepped off the train platform and moved into the interior of the old rail station. It was the first time he'd ever been in the old building. It had been closed up during the years he had lived in Jamestown, but had been refurbished and brought back onto line and life with federal grant money given to the state for downtown revitalization. He had to confess the interior of the building was amazing. It had been built at the turn of the century when high, wood-paneled ornate ceilings were the style. The rich dark paneling lay between heavy wooden beams, crowning over huge marble tile flooring. The remodel had been true to the original design, all the way down to the awning-covered ticket windows and the diner counter with red leather barstools hosting the morning breakfast crowd. He almost felt like he had stepped back in time to see it like this.

Grabbing his roller suitcase handle with one hand, and his oxygen roller tank with the other, he headed toward the exit. In truth, the stop to admire the interior architecture had been as much too catch his breath as to admire the refurbished interior. Even with the continuous flow of oxygen from the trailing green tank, he still struggled to walk very far or fast. And then, it was more of a slow shuffle than a walk. He was not who he had been once, for sure— and he hated who he had become now. Moving more than a few yards triggered a pounding in his chest as he struggled to make use of the oxygen supplied by the tank and its tubing. His legs were constantly swollen with fluid, and he felt like he was walking on wide redwood stumps. It crossed his mind that it'd be nice to be refurbished like this old station had been, to what and to whom he had been once before. Well, so much for wishful thinking. The pounding in his chest subsiding for the time being, he resumed his shuffle toward the exit.

When he stepped outside, he searched for the driver his

daughter had set up for him while he was back in town for his 55th high school reunion. He hadn't planned on making the trip at all. It'd been 40 plus years since he had left Jamestown, and the idea of coming back, especially for a reunion, was not anything he was interested in.

But his daughter had insisted he make the trip. "Rekindle friendships, visit the hometown, embrace old memories," she told him. She had been adamant during his recovery from his last hospital stay that he begin a renewed lease on a more active life that had been missing for some time. "The high school reunion is a great place to start," she said.

To that end, she had made all the arrangements, booking a hotel for his stay, confirming the reunion activities, and somehow arranging for a full-time driver during the time before she herself arrived the next day. She had never been to this part of the country, and wanted—no insisted—that she be his 'companion' for the reunion dinner and dance. He knew that she knew he'd bail on the dance, actually on all of it, if she didn't come along. He only acquiesced because he knew it was her attempt to further bond with him after years of a distance that sometimes, maybe usually, occurred when families live apart in both distance and lifestyle. She had her own family and her own life to lead. He knew that. He accepted that. It was what his life had been when he was younger himself. Well, whatever, it was nice to have her closer in his life again. No, it was more than nice. He had been drowning in what his world had become, and she had reached out and given him—what? Renewal, is what she called it. He called it respite. Regardless, he was appreciative of her efforts and was looking forward to their reconnecting.

He walked out thru the automated door and felt a blast of cold air as he stepped out to the street. He had not forgotten how cool it can get up in this part of New York in September, and in anticipation had worn his old Carhartt hunting jacket. It fit a lot looser now in his later years, but it still should deflect a lot of the anticipated cold. The truth was, he hadn't really been warm in a couple of years regardless of what he wore. He just couldn't seem to warm his core up. Even while he had been living in Florida, he usually felt cold, but this belt-strike of cold bit deeper than he expected.

"Shit it's cold!" he said to no one in particular.

"Mr. Miller? Mr. Tom Miller?"

Turning in response to his name, he saw a younger woman—a girl on closer inspection, smiling at him. The shoulder-length hair cascading down one side was blondish with blue and pink streaks. A small thin nose ring rested just above an incredibly friendly white-toothed smile. She was dressed in a red and blue flannel shirt hanging out over faded blue jeans.

"Mr. Miller? Hi. I'm Kayla. You daughter hired me to drive you around today, and both of you around for the weekend. How ya doing?"

"Uh, hi. You're my ride?"

"Yes sir. Can I take your suitcase for you?"

"So, you're like a driver for the entire weekend?"

"Yes sir. Your daughter said to pick you up and show you around before you check in to the hotel. She described what she thought you might be wearing and sent a text with your picture to help me find you. I gotta say, she was spot-on with the clothes description. How was the train ride?

"You know, you can't check in until after one o'clock. I already checked with my mom. She works on the hotel front desk, and kinda that's how she recommended me to your daughter to drive for you guys during your stay this weekend.

"So you have a couple hours to kill. Your daughter thought you might like to drive around the lake and see some sights. You know, since it's been so long since you've been here, though I bet a lot of things haven't really changed all that much. I can take you around the lake—or say, have you eaten yet? Your daughter said you might not have eaten since it's still early. Want to get something to eat? I know...blah blah blah."

Jesus...does she ever stop talking long enough to breathe?

"Ah, yes. I guess I could grab something. Are you hungry and do you know—"

"Know a place? Sure, I know a great place up in Ellery. Do you know Ellery? Your daughter said you were here for, like a high school reunion or something, right? So you probably know Ellery if you went to high school here. We can—"

"Yeah, great", cutting her off mid-sentence. "That'd be great. I didn't know Ellery had any places to eat, but yeah, that'd be fine. Thanks."

Grabbing his suitcase handle, she turned and walked up the hill ahead of him, while he pulled the mini oxygen tank behind him in pursuit of his chatty driver. She continued to talk about something, but he focused on just breathing and hoping he wouldn't have to stop to catch his breath before he reached her vehicle. Luck—or fate— provided a brief respite, as her vehicle was only about 25 feet up the hill. Still, when he arrived at her car, he was breathing hard and needed to focus just to breathe. He was still getting used to being tethered to an oxygen tank, and he hated that they were so cumbersome. Still, he guessed he wouldn't be breathing without it. And since he wasn't ready yet for the alternative, he'd adapt.

The conversational driver loaded the suitcase in the trunk, and walked around to the driver's side. "There's room in the front seat for your tank, Mr. Miller. My grandma has one just like it and she leaves hers in front of her when I drive her around. The seat is set way back."

Maneuvering the tank in ahead of him, he was surprised to see there really was enough room for both himself and the friggin' tank. Still trying to calmly suck in enough air, while trying to not look too air-spent, he settled in and checked the dial on the regulator to make sure the setting hadn't moved. It hadn't, but he opened it up just a bit more anyway. It couldn't hurt.

Downtown hadn't changed much in the 40 years since he had left. It had been a poor town back then, and efforts to revitalize it had for the most part proven unsuccessful. Perhaps the newly refurbished train station might jump start it. It didn't really matter to him; this would be his last visit back here.

His thoughts rambled almost as much as Kayla's babbling as he looked around at the passing reminders of that time long ago when he had lived here. All in all, though, it was fresher in his mind than he had supposed it would have been when he first agreed to return for the reunion.

"Mr. Miller? Mr. Miller?"

"I'm sorry Kayla, I didn't hear your question. Bad hearing," he lied. "From the war."

"No question. We're here".

Jesus, what had he actually been looking at or thinking about during the drive up here to the restaurant? He didn't normally zone out like that. Setting his tank out first, he pulled himself out and looked around. He knew the building. He had driven past it almost every day for over a year when he had been with 'her.' From the outside, the building didn't seem much different from what it had appeared like back then. Repurposed now, apparently.

Kayla was talking again about something as she held open the door for him. "My aunt owns the Ellery Cow now, and it's the best breakfast you'll find in the whole county."

"Well, alright then. Thanks for suggesting it," he said as he walked in.

Whether it was as good as Kayla had bragged or not seemed to slip by him as he ate, as did the constant babbling that the young but genuinely friendly girl kept up in a machine gun pace. His mind was wondering about other times. Kayla seemed to be okay with his occasional nod or a "Really?" from her new charge, and didn't seem to notice his lack of focus to her babblings. The restaurant building itself had triggered long suppressed memories about 'her' and the life he had walked away from so many years back. The emotions began a hurt deep in his chest as they washed over him. He had never really planned on being in this area—no— he was NOT coming up to this part of the county when he agreed to come back for the reunion. But here he was, and with his arrival here came all the memories and repressed emotions he had buried in the past about the life he once had here.

Kayla was droning on about a boyfriend or a brother, or some guy doing something with a truck when he interrupted her.

"You know anything about the old Preston farm down the road a bit?"

"Sure. Miss Preston was my favorite history teacher when I was in high school. Her family has owned the property for, gee, like about a hundred years, I guess. It's for sale now. She died a few years back. She was the last of her family, so the bank has been trying to sell it for—I don't know, about a year, I guess. Did you know her?

"Mr. Miller. You okay? Mr. Miller?"

"Yeah. Yes, ah, no, I'm fine. It's my tank, I think. Sometimes it just doesn't push out enough air. No. Really I'm fine."

"Well if you need to rest, I can call my mom and see if they can get the room ready earlier."

"No, seriously I'm fine. You said she was your favorite teacher? How so?"

Having asked an actual question to the chatter machine that masqueraded as his driver, and then showing a genuine interest in what she was saying, really ignited Kayla's continuous banter. For the next 30 minutes and two cups of coffee, he listened to her talk about 'her.' When she ventured off point, he gently brought her back to her former teacher and apparently later friend. And all the time he sat there and listened. The watershed of emotions he had told himself he would ignore while he was here for the weekend now breached inside him.

"Kayla, the breakfast was as good as you claimed, and the company was excellent. Thanks for suggesting your aunt's place. I've got the bill. Say, since we're up here already, mind swinging by the Preston place? We still have some time to kill, and I'd like to see it again."

"Sure. It's just up the road. I'm pretty sure it's still for sale and empty."

Tom climbed back into the front seat of Kayla's car and once again examined the dial on the tank. It showed it was nearly half full, but he still struggled to get air, and his chest pounded from the effort to breathe. Even though he had only been sitting at the table his chest had been pounding. He adjusted the nob a bit higher.

Kayla left the restaurant parking lot and pulled into the driveway of the old farmhouse a quarter mile down the road. Turning left, she started up the gravel-gutted road.

"That's all right. Here is fine. I'd like to get out and just walk up the driveway a bit if you don't mind."

Kayla looked over at her passenger, "You sure? I can drive right up to the house."

"No, here is fine. I'm only going to walk to that granite boulder up there on the right. I'll be fine."

At that moment, Kayla's phone rang and Tom could overhear some guy talking to her about something going on with a truck. He took the opportunity to open the door, ease the oxygen tank out, and maneuver himself out of the passenger seat. With Kayla now fully engaged with some other poor soul's ears, Tom headed up the drive. The property wasn't the well-maintained landscape it had been when he left all those years back. The growth in the front pasture belied its former care. Tom took into account the flower beds in front of the fencing had grown to wild seed. By the time he had gone the 50 feet or so to the pink granite boulder he was again struggling to catch his air; his chest again pounding trying to capture air that continued to elude him. He sat down facing Kayla and her car, and reintroduced himself to the valley beyond.

God, he had forgotten how much he had loved sitting here and looking out at the patchwork of trees and bushes that ran down to the lake shimmering below. This boulder, and its accompanying view, had been their favorite spot on the whole property. Countless glasses of wine, hours of dreams being planned, and whispers of love as the sunset painted the valley below were all once here, a long, long time ago.

His breathing evened out, his chest stopped pounding, and he turned to face the house. The once white picket fence in the front was now a time-weathered grey vestige of itself that was missing more than a few pickets. The front of the house had fared no better. Originally rich, deep brown stain had given way to neglect, and now was a grey shell over the building. Still, he half expected the front door to open and have her walk out, with wine glasses in one hand, and an open bottle in the other. His eyes began to water, blurring a picture of what never should have become a buried memory. He dropped his head and noticed the wild yellow lilies still fighting to live in the shroud of weeds that ringed the base of the rock he sat on. She had planted lilies like these here, back when they had spent time on this rock, sharing dreams, and wine, and love. She said they'd always come back when she chose them to be planted there. Again, his eyes blurred with the memories and the emotions.

He looked back up at the house; the perfect white picket fence bordered with multi colored pansies and red geraniums standing in front of the dark-stained siding. The warmth the house held of those times and emotions radiated out to him. The expectation that the front door would open literally pumped his chest with anticipation. As the door opened he struggled with his air...

"Mr. Miller? Hey, Mr. Miller."

Kayla's voice snapped him back from another time he so desperately wanted to regain. His damn machine must not be working right. He just wasn't getting enough air! As he turned and looked back at her, the passing glimpse of the dilapidated fence and faded house again unleashed the flow of tears.

Kayla was waving her phone at him. "It's my mom at the hotel. She said your room's all prepared. I can take you back whenever you're ready."

"Five more minutes. Just catching my breath. I'll walk back in five more minutes."

"Need some help? I can drive up."

"No, really I'm fine."

He looked down at the lilies, with eyes that were so filled with tears that the flowers were just a glob of gold.

"Hello Tommy."

He raised his head. Her auburn hair hung curled down to her shoulders, as it always had. Her sea-green eyes had always given way to a look of bemusement when they would meet, just as they were looking at him now. And her smile. Her smile had always been what he had loved the most about her. It was what he had missed the most.

"I—I— I always meant to come back. It's just...."

"Shhhh. I know. It's okay Tommy. I know." She placed a finger to his lips to stop his lament.

Her finger's touch brought him to his feet. Behind her, the breeze brought the flowers into a soft dance that was in concert with the flow of her hair. When he stood, she moved closer to him and wrapped her arms around his neck and pressed up against his body. She was so warm. He remembered the warmth her embrace always brought, and the cold at his core melted. For the first time in years, he wasn't cold. She looked deep within him, smiling that smile that he had fallen so deeply in love with in another time.

215

Wanting to kiss her like he once had, he pulled the oxygen tube from his nose and let if fall back to the useless tank it was tethered to, freeing him at last. His chest pounded with all the emotion he had repressed and forgotten until then. With the tubing gone the rush of her intoxicating scent left him as light-headed now as it had those many years before. She smiled again, and leaned in and met his lips with hers. God he had missed her.

Turning around from the valley view, Kayla was still talking on the phone to her mother at the hotel, "He said he had known Miss Preston a long time--OH MY GOD! Mom call 911! He's on the ground and he's not moving!"

# HUMOR

# Handcuffs

## by ML Condike

"You okay, Sara?" Paul mumbled.

"If the guy in this book rolls his eyes once more, I'm going to vomit." Dropping the paperback, I threw off the blankets and groused all the way to the bathroom. Paul was reading *War and Peace*. Why anyone would read Tolstoy is beyond me. He likely wants to brag he's read it. What a literary snob!

Once back in bed, I resumed reading *Fifty Shades of Grey*.

"It's unbelievable. The neighborhood women are ranting about this book. It's the poorest written trash I've ever read."

Paul grunted and turned out his light. "I've had enough. Read as long as you like. A brass band couldn't keep me awake after that last chapter." He snored before I'd turned the page.

* * *

I finished the book by dawn and headed to fix breakfast.

"Garbage." I tossed the paperback into the trash.

"What's garbage?" Paul strolled into the kitchen, smelling of Stetson aftershave and looking sexy in his police uniform. He peeked into the trash without saying a word, but his eyebrows nano-arched.

"Court today?" I said, hoping to distract him from the book I'd chucked into the bin.

"Nope. I'm inside, writing reports. Back on the streets tomorrow."

Paul didn't like to write, even though he loved reading.

He glanced into the trash again and smirked. "Some of my reports read like that book, including the handcuffs and the whips."

"It was disgusting. I can't believe Janis recommended it."

He grabbed the newspaper while I served breakfast.

"More coffee?" I watched him mop the plate with his toast.

"Not today. The reports I'm writing should keep me awake." The corners of his mouth twitched. "But I can't disclose the details."

His car barely disappeared from the driveway when I noticed his handcuffs on the counter. I stared at them and recalled a scene in that god-awful book. "Hmm..."

Sauntering over to the island, I snatched the silver manacles and rubbed them on my neck. The metal cooled my hot skin. I shivered.

"Whew! I'm hot! It's this damned polyester bathrobe." I ripped the garment off with the flair of an over-the-hill stripper while I twirled the handcuffs over my head. My saggy boobs drooped beneath the satin top of my babydoll pajamas. I didn't care. I slithered out of them and tossed them aside while my libido took over.

What did that god-awful book say? Were the handcuffs a part of the crouching dragon position or the other one? What was it called?

"Oh, hell. The way Grey described it, I'd bet a contortionist would pull a muscle."

Dropping into a squat, I slipped one ring of the handcuffs onto the leg of the glass-topped table. And of course, in my excitement, I immediately clamped the other ring to my wrist, tightened it, and flopped onto the tabletop.

The smooth glass chilled my belly, causing me to squeal and giggle with delight.

"Watch this Mr. Grey!" I writhed naked on the table, fogging up its surface. With one arm still hooked to its leg, I was about to slip off and swing into a bumpy-grinder dance when my phone rang.

My motherly voice on the answering machine broke the spell. *I'm sorry. I can't come to the phone right now. Please leave your name, number, and a brief message. I'll return your call as soon as possible.*

"Sara, it's Paul. I forgot my handcuffs. Kavanagh will be over at eight to retrieve them."

"Oh, Christ." It was ten minutes 'til. Panic struck. I'd have peed my pants, if I were wearing any.

"Get off the table you horse's arse and unlock the cuffs." I peeked under the table for the keys. Paul always clipped them to the chain when he removed the cuffs from his service belt.

"No keys! On the counter!" I craned my neck searching for my means to freedom. I spotted the keys on the floor by the refrigerator. They must have flown off during my wild bathrobe fandango.

My sweat glands shifted into overdrive. The loose skin on my belly stuck to the smooth surface, sounding like a farting walrus with each move as I wormed to the edge. Worse still, I left a slightly smeared, but visible body print of Moby Dick on the tabletop.

I reached for my robe. "Shit. Two inches. That's all I need." I could almost touch a sleeve, but not quite. And forget the baby dolls. They were hanging from the kitchen fan. And the damnable keys might as well have been in Kansas.

When the doorbell rang, terror grabbed me by my nakedness, all 190 pounds of it. "Just a minute."

I stretched a leg toward the bathrobe, snagging it with a toe. I managed a few inches.

The doorbell rang again. This time the door open. "Sara? It's Kavanagh. You in there?"

"I'm not decent. Just a minute." I controlled my voice, but sweat poured into the crack of my butt. "Jesus. Another inch." At last, I got it, stuffed an arm into the sleeve, and wrapped the bulk of the robe around my oversized torso. "In here..."

"What happened?" Kavanagh's eyes rounded like a glass-eyed Beanie Baby.

"The key is over there." I gestured toward the refrigerator.

While retrieving the key, Kavanagh happened to glance into the trash, then asked, "Do you play with handcuffs often?"

"Almost never. The last time I trapped myself in cuffs, I was seven-years-old, playing Annie Oakley."

"Who were you playing today?" Kavanagh's face remained stoic.

I stared at the floor.

"Never mind. I can guess."

Kavanagh's phone rang.

"Hey, Paul. No problem. My pleasure. They were in the kitchen, but not on the counter. I'll tell you at the station."

"Tell him what?" I slumped into a chair.

"To add another 'remove shackles' incident to his report. We've rescued a dozen women since..." He gestured to the wastebasket, "...Since that book came out."

"Damn." I said, and then rolled my eyes just like the guy in the book.

# Another Day with Bubba

## by Dan Vanderburg

Bobby Earl sat on his couch in the trailer with his feet resting on a laundry basket full of dirty clothes. He had been on his way to Sparkle Kleen, but got caught up watching *The Dukes of Hazard*. He was thinking the laundry could wait when he heard the gravel crunching out front. Peeking through the broken window blinds, he saw Bubba open the door on his Ford Falcon station wagon.

*Oh Lord, what's he doing here? I'll ignore him and hopefully he'll go away. I'll just scrunch down here on the sofa. Maybe he won't see me.*

That's when the banging on the door started.

"Hey, Bobby Earl, open up. I got some good news." *Bang, bang, bang.* "You're not still mad at me, are you?" *Bang, bang, bang.* "We had that one little mishap, that's all. Come on, open up. You can't be mad forever. Hey, I got a six pack. Open up and let me tell you the news. You're gonna like it. We don't need that old job anyway."

"Alright, that did it," Bobby Earl muttered, shaking his head. He pushed himself off the couch, strode four steps across the trailer and yanked the door open.

"What do you mean, I don't need that job? That's the only job I had."

"Well, that was a sorry job anyway. How was I supposed to know that big old cart with all them trays of plucked chickens was top-heavy? I sure didn't intend to trip and knock it over and let them birds fall on the conveyor belt all at once. Then when I stumbled into you causing you to accidentally flip the conveyor speed lever to high, why that was just a freak accident. That coulda happened to anybody."

"Yeah," Bobby Earl said through clenched teeth, pointing his finger at Bubba's nose. "But that freak accident of yours set off a chain reaction along the whole cutting line with naked chickens flying down the conveyor about ninety miles an hour. That line of cutters looked like a combination of ninja warriors on steroids slicing and dicing, and Lucy and Ethel at the candy factory."

"Yeah, I kinda got that picture stuck in my mind too." Bubba shook his head as he pushed past Bobby Earl through the door, twisting a beer out of the box. Setting the box of beer on the kitchen counter, he pulled the tab on one and handed it to Bobby Earl. "But ya know, I think we coulda got out of all that if it wasn't for ol' Luther Ray coming out to check on the cutting floor when he did."

Bobby Earl turned the beer up and chugged about a third of it. "Yeah, that was terrible timing for the boss to come check the line."

"You know, it's amazing how slick a concrete floor can get with all them carcasses falling off the conveyor and sliding around there on that slippery floor. You think Luther Ray really did break his tailbone?"

"I guess we'll never know, now will we?"

"I reckon not." Bubba's face brightened. "But none of that matters no how."

"What you mean, 'it don't matter?' I'm still out of a job."

"Well, I'll tell ya." Bubba reached for a beer on the counter and rocked his head back and forth from side to side, looking all smug. "It don't matter because—" He popped the pull tab. "We got us a new job!"

"What you mean, we?"

"We—you and me. I got us a new job."

Bobby Earl looked at Bubba for a long stare. "Naw." He lowered and slowly shook his head. "Naw, not again."

"Now wait just a minute." Bubba looked hurt. "How 'bout a little appreciation here? Now here you are standin' around whinin' 'cause you ain't got no job, and then your very best friend in the whole world goes out lookin' all over town and finds you a job—because he's lookin' out for your welfare, because he cares about you. Then he brings you beer to celebrate and all he gets is, 'Naw, not again'?"

"I really appreciate your effort, I really do, but—seems like these jobs that you come up with just sort of have a way of not working out."

"Aw, that was just a run of bad luck. This here's different." Bubba's face was aglow with enthusiasm. "Come on, I know you wanna hear about it."

"Alright." Bobby Earl reached for the six-pack, pulled one out and straddled the stool next to the bar. "Tell me all about it."

"Well, I'll just skip to the bottom line. We're fence contractors!"

"We're what?!" Bobby Earl lifted several inches off his stool.

"You heard me. Fence contractors. We build fences." Bubba wore a look of smug satisfaction.

"Bubba, just tell me how in the world you came up with this scheme? We've never built a fence before in our whole lives."

"Yes we have, or you have anyway. Remember when we were fourteen, you helped your Uncle Leo replace the gate on your grandma's old wooden fence?"

"All I did was hold a dang board or two while Leo nailed it on. I had no idea what he was doing. Besides, that was eight years ago. And as far as I know, you don't know the first thing about fence building either."

"Well it can't be too hard. We'll figure it out as we go."

Bobby Earl closed his eyes and sighed. "So, tell me more about this fence building business."

"Well, I was down at The Home and Pro store this mornin' just mostly goofin' off, lookin' at fishin' tackle. I wandered through the tools and fencin' area and there was a big ol' sign up there, said, 'Fencing Contractors Needed'. Now, I'll tell ya, that sparked my interest.

"There was this kid workin' there, you know, like a teen-ager. I asked him what the job was all about. He said there wasn't much to it. Just put up wood and chain link fences for customers that buy the fence material at the store. So, I went and talked to the manager. He said the fence sales are boomin' this spring and they can't get enough installers to put 'em up. They got a list of customers as long as your arm waitin' for their fences to be built. After I convinced him that we could do it, he hired us."

"You lied to him! We don't know nothing about building fences."

"Oh, I got that covered. I drove around a new construction neighborhood today after I left the Home and Pro and found some Mexican fellers puttin' up fences. I just watched 'em for a while. Piece of cake. If they can do it, we can do it."

"So, what about tools and equipment and a truck? We don't have any of that stuff."

"I got that covered too." He tapped the side of his head and grinned. "Here comes the good part. When I was finishin' up talkin' with the manager about the job, he asked me about tools. Well, you know how quick I think on my feet. I just told him that all my tools had been stolen and I needed to get all new stuff but didn't have the money till after I got paid, so he gave me a temporary store line of credit. He actually gave me credit! Can you believe that? All we have to do tomorrow morning when we go to pick up our job orders is to shop for whatever we need. No problem."

"That still doesn't answer the truck issue. Bubba, we—have—no—truck!"

"Yes, we do." Bubba drew his mouth to one side and shook his head. "What's the matter with you? You gotta think outside the box. There's a perfectly good little truck sittin' right outside your door."

"What are you talking about? There's just my VW Bug and your old beater Ford Falcon station wagon out there."

"Right on!" Bubba lifted his finger in the air. "That fine little piece of Ford craftsmanship sittin' in your driveway is gonna serve us well. All I have to do is take the back seat out and open the tailgate and we can haul anything in it that we could carry in a truck. Plus, we can lock it up at night with our tools inside. That's something you can't do with a regular pickup truck. I'd say we have work transportation much better than a truck."

"What about all the materials—the posts, and chain link, or wood pickets, and stringers, and all that stuff? We can't carry it in your Falcon."

"That's the best part," Bubba grinned. "The store will deliver all that to the job site before we even get there. It will all be there waitin' on us. All we have to supply are the installation supplies like nails, bolts and concrete. Then we just put it up. Simple as that."

"What about the pay? How are they going to pay us?"

"By the job. The more we do and the faster we do it, the more we get paid. I'm telling you, we're gonna make a fortune doing this." Bubba cracked two more beers and slapped his friend on the back. "Don't it feel good to have such a great business partner as me?"

* * *

Bobby Earl answered the door at 7:30 the next morning to find Bubba standing on his little porch with his lunch box in one hand and a carpenter's hammer in the other.

"Where's the Falcon?"

"Wouldn't start." Bubba's exuberance from the night before was as flat as the look on his face.

"Why not?"

"Don't know. Tried everything. The starter kicked over and there was juice in the battery but it just won't start.

227

We're going to have to take your Bug."

"Why don't we just go back over to your place and try to fix the Falcon?"

"Don't have time. I told the manager that we'd be there when they open to get our tools and work order and then head out to the job. We're already late from me trying to get the car started. We need to make a good impression, so we gotta get down there as soon as we can. We can work on the Falcon tonight. Come on, get your keys, we gotta go."

\* \* \*

"Are you sure we need all this?" Bobby Earl asked as he pushed the shopping cart down the aisle while Bubba pushed the wheel barrow.

"It's what we put on the list last night. It really ain't much. Let's see here—we have another hammer, all these nails, two five gallon buckets, a long level, a measuring tape, a bubble level and string, a post hole digger, two shovels, a circular saw, a hack saw, saw blades, bolts and nuts, a long garden hose, 100 feet of electrical cord, that heavy rock breaking bar, a wheel barrow, and according to the job order, we're going to need enough bags of concrete for thirty-five holes."

"We can't haul but a few bags of that ready-mix concrete at a time." Bobby Earl said. "We'll have to make several trips. Come on, let's check out and get to the job."

\* \* \*

Soon they were in the parking lot with the Volkswagen front trunk lid up, organizing their load.

Bobby Earl looked from the wheel barrow and cart to the car. "OK, genius, how are we going to do this?"

Bubba grinned. "I got that figured out too. You're such a worry wart. We'll put what we can in the back and passenger seats and the rest will go up front in the trunk."

"Where are you gonna ride?"

"Why, up front of course."

Bobby Earl closed his eyes, sighed and slowly shook his head.

After loading three bags of concrete, the posthole diggers and the rock bar in the rear passenger seats and floor, they started shoving material into the trunk around two more bags of concrete. Then Bubba turned his baseball cap around backwards and carefully crawled into the trunk under the open lid and sat cross legged all hunched over in front of the bags of concrete with tools nestled around him. All that was left outside was the wheel barrow. The overloaded Bug was squatting close to the ground and the tires looked like they could pop at any minute.

"OK, roll the wheel barrow over here to me," Bubba said, reaching for the handles.

"Again, are you sure you want to do this?"

"No problem," Bubba smiled his lop-sided smile. "It ain't far. Just stay on the side streets to avoid the cops and stick your head out the window so you'll be able to see okay, and I'll holler directions for what you can't see. You drive the car and I'll drive the wheelbarrow. Just foller my directions."

Bubba's coordination of the turns on the wheel barrow in relation to the car direction was a little tricky at first and he almost had the barrow going one direction with the car going another, but he soon got the hang of it. The trouble started when they got on the side streets and Bobby Earl picked up speed. Bubba hollered loud enough for Bobby Earl to understand right and left, but stopping was a problem. The first time they came to a cross street, Bubba hollered something and Bobby Earl couldn't tell whether he said "go," "whoa," or "Oh No!" He panicked and slammed on the brakes, sending Bubba flying forward and sliding into the middle of the intersection, still hanging onto the wheel barrow. Luckily there wasn't any cross traffic, and the only damage he could see were holes in his jeans and the toes of his sneakers ripped out. After Bubba found he had no broken bones or major scrapes, he settled back onto his perch with a better-defined set of verbal instructions about the orders to proceed and stop. Bobby Earl kept the speed to below twenty miles an hour for the rest of their trip.

\* \* \*

Soon they arrived at the job address where all the materials for the six-foot high wooden fence for the backyard had been stacked in the driveway. Walking to the back of the house, they saw a series of metal stakes pushed into the ground with red flags attached indicating the fence line and gate location.

"Oh my gosh," Bubba said, standing with his hands on his hips, shaking his head, looking over the yard. "Sure gonna be a lot of holes to dig. Each of them gotta be over two-feet deep. We'd better get started."

After measuring and marking off a couple of hole locations, Bubba grabbed the posthole digger and started thrusting it in the hard, black clay, removing grapefruit-sized chunks of dirt while Bobby Earl flagged the other places to be dug.

Bobby Earl then unloaded the tools and wrestled a couple of 50-pound bags of concrete close to the first hole. He dropped the last bag next to Bubba. "How's the digging going?"

Bubba stretched his back and wiped sweat from his face with his bandana. "Lordy, this ground's hard." He looked at the palms of his hands to see the beginning of blisters. "It's gonna take forever to dig these holes. We gotta find a better way."

"We could use a power digger, I guess." Bobby Earl offered, pushing his baseball cap to the back of his head and flinging sweat from his brow with his thumb.

Bubba's face brightened. "Why didn't we think of that earlier?"

"That don't matter now, I reckon. You know, there's that tool rental place around on the back side of the Home and Pro. They ought to have a power digger we can rent. I'll just run back there and rent one for us when I get another load of concrete."

"Bobby, Earl, I'm sure am glad to have you as my partner. You think of everything."

* * *

When Bobby Earl returned, Bubba had completed only three more holes. He was shirtless as he labored over a hole, his sweaty back glistening in the sun.

"Lookie here, Bubba," Bobby Earl said turning the corner of the house carrying the one-man digger. "This thing's perfect for what we're doing. You'll be zipping in and out of them holes in no time."

"I'm sure glad to see you. I'm runnin' into rocks down there. Really slowing me down." Bubba eagerly eyed the power digger. "How does it work?"

"Easy as pie. You put the auger where you want the hole, point it straight down and pull the rope to start it. Here's the switch. This lever over here next to the right handle is the throttle. You adjust the speed by squeezing it. See, it's got two handle bars here, just like a bicycle, so you only need one man to run it."

Bubba's eyes were wide with amazement. "Dang, what they gonna think of next?"

"Go ahead, give her a try. I want to make sure you have the hang of it before I go back for another load of concrete."

Bubba went through the start-up routine and within a couple of minutes had a hole completely dug and was ready to move onto the next one. "Now ain't that slick as a whistle?" he said with satisfaction.

"Looks like you got it," Bobby Earl said, "I need to make a couple more runs to the store and I'll start setting poles."

Bubba was gleefully digging away before Bobby Earl turned the corner of the house.

It only took Bobby Earl about thirty minutes for the round trip this time because he didn't have to mess with the digger rental like the first trip. He was about five or six blocks away from the job site when he had to pull to the curb for two fire engines that were roaring past with their lights flashing and sirens blaring. *Humm, wonder where's the fire?*

He pulled out after the fire trucks passed and followed them two blocks when they turned onto a residential street to the right. *Wow, must be right here in the neighborhood where we're working.*

He made the right turn behind the trucks and followed them three more blocks until they pulled over.

*Uh-oh, this can't be good!* The fire trucks stopped directly in front of the house where Bubba was working.

Bobby Earl followed about a half-dozen firemen to the backyard to find Bubba in the far corner of the yard squatting on his heels with his shoulders scrunched up around his ears and his hands over his head, like he was waiting for a major explosion. The power digger was turned off and lying on the ground next to a hole with a loud hissing noise coming from the hole, smelling like natural gas.

Bubba and Bobby Earl stayed out of the way while the firemen, gas company and plumbers did their work to close the gas line, patch the hole, and test the line for leaks. Then they used a gadget that looked like a metal detector to find the gas line underground and marked it with red paint on the grass.

"All right fellas," the fire lieutenant said before they left, "just remember to call 811 before you dig anytime in the future and somebody will come out and mark the line location crossing through the yard so you can avoid it."

"Yes sir, we'll do that for sure," Bobby Earl said, shaking the fireman's hand.

"Whew! That was close. Thought I was a goner," Bubba said after the firemen left.

"Why don't we take a little break over here in the shade and eat our lunch and let your nerves settle before we get back on it? It's lunch time anyway."

After lunch, Bobby Earl rose from their spot under the shade tree. "Well, there's still a bunch more holes to dig. Think you can handle it while I make the last run for concrete?" He looked at Bubba skeptically.

"Oh yeah, no problem. I got it now."

"I'll try to get back soon as I can. Be careful."

Bubba waved and gave his carefree grin as Bobby Earl headed once again to the Bug for his final trip for ready-mix.

About thirty-five minutes later, Bobby Earl rounded the corner carrying a bag of concrete and found Bubba sitting under the shade tree holding his head in his hands.

*Oh no, what now?*

He dumped the heavy bag next to the digger which was sitting upright in a hole. He noticed the ground and grass was all torn up around the hole. "Hey, what's going on?" He asked, walking toward Bubba.

Bubba slowly raised his head to reveal a huge swelling and bruise forming under his left eye. He had a golf ball sized knot on his right forehead and was bleeding from his lip, which was also beginning to swell. He had red abrasions and bruises and swelling all over his torso and arms.

"My God, Bubba, what happened to you?"

Bubba looked at him with the most pitiful look he'd ever seen. "You know I been workin' hard all mornin'," he said around swollen lips, "first with the post hole digger and then the power digger and I was gettin' mighty tired. I was beginnin' to cramp up in my right hand and forearm from squeezing the throttle. Well, I decided to just tie it down with a piece of wire. Everything went along well till the auger got all wedged up between a couple of big ol' rocks. With the auger wedged and not budging but the engine still running full speed and the control lever wired down all the way, the top part of the machine was going around in a circle—real fast." Bubba hesitated and shook his head thinking about it. "I did my best to keep up with it and ran around the machine fast as I could holding on to the handle bars trying to get it un-wedged. But after a few seconds I couldn't keep up with it. I was flying around in a circle with my feet draggin' on the ground, still holding on to the handle bars. Finally, I had to let go. The digger was still spinning round and round.

"Well, I knew I couldn't just let it stay like that. I had to somehow unwire the control handle. I started reaching in about every third time it came around to try to undo the wire. That's when I got tangled up in the machine. It knocked me around with the handle bars and beat the living tar out of me till I could finally break loose. I guess it would still be going around in circles if it hadn't run out of gas just a couple of minutes ago."

"Do you need to go to the hospital?"

"No. I don't think I broke anything. Just hurt—all over."

Bobby Earl looked down at the whipped Bubba, took a heavy sigh and said, "You sit there and take it easy awhile and I'll try to catch up with the work."

* * *

Bobby Earl hadn't been working more than 30 minutes when a man in a dress shirt came into the back yard. He was the manager of the contractor department at the Home and Pro.

"Hey, boys, come on over here. We need to talk."

Bobby Earl joined him under the tree where Bubba was still nursing his wounds.

"You gonna live?" the boss asked Bubba.

"I think so." Bubba sheepishly looked at him through his one good eye.

"Well guys, I had an interesting phone call from the home owner here who's been watching you from her windows. She's quite concerned about your well-being.

"Fellas, I don't think the fencing business is for you. I want you to pack up your gear and head on out. There's another crew that's coming over here in a few minutes to finish the job. And for God's sake, leave the wheel barrow here. I'll have the other crew return it to the store. You can pick it up whenever you have a way to haul it. We'll settle up on what you've done then."

* * *

They didn't have much to say to each other on the way back to the trailer park. Bobby Earl stopped at a convenience store and got Bubba a cup of ice from the soda machine and an empty plastic bag from where they sell donuts. Most of the way home, Bubba slouched down in the seat and leaned his head back with his good eye closed, (one he couldn't open anyway) and rotated the ice from one bruise to another. Bobby Earl felt bad for Bubba's injuries, so he saw no point on browbeating him about costing them their job. He'd been beaten up enough.

* * *

Three days later, Bobby Earl was watching NASCAR, eating Cheetos, and licking the orange Cheetos residue off his fingers when he heard gravel crunching outside the trailer. Within a few seconds he heard knocking on his door. He knew there was no point in trying to avoid Bubba if it was him outside, so he answered the door. Sure enough, there stood Bubba holding a six pack. He peeked through the big purple and blue shiner over and under his eye and gave Bobby Earl his crooked grin around the swollen lip.

"Guess what Bobby Earl," he said exuberantly. "We got us a new job!"

# A Guy Walks Into a Bar...

## by R.L. Sykes

I sat down on the wooden barstool and threw my tie down next to the bowl of pretzels. What a beating it had been with the market thrashing about. Phones rang off the hook, and I felt like a bookie during a Las Vegas fight. Sell, buy, who the hell cared? My entire team was drained once the bell rang in New York. Another day in the world of stocks and bonds.

I had emerged from the elevator to head home, but the smell of popcorn grabbed my nostrils and I parked my butt on the barstool at Margin Call, downstairs from the trading floor. I swear Martin, the owner of the bar, knows how to draw us in with a scent of butter and cold liquid to end the day. I settled into my stool and hunkered down with the hope no one would interrupt my work detox. With the top two buttons of my dress shirt opened, my suit jacket on the stool next to me, I felt the day come to an end.

I grabbed a handful of popcorn with one hand while my other held the chilled glass of Tom Collins and vodka. Stacey, the afternoon bartender, knew what I liked. Televisions above the bar could have been announcing the world was coming to an end. My brain turned to Jell-O, and I couldn't care less.

Noise filtered around me. I could hear traders swapping their daily horror stories of stock prices dropping, bosses yelling, and clients cussing. I wanted none of it. I tuned out.

"Hey man, where'd you get the popcorn?" A cocky young guy sat next to me. I imagined my invisible shield must have lost power and I swore under my breath.

My head turned toward this annoyance, and I found myself unable to stay silent, "The bartender." I turned back to the TVs in hopes the guy would get my drift that his audience of one was less than fastidious.

237

"Yeah what a day," he went on. He ordered a beer on tap and inhaled the popcorn Stacey delivered with his drink order.

Out of the corner of my eye, I could see popcorn spilled around this slob. Do I move? Do I care? Let the idiot eat his popcorn. He'd be gone soon.

"Exciting, though!" He gulped his beer and ordered another. Some dribbled down the sides of his mouth.

*Geez, take it easy, kid.*

"Do you work around here? Truth be told, I may be up for a promotion before I even start the job!" He chuckled at his announcement.

I signaled for another drink to knock back, and told myself to take it easy. I didn't have plans to go anywhere for a while.

"I had this interview today right before the market went wild." He chomped, while more popcorn hit the bar than his mouth. "I went home afterward and wondered if I would hear back soon."

Raucous laughter had broken out to my left. A group of young guys in suits huddled over someone's phone. Some stupid Facebook post or Snapchat. Kids. At forty years old, I'm too old for that social media crap. I've got too many other things to deal with. Who gives a—well let's say once you've seen one half-naked girl, you've seen them all.

He leaned in toward me like I was the one chosen for some kind of secret confession.

"And then, I got called in for a second interview right after the market closed." He used his sleeve to wipe his mouth. Genius.

Interviews. My least favorite subject. My boss was a hardass, but to be fair, I respected the tyrant. I admired all that tenacity and drive. I just wish I could be left alone some days. You're damned if you get good numbers one day because it's expected every day. I drank.

238

"Let's just say that the second interview did not go as I had planned." He chugged the last of his beer and ordered another. His words began to slur.

While listening to this moron, I pondered the latest rumors that my boss' interviews were brutal these days. I wondered who the kid had interviewed with. Numerous hedge funds and trading groups filled our office tower. I grabbed a handful of popcorn to keep my mouth full. I really didn't want to prolong a conversation with this guy.

"Oh yeah?" The words escaped me. I cussed inside.

"I walked in, ready to be hit with more questions." This guy had really taken this interview thing seriously.

"This time it's just the one interviewer." His drunken whisper could have been that of a small child during church. Loud. "And this time we meet in a smaller office, no windows."

My eyebrows shot up. Intrigued, I relented and turned toward him. He had hooked me.

"A few questions are asked, like what hours do I prefer to work, and something about salary and bonus structure," he said.

"Sure, that's typical for second or third interviews." I blew off his explanation of what anyone in the industry knew. I finished my second drink and decided I had enough. I popped a few pretzels into my mouth and pulled my wallet from my suit jacket's inner pocket.

"The next thing I know I'm tangled up and we're all over the desk."

The pretzels flew out of my mouth and scattered over the bar. I wondered if I hit the maraschino cherries and limes that I knew Stacey kept under there.

"Excuse me?" I used the two white bar napkins to quickly clean up before I owed Stacey a bigger tip.

"Yeah, she was all over me." He shook his head like he

was reliving the fantasy in his head. "Her hands tore at my clothes before I could ask what percent my bonus would be."

My eyes blinked several times. Now, I had to know more. "What company did you interview with?" My grin grew like the Grinch on Christmas Eve.

In a nonchalant tone, he said, "Warren and Warren. I just hope I nailed it!" He burst into laughter, proud of his comment. He took a drink.

My days of playing poker benefitted me well at that moment. I knew that company well. I refrained from giving that away and kept my composure. I stood and paid the tab—both his and mine. I had not expected my day to end like that, but what a story.

I wished him good luck and left. I pondered how I should handle this revelation about the company I worked for. My morals told me I needed to say something, but my brain said to keep my eye on the ball. It was just work.

I reached my Porsche 911 as cars whizzed by me through the underground garage. I shook my head. With the roar of the engine, I emerged back into the world. City lights surrounded me. The Fort Worth skyline reminded me I did love my life.

I turned down 6th to head home to my condo. My phone rang.

"Hello, Mother," my tone less than enthusiastic. She called me every day around that time.

"How was your day, son?" I could hear tinkling glasses and muted conversation behind her voice. "I'm at the bar at Giovanni's if you want to meet for dinner."

I merged onto West 7th.

"Sure Mom," I said, too tired to say no. "When I get there, let's talk about your interviewing techniques."

# Lucky Underwear

## by ML Condike

"Mark, can you grab that? It had better be the guy calling with the address for this reception." My heart pounded. I had less than two hours to finish the food prep and deliver the buffet.

Mark mumbled something about Barnstable Road and waved a scrap of paper in my direction. "Here's the address where the order's going, Frank. The guy sends his apologies. It slipped his mind."

"Talk about last minute. You map the directions, and I'll finish up here." My gloved hands dripped with onion juice, making my eyes sting. "I can't stop or we'll be late."

"Sure." He disappeared into the van.

Sniffing the Swedish meatballs, I added a pinch of allspice. My mouth watered as the steam carried the pungent aroma into my nose.

Moving from station to station, I taste-tested each entrée and fussed over the extra fluffy éclairs, stuffing each with fresh vanilla cream filling. Once filled, I dusted the pastries with powdered sugar and packed them single-layered to keep them neat.

Mark returned. "Ready?"

"Ready as I'll ever be." The sweet powder floated up my nose as I removed my gloves.

Ten miles out of town, I turned onto a narrow tree-lined road leading toward the river.

"Are you sure this is right?" Mark asked. "There isn't much out here."

"It's where the GPS says to go. You loaded the address."

"I know, but…" Mark opened his phone. "We're heading toward 'Wearing as Born.'"

241

"I'm going to check my order slip." I pulled over and grabbed the order book from the back. "Hmm. Some guy named Burns placed the order months ago and gave me his credit card. My note said he'd call with the address." I glanced at my watch. "Cripes."

"Relax Frank. We'll make it. We're not serving for another half hour."

"You're right." Trees blurred as I sped along the GPS route, passing a small unmarked road not on the map. "Looks like we're headed straight into a church camp."

I checked my watch, again. My heart raced. I didn't want to mess up a fantastic order. We'd make at least a grand on it.

"There it is." Mark pointed to a gated compound.

A tasteful sign indicated 'Wearing as Born' and an arrow pointed straight ahead to an entrance. The gate was open, so I proceeded at a crawl.

"There's a building over there and the door is open." Mark looked for other options. "That's got to be it. Nothing else is big enough."

"Okay." I swung around and backed up to the door. "Come on. Somebody inside will know where to set up."

Sweat dripped down my brow, but my anxiety had turned to relief.

As I approached the door, a man without a stitch of clothes stepped out. "May I help you?" His skinny legs supported a turnip-shaped body with a hairy chest and a round belly drooping down like a loincloth hanging over his privates.

After I cranked in my eyes, I blurted, "We're here to serve dinner, and we're running late. Where do we set up?" I averted my gaze and stifled a laugh.

"Follow me." He hustled us inside to a well-lit kitchen, his rotund body shaking like a bowl of Jell-O.

Mark's mouth contorted and his eyes bulged. "Right.

Let's look around."

I gestured for him to simmer down as I repressed a smile.

"Is it a buffet?" the man asked.

"Yes, of course." He'd placed the order. *Why didn't he know?*

An attractive naked woman waltzed into the room. Her firm slender body glowed in the natural light. "What do we have here?"

Stunned by her perky breasts with nipples rolling like eyes as she walked, I nearly swallowed my tongue. I forgot my question. "Dinner," I croaked while surveying the room.

The kitchen smelled of institutional cleaners and the counters sparkled. Still, after glancing at a mob of unclothed bodies outside the row of windows, I sprayed a coat of odorless disinfectant before rolling out butcher paper. "You bring the food in from the van, and I'll arrange the tables."

"Got it," Mark chirped and hurried out.

"Is it acceptable to remain dressed?" I asked, ignorant of nudist etiquette.

The buck-naked man smiled. "Absolutely. Food servers may wear whatever they desire. Give a holler when you're ready." He joined the throng outside. Sunscreen glistened on their birthday suits.

It took us twenty frantic minutes to set up.

Several people stuck their heads inside and remarked at the enticing aromas.

Mark fanned his face. "It's bloody hot in here. There's no air conditioning. I'm stripping to my underwear. I won't stand out in this crowd." He shed his outer clothes and slipped into his whites.

I contemplated shedding my clothes too, but I'd worn my lucky boxers, the ones with the hearts and arrows on them. The red pattern would show through the whites.

Besides, I was used to hot kitchens.

The temperature skyrocketed when the sun hit the bank of windows.

"It's unbearable!" I said. "It's a hundred and fifteen and climbing." I mopped my brow.

Grinning, Mark said, "I'm comfortable."

"Aw crap." I stripped to my boxers and slipped on my whites.

Giggling like pre-pubescent boys, we donned our chef hats.

Mark shouted, "Food's on!"

A steady stream of naked men and woman filed in. Everyone carried a towel over his or her shoulder and placed it on the chair before sitting.

"I wonder which one's the bride?" Nobody seemed pink-cheeked and giddy, although there were a lot of cheeks on display. And nobody was hanging off the arm of a handsome, young dude wearing a bow tie.

"Maybe nudists don't wear gowns." Mark winked.

"Anything's possible."

The line continued for what seemed an eternity. All sizes, shapes, and colors of bare bodies moved past. It wasn't easy, but I managed not to stare. About thirty minutes into serving, and three refills of the warmers, my phone rang.

"Who's calling me now?" I hesitated to answer, but the number looked familiar.

"Hey. Where are you guys? You were supposed to be here an hour ago." The man's voice had an edge to it.

"What do you mean?" My heart plummeted past my shorts, and landed at my knees. "Who is this?"

"It's Joe Burns for Pete's sake—we have a whole damn wedding party here waiting for food, and you haven't shown."

"Where are you?" I looked at Mark in alarm. "We're serving at Ninety-eight Barnstable Road."

"I'm at the 'Wedding Barn' at Eighty-eight Barnstable Road." His loud voice bounced off my eardrum. "It's at the end of that small unmarked drive a quarter mile back."

I covered my phone. "Shit. We're supposed to be at the 'Wedding Barn' at Eighty-eight" not 'Wearing as Born' at Ninety-eight. It's a block back the other way."

"Please tell me you're coming! I have two hundred hungry wedding guests and no food!"

"I'm not sure how to say this, but there's been a major mix up." My underwear didn't feel so lucky now. In fact, I was fighting to keep them clean. "We served the food to another group." I hesitated. "I'll send over fifty pizzas."

"Well make it fast." The line disconnected.

"Call all the Greek and Italian places in town and order pizzas."

Mark stared at me, his mouth fighting a grin. "Sorry, Frank."

"And get dressed!"

"I was just getting comfortable." Mark lost his fight and grinned broadly.

The flaccid man who'd greeted us strolled over. "Is everything okay?"

"No. It's not."

"By chance, were you headed to the Wedding Barn?" He asked.

My neck heated like a Bunsen burner. "Yes. Don't tell me you knew?"

"Don't feel bad. We get a great meal about once a year this way." He turned and raised his hand. "Quiet, please. Let's give well wishes to the bride and groom, and offer them thanks for their generous donation of such a fine meal." The crowd responded, "Amen."

"Wait a minute. There's no way Joe Burns is going to pay for this." I seethed.

"Did you hear that folks? Joe Burns' daughter got married." He raised both arms to the ceiling. An applause ran through the crowd like a wave at a ballgame.

A voluptuous woman stood. "Shall we give thanks?"

A grin appeared on Mark's face. I wondered what he expected would happen next.

As if rehearsed without another word, the crowd stood, grabbed their towels and left.

The naked woman pointed her finger at me. "You wait here! We'll be right back."

Where was I going? I still had cake and 200 éclairs in the kitchen.

Within ten minutes the crowd returned, each nudist waving cash.

The buck-naked lady collected the bills as they re-entered the building. When the line ended, she handed the stack of hundreds to Mark. "Here's four thousand dollars. It should cover your costs, including the pizza, and give you a little profit."

Someone from the back shouted, "Use it to buy new underwear. Yours are showing."

I shook my head. "Not a chance. These are my lucky underwear."

Just then, seven naked men emerged from the kitchen, carrying the wedding cake and six trays of éclairs. Their leader shouted, "Come on folks we have a delivery to make."

A line of flashing, jiggling, exposed bodies exited the hall singing, *We Will Rock You.*

# Playa

## by Rick Anderson

I heard the bell ring on the small sample elevator that brought beer samples from the production floor up to the 2nd floor lab. I was just finishing up the sample analysis on the aging tank samples pulled from the brew house earlier, so I knew I had some extra time to help Maria with her analysis of production line samples.

"I got it Maria!"

"Thanks, Rick."

Maria and I had been lab partners for about a year. Chemistry analysis in a brewery can be pretty fast-paced and stressful. Having the right partner with the right attitude to adapt to that environment was critical to being successful. Maria was both. Those qualities plus the bonding that a high stress job can create, had become the foundation of a pretty tight friendship.

I left my side of the lab, moved over to the elevator, and slid up the elevator door. Doing so triggered a memory of the old 'grey' movies from the 30s I used to watch as a kid, where the butler would retrieve food from a dumb waiter.

I pulled the sample-laden basket of cans and bottles from the elevator, and sent the elevator back down to stage the next round of samples.

I looked over at Maria focusing on her own samples.

"I'll get started on these."

Maria looked over at me. "Great. So, are you excited about your date tonight?" Maria had followed the saga of my divorce and the subsequent less-than-successful progress into singlehood with empathy and occasional advice.

"Excited? No, not excited," I lied. "You know, I have been on dates before." Well, that might have been a stretch. But in all fairness, I had talked to women on occasion, and

247

this one had actually responded with the offer of a 'home-cooked meal.' Even if it went no further, it was a guaranteed meal that I didn't have cook. Yep, this was already a win.

"Yeah, I know you have." She paused and looked up from the computer. "So, not counting the ones before you got married, have any of them been since your divorce?"

"Well—not that many I guess."

Maria pressed further down an awkward subject. "So not counting the sit-down lunch with your ex-wife, how many?"

I didn't know that didn't count as a date. I would have to remember that in the future should a date tally be the topic of conversation. "Okay, so this is—well—maybe the first one. Why?"

I suspected what would be next. I appreciated her efforts in offering me what I knew to be coming—advice. It wasn't the first time she had offered insights into the world I was now a part of, that of being newly single, and her advice was normally pretty spot-on. I didn't always take it, but I always listened.

"You got married at nineteen, right?" Without waiting for the confirmation that she already knew, she continued. "I recall you saying you hadn't dated much before that. Sooooo....... A lot of things have changed in the dating world since the Dark Ages, my friend."

Maria, single and in her mid-twenties, just might have had a better understanding of current social settings and dating than I did, true. But damn, I was a grown-ass man. And now that I was out and about on the town, so to speak, I bet I could figure all this stuff out. I was a child of the sixties after all. You know—free love, drugs, orgies—not that I had ever been a participant in any of it. I may have been one of the shyest of the sixty's children, plus I had spent part of that 'free love revolution' in the Marine Corps—not the most free-spirited of institutions. But I had heard about it all.

"Well, I doubt it's changed that much," I said. "Your

point?"

She looked up from her computer and flipped back her dark hair. Her amused smile was friendly, but a bit condescending. "Okay. So, you're bringing 'protection' on this date tonight, right?"

Okay, then. Not what I had been expecting. Honestly, I hadn't given it any thought. It had been a spur of the moment invitation for a home-cooked meal that I had accepted with the hope something more might happen, but it was more hope than expectation.

"Well of course I am!" Perhaps I might have stated it with more overconfidence than reality might support. I had never even bought one before, nor really had been in a position to use one. Well, I had been in a position in my youth, but had been a bit careless I guess, looking back on it now after Maria's query. She was probably right, though. I'd swing by Walgreens and pick one up when I left the house tonight. Now, though, without further comments on my single life challenges, I—we—needed to focus on work or I'd never get out of there.

* * *

Evening came, and driving out of town to the much anticipated 'date,' I saw Walgreens and thought of my earlier conversation with Maria. Okay Rick, just pull in and pick one up. You never know—maybe you would get lucky.

I looked at my watch when I walked into the drug store. I knew I was going to be a little late already, but I'd blow that off to traffic. This wouldn't take too long. It was still dusk, so timewise I should be fine. A young girl at the register greeted me with a friendly and somewhat innocent smile.

"Can I help you find something?"

"Ahhh—no. I'm good. Thank you, though." I doubt she'd be helpful with finding what I was looking for anyway. Nope, I would find one myself. Wait, do they sell them individually? Maybe I should buy more than one. You never know—this could be a great date. Yeah. I'd buy—wait. What do they come in? Like a 2-pack? Well, I'd have the answer to that in a minute. Just have to find them first. I gazed around, and not seeing an aisle sign prominently directing, 'CONDOMS HERE' like a blue light special for single guys on a Friday night, I proceeded to go up and down aisles of cards, chips, hair products—anything and everything that someone else might need—but not what I needed. And time was now becoming a factor.

"Sir? Can I help you locate something"? I turned to the voice and saw Miss Royster, my seventh grade Algebra teacher. Actually it wasn't really her, but she sure could have passed for her. Heck—she was like 100 years old back when I took her class in junior high school. But dang, the lady before me looked just how I remembered Miss Royster. Short silver hair, and round puffs of red rouge on her cheeks that somehow always matched her lipstick. Small gold-rimmed glasses positioned halfway down her nose were overseen by remarkable blue eyes, even at her age. Dang, it was Miss Royster incarnate.

"No thank you Ma'am, just looking." I'm not sure Miss Royster would have approved of me buying condoms back then—or now. My sense was I didn't need to shock this Miss Royster about such a purchase now, either.

"Well if I can help you, let me know." She smiled and moved off somewhere.

"Thanks." I doubt they even had condoms back in her day. How much help would she have been anyway? I needed to refocus on my quest, as now I had spent waaaay more time than I should have looking for the 'grail of sin safety.' If I delayed much longer, the chances of getting laid would definitely decrease. After going up and down every friggin' aisle, I made my way back to the pharmacy section, and there they were—safely secured behind the counter.

Why would they be behind the friggin' counter? I mean, this was the 80s for crying out loud! Shouldn't something as vital to Friday nights as condoms be built up in an aisle of their own? Displayed like those towers of beer cases you can't hardly maneuver around? I stared over the counter trying to get some idea of what I needed to get, when 'Miss Royster' stepped in front of me—now behind same said counter that was beginning to loom like that last wall at the Alamo defending my sought-after prize.

Still masking that pleasantly helpful do-you-understand-the-Pythagorean-Theorem-young-man? smile, she said, "Did you find what you're looking for?"

Well, crap. I know I shouldn't have been embarrassed by asking for a condom, condoms, whatever—I was a grown-ass man, remember? But somehow I was. And I damn sure didn't want to buy them from the Miss Royster clone. It was like trying to buy beer again when I was underage at the Palace market. I felt that same insecure, nervous anxiety building up when you're doing something not quite on the up and up. Yes, I was an adult attempting, key word, attempting to buy a legal adult product. Do they ID you for condoms like liquor? Focus damn it! Focus!

I needed a plan. And more time for a guy to return behind the counter—definitely not Miss Royster.

"Ahhh no Ma'am. Still just looking." And I stepped away from the counter, like the Mexican legions that were repulsed in the beginning of the Alamo siege.

Thinking of the Palace market, I seized on the same strategy that sometimes had worked back then. I was desperate. I shouldn't have been, but there it was—I was nervous and embarrassed. It's Friday night and this guy strolls in and buys—a condom. Or condoms—or however they friggin' come packaged. You know what he has on his mind. That's why he's buying one. Or them. Damn it! If I don't hurry up and get on my way, that's all it'll be, on my mind. Stupid Maria!

I walked away from the counter and put the aforementioned Palace Market strategy into action. It was the old decoy ruse. I walked down the nearest aisle and grabbed goods that would mask the true prize of my purchase.

I grabbed a bag of potato chips. Kind didn't matter for this ploy. I pulled a soda from the refrigerator section (my mouth was now dry as a desert so this, I could use). I grabbed a bottle of aspirin, which at the moment I was beginning to feel I could use as well. And shoe polish. Considering I had no polish-able shoes, I admit this was not as well planned out as my Palace Market escapades had been, but I needed the props, and time was now a critical factor. When I returned to the counter, I initiated the master plan.

Miss Royster re-appeared behind the counter's ever towering wall with that same sweet-old-lady-forget-your-homework-again? smile.

"Find what you were looking for?"

Damn it! Courage and focus!

"Why, yes. Yes I did. May pay for these here?" I obviously was not going to get a man to sell me what I needed, so I needed to 'suck it up Sally' and put the plan into action.

"Of course you can, sir."

The only thing missing was the 'young man' admonishment to replace the 'sir' she used. As I reached for my wallet and she began ringing up my purchases, I looked up at her June Cleaver smile. (Where was all this coming from? June Cleaver? Geeze, I must be more nervous than I thought. And I knew I was nervous).

"Oh, and may I have a condom please instead of the shoe polish?" I about choked spitting out the word 'condom' to the sweet old lady behind the counter, but there it was. I only hoped she didn't collapse at my vulgarity! Or worse, recover enough pull out a ruler and wave it like a rapier at my sinful countenance. Well, at least my quick catlike mind saved me from the shoe polish purchase. Sweat was beading around my forehead like I had just finished running a marathon. Hell, I hoped I didn't collapse! My heart was pounding! Now if I could just grab all my groceries, including the prized condom, and get out of the now sweltering drug store, it would all be worthwhile. Damn it's hot in here!

Surprisingly unfazed, she said, "Certainly sir. Which brand would you like?"

They have different brands? I thought they were all Trojans.

"Well, Trojans? Ahhh...better make it two." Yep, two. Letting Miss Royster know little Rickey was all grown up now and was a "playa".

The Miss Royster clone looked at me for a minute. It was that same look that she gave me umpteen years ago after I had given her my version of the Pythagorean Theorem, a version still unaccepted to this day.

"Sir, they come in multi-pack boxes."

"Oh, sure, that'll be fine."

Smiling sweetly, she inquired, "Latex or sheepskin?"

What the hell is sheepskin? "No, the regular will be fine." I wished I had recognized either the slight smile growing at the sides of the red lipsticked mouth, or the amusement in her still, so very blue eyes.

"Lubricated? Or non-lubricated?"

What the hell? "Ahhh—regular is fine."

"Ribbed or...?"

"Just the regular ones will be fine. I'm in a bit of a rush." I felt like Perry Mason was in the middle of interrogating me into confessing the dark recesses of a crime the evidence in front of me suggested I intended to commit. Yes Miss Royster, I hope to get laid tonight, but if you don't ring up my condoms that is not likely to happen in this friggin' decade!

Still sweetly smiling, she said, "Of course sir. And size?"

Now the pressure was getting to me. Damn it was hot in here! Do they not understand the concept of air conditioning? Size? They come in different sizes? Jesus, how complicated is this anyway?

"Regular. Regular size."

"Of course." The Miss Royster clone began ringing up the last, and most significant, of my purchases.

"Oh dear. This isn't marked with a price."

I wasn't really paying that much attention to what she was saying, only focusing on how I wished this was the Palace Market again instead of Walgreen's den of torture.

*"I need a price check on a Trojan multi pack."*

What? That just went out over the loudspeaker? Can they actually say that over the airwaves? I began looking around guiltily to see if anyone else was around to bear witness to this whole debacle. Some voice responded over the loudspeaker *"Which one?"*

*"The lubed, medium."*

"Large. Large. I wanted the large. Definitely the large!" Again, I did a spin to see if anyone might be standing around that would recognize me.

*"He now says large."*

A price came over the airwaves but honestly, I didn't care what it was. Whatever it was, Miss Royster rang it up, handed me my bag of items, and I paid for it.

I'm sure she said something to me, I don't know exactly what. I muttered a thank you in response to whatever it was, but being polite was really not on my mind at the moment.

God I am glad that's over! I can't wait to open that soda. It was like I had a sock in my mouth that had been left in a sand box all day. I looked at my watch.

Damn it, I've already been here 45 minutes! I need to go. I gave a nervous smile to the young cashier I had seen earlier as I rushed by and made my way out thru the front door.

"Good evening sir. Come again."

Fat chance of that happening. My face is probably already being typeset on posters to be taped on the front of buildings, "THIS MAN BUYS CONDOMS ON FRIDAY NIGHTS!"

*Ding dong...ding dong...ding dong.*

"Sir. Sir! I am sorry sir, something in your bag triggered the alarm. I'll need to check it, sir."

What? Good lord, is this nightmare ever going to end? I turned around and returned to the young cashier.

"I paid for it back at Pharmacy. Here's the receipt," I stuttered. Innocent! I'm innocent! I was beginning to wonder if a crowd would be waiting outside for me, intending to sew a scarlet red letter "C" on my sweat-soaked shirt, raising a chant of, "He's buying condoms! He's buying condoms!"

"Sorry sir, store policy. May I see your bag?"

"Ahhh...of course. Here's the receipt," I repeated.

Handing her the bag, I noticed Miss Royster was now moving up to man the other register, still smiling that sweet-old-lady smile. Wait a minute. It didn't look quite as sweet now. It had more of an amused, entertained look to it. And it definitely looked a lot wider. With the alarm raised from my attempt to apparently breach protocol and abscond with ill-gotten gains, an assistant manager came over to assist the younger cashier.

She introduced herself. "Good evening sir. I'm Jan Stevens, the assistant manager. Sorry for the inconvenience. I am sure we can clear this up in no time." I recognized her voice as the price resource voice from over the loudspeaker.

This never happened at the Palace Market.

Laying the assortment of goods on the counter, Ms. Stevens discovered the culprit for the alarm trigger was in fact the multi-pack of condoms. Of course it was! Glancing over again at Miss Royster I was not surprised to see an even bigger smile, and I think I heard a chuckle as she turned and faced in the opposite direction.

Ms. Stevens looked up at the Miss Royster clone. "Lidia,

remember you've got to scan the condom box so it won't trigger the security poles at the doors."

"Oh, dear me. I am sooo sorry."

The assistant manager resolved the register issue, repacked my bag and with an apology for the inconvenience, bid me *adieu*. As I approached the door, I happened to catch Miss Royster's eye.

"Good night sir. I'm sure you'll have a great evening." I could have sworn I heard an accompanying cackle as I passed thru the door.

Walking to my car I thought to myself, when these condoms are gone, I'll just become a monk!

# Old Gus

### by Dan Vanderburg

We all knew about dog laws in our little Texas town in the early 1950s, but nobody except the dogcatcher cared much about them nor did much of anything to abide by them. There wasn't an actual, real, full-time dogcatcher in town. If the sheriff got a complaint about a dog, he'd get Hubert Gene Perkins to be the dogcatcher for an hour or two.

Hubert Gene was a middle-aged guy that swept up the court house and the jail to pay off his bail. He seemed to be a regular there for enjoying the cheap wine he bought from the bootlegger across the tracks. He wasn't a real criminal. He just drank too much and sang too loud on the courthouse steps on Saturday nights. He was a skinny little man that walked kind of bent over, looking at the ground most of the time. We kids thought it peculiar that such a small man would wear such oversized pants all bunched up and belted a few inches south of his armpits. He was shorter than most grownups. When he stopped on the street to talk to folks, he stood there, hunched over, with his head tilted up, peering through very thick glasses under his dirty, sweat-stained hat as he talked.

On the occasions when Hubert Gene became dogcatcher, Sheriff Eads gave him a badge that said, 'Dog Catcher.'

The story goes that the sheriff found that badge at First Monday Trades Day over in Canton when he went one weekend to sell pigs. Hubert Gene wore that badge pinned to his shirt with pride. There wasn't much Hubert Gene took seriously, except getting his bottle of wine, but when he put that badge on, his whole attitude changed. It was as if he became the Captain America of dogcatchers. He was out to save the world from stray dogs that simply wanted to sniff trash cans and each other's butts.

Of course, the sheriff had to give Hubert Gene a sobriety test before he'd give him the keys to the county truck. Then Hubert Gene had to take out the tools that the cesspool maintenance crew left in the old International truck, and put the wire cage in the back of the pickup before he could go out in the neighborhood and troll for an errant dog or two. When his dog catching workday was over, he had to give the badge back to the sheriff.

Seldom did a dog actually pose a real threat to the community, but the sheriff felt an obligation to respond when he got a complaint. A typical call would be like the day a stray jumped Miss Lucy Hopkins' fence and had his way with Sugar Bell, her yappity little poodle. It took the sheriff fifteen minutes on the phone to talk Miss Lucy down from her heightened state of distress when she discovered the stray dog doing what came naturally with little Sugar Bell out in Miss Lucy's petunias. The stray was back over the fence and well on his way to peddle his wares somewhere else by the time the sheriff found Hubert Gene, verified his sobriety, and sent him out to incarcerate the offender.

Then, there was the time Oscar Blount's bulldog took a bite out of Elmer Slidell's backside when Elmer tried to slip through Oscar's yard and in his back door to visit Mrs. Blount while Oscar was over at Mount Pleasant taking care of business for the day. Mrs. Blount wanted to keep the whole business quiet, but word got out pretty fast around town when Elmer was seen busting through her backyard picket fence, running down the street, trying to hold his pants up with Oscar's dog hanging on to the seat of his britches like a snapping turtle and Elmer hollering, "Get 'em off! Get 'em off!"

But dogs were a normal part of the neighborhood. Oh, some people kept their dogs inside fenced yards if they could be considered a nuisance on the street, but many dogs sort of hung out, doing what dogs do, napping in the shade or following kids around, looking for a handout. One of those dogs was a neighborhood pooch we called Old Gus.

Gus was a member of our group of kids that goofed off

together in the summertime. He was a medium-sized mutt with bushy, gray hair, floppy ears and jowls, and a tail that always seemed to be in perpetual motion. He had soft, brown eyes that could melt you into giving up half your ice cream cone from the drug store's soda fountain, if you had a dime to buy one.

There were six of us, all between eight and eleven-years-old that hung out together in the summer. Gus always knew when and where we would gather, and wanted to participate in whatever activity we had planned for the day. Sometimes we roamed the woods back behind the old cotton gin, fishing for crawdads in the creek. Frequently we sat and counted freight cars rolling along the tracks on the other side of the highway, speculating as to what they held and where they were going. Other times we did nothing more than sit in the shade on the sidewalk in front of the barber shop and pass the time of day listening to baseball games from the radio through the open window.

At least twice a week we played baseball. There was a vacant lot at the end of Main Street, on the corner beyond the abandoned blacksmith shop. We put a few hours in every spring picking up trash that accumulated during the winter and mowing the weeds with Harlan Jinkins' papa's reel-type mower. It wasn't much of a baseball field, but it worked for us.

We never seemed to have enough players to field a complete team. Most of the boys we went to school with lived in the country on their family farms. My buddies lived in town and we only had a pitcher, batter, catcher and three basemen. Old Gus rounded out the roster. He played outfield.

I don't remember anybody ever teaching Gus how to play. He just liked to chase baseballs. At first, we had trouble getting the ball back in play after he ran down a fly ball. He wanted to take it to a corner of the field, lie down and chew on it. It took some coaxing to get him to return it. Finally, he caught onto the idea that if he ever wanted to run down the ball again, he'd have to get it back to the infield. He usually did a good job, but sometimes the game got more than lively when he wanted to make up his own rules by playing keep-away and darting back and forth between Frankie at first base and Albert at second, with the slobbery ball firmly in his mouth. As soon as one of us got close enough to almost recapture the ball, he'd scoot away. He'd eventually give it up so play could resume.

It was one of those days after a hot afternoon of baseball that we almost lost Old Gus to the dogcatcher. We were all sweaty and thirsty after a spirited game. After we pooled our money for cold drinks, we found a total of thirty cents. So, we walked down to the filling station on the main farm-to-market road for a round of Big Red soda pops rather than chugging from the water hose behind the cabinet shop.

The ice water inside the bottle cooler box felt so good when I raised the hinged lid and let my hand linger there awhile, swishing the water around. An empty Dixie cup filled with cold water from the soda box suited Gus just fine. We settled down in the shade of the awning over the gas pump to enjoy the cold, sweet flavor of the soda pops.

Traffic was slow along the farm-to-market road on that steamy summer afternoon, with only an occasional farm pickup or dusty sedan kicking up a hot breeze as they passed. Then we saw the old International pickup truck with the wire cage in the back as it turned onto the pavement several blocks west of us, down by the Methodist Church and headed our way. Hubert Gene was on the prowl. He drove slowly on the shoulder, looking to his right and left for any canine culprits foolish enough to be running loose in his jurisdiction.

"Uh-oh," I said. "Looks like old Hubert Gene's on patrol."

"Better hide Gus or put him on a rope," Albert said.

"Anybody got a rope?" I asked. We all looked at each other, shaking our heads.

"Quick, Harvey, give me your shirt." I said to the littlest

guy in our group.

"Why?" Harvey asked, protesting.

"Just give it to me. Hurry!" I watched as the rusty, gray truck rolled closer, still about a block and a half away.

Harvey wiggled out of his green and orange striped T-shirt and handed it to me. He didn't look out of place, sitting there naked from the waist up. Albert had taken his shirt off while we were playing ball and had it wadded up in his lap.

Within seconds we were ready for the confrontation that we knew was coming from Hubert Gene. Sure enough, when he saw us lined up on the curb next to gas pump facing the road, he cut diagonally across the farm-to-market and pulled up next to us.

We looked like six innocent cherubs, with shaggy summer hair, sweaty dirt necklaces, smudges of baseball dust on our faces, arms, and legs, and baseball gloves in our laps drinking soda pops. The only thing clean on any of us was Harvey's chest and belly, glowing white in contrast to his sunburned arms. We sat as close together as we could get on the curb. Old Gus was jammed in with us, right in the middle. Only his chest and head were showing. He looked quite spiffy in Harvey's orange and green striped T-shirt and my faded Fort Worth Cats baseball cap pulled down tight over his ears. Frankie and I, who sat on either side of Gus, held him snugly with our arms behind his back, securing his tail so it wouldn't move.

"Howdy do, boys," Hubert Gene said after he pulled up next to us. He squinted through those thick glasses. "Seen any stray dogs today?"

"Not a one," Albert said with a straight-faced look. "How 'bout you? Looks like that cage is still empty."

"Naw," he drawled, "none yet, but my day ain't over." He craned his neck, leaning his head out the open window squinting at us. He wrinkled his nose and lifted his upper lip as he tried to focus his gaze on Gus. "Now I know all y'all, 'cept I can't say that I've met that feller in the middle there."

261

"Oh, that's my cousin, Gus," I said, smiling at Hubert Gene. "He don't live here. Just stopped by for a visit. I'm surprised you don't recognize him. He's actually pretty famous. Gus here's a midget. Works in the side show at the circus. You ever go to the circus over in Texarkana when it comes to town, Hubert Gene?"

"Uh, naw, can't say I have." Hubert Gene pushed his heavy glasses up on his nose and scratched the stubble of whiskers on his neck as he studied Old Gus.

"Aw, that's too bad, 'cause I'm sure you'd recognize him if you had. He's the star of the show. He has a condition that makes hair grow where it normally don't on people. The circus likes 'em to have fancy show business names. He goes by Jojo the Dog-Faced Boy."

Hubert Gene stared hard at Gus. Then a smile started to crease his face. "Come to think of it, by golly, I think I have heard of him. Howdy do Mister Jojo?"

I leaned toward Hubert Gene and put my open hand beside my mouth between Gus and Hubert Gene. "Gus here don't talk much," I said in a harsh whisper. "Has a speech impediment." I tilted my head toward Gus and cut my eyes his way. "He's a little sensitive about it."

"Well, that's too bad," Hubert Gene said. "I guess he don't have to talk much in the circus though. Just lets people look at him, right?"

"Yeah, that's about it."

"Well, guess I better get back to work. We could have a big ol' invasion of stray dogs if I don't stay on top of it."

Hubert Gene started to pull away but abruptly stomped on the brake. Leaning back out the window, he squinted and said, "Oh, by the way, Mister Jojo, you wouldn't happen to have an extra ticket for the next time the circus comes to town, would ya?"

# NON-FICTION

# The Tube of Torture

## by Connie Lewis Leonard

This wasn't the first time I'd been trapped in a Tube of Torture. Exactly three weeks prior, I showed up for my first appointment, confident I could meet the challenge. After donning the frock for the fat, I met the technician.

I lay down on the cold slab. The technician asked if I would like a blanket. I nodded because the room was as cold as a morgue. She asked if I would like head phones to listen to music. No, elevator music annoys me. She asked if I would like to cover my eyes. No, I like to be aware of my surroundings.

She jammed my shoulder into the appendage of the machine. "Don't move."

Move? How could I move? I was constrained in that contraption.

"Once we begin, lie perfectly still. Don't take deep breaths." I heard the door close as she left the room. The slab slid inside the monstrous machine.

The slab stopped, and I opened my eyes. Shrouded in darkness, mere inches separated me from the oppressive cocoon that encircled me. With my shoulder bound down, I had no room to move, even if I could, which I wasn't supposed to do.

Then the noise came—like blasts from atomic bombs. My legs and feet extended outside the cocoon, weighted down by the heavy blanket. The world could be disintegrating while I was trapped in this tube of torture.

Pray. *Yes.* "The Lord is my shepherd..." *Take my hand Lord Jesus. It's trapped in here. I can't reach up to You.* "I shall not want..." *I want out of here!* "He maketh me lie down in green pastures..." *Visualize green pastures surrounded by mountains—mountains—I feel like the mountains are crumbling on top of me, burying me alive.*

265

"He leadeth me beside the still waters..." *Water, oh God, is this what it feels like to drown?* "He restoreth my soul: He leadeth me in the paths of righteousness for His name's sake..." *God I'm trying to follow, to keep up, but my racing heartbeat is echoing, louder than the exploding noise.* "Yea, though I walk through the valley of the shadow of death..." *God, I'm in the valley of death. I can't breathe. I'm not afraid to die, but I don't want to suffocate, not today, not in here.*

"Stop! I want out of here."

The slab slid out. The technician reappeared. "What's wrong?"

"I can't move. I can't breathe."

"Do you want to take a break for a few minutes and try again?"

"How much longer will it take?"

"About forty minutes."

"No, I've had lots of CT scans, and they didn't bother me. I had an MRI on my knee, but I can't do this. It's too confining. I can't stand to be bound down. I cannot breathe!" I threw off the cover and sat up.

"You didn't tell me you're claustrophobic." She frowned.

"Well, I am a bit claustrophobic, but not bad. I have no trouble functioning in everyday life, but I felt smothered, like I was about to asphyxiate."

"Maybe your doctor can prescribe anti-anxiety meds."

I stood up and slipped on my shoes. "I don't do well on drugs."

"Well, call your doctor and see what he says."

* * *

That was three weeks ago. My doctor set up an appointment for an open MRI, and here I am.

Wrapped in the frock for the fat, I stared at the Massive Monster MRI. It wasn't a Tube of Torture, but it was still

266

imposing. It looked like the *Star Ship Enterprise*, or perhaps an enemy spaceship. The top would still be inches above my head. But the sides are open. I could stretch out my arm. I told the technician about my previous experience.

"You had a panic attack. That happens to a lot of people."

"I've never suffered from anxiety or panic attacks—before."

"Anxiety seems to increase with age. You want to give it a try?"

I nodded, kicked off my shoes and lay down on the cold slab.

She slipped my right arm into a shoulder attachment. So far, so good—not as tight or confining as the other contraption.

"Would you like a blanket?"

"No, thank you." I would rather be cold than smothered.

"Would you like a cloth over your eyes?"

"Yes, wet, please."

"Wet?" When I nodded she left the room and returned with a wet wash cloth. "Are you ready?"

I swallowed hard. "My mouth is really dry. Could I have a drink?"

"All I have is water. Is that okay?" I nodded and she returned with a cup of water and a straw. She held it while I took a sip. I swallowed and took another drink. "Are you ready?" She asked in her calm, quiet voice.

I nodded and placed the cloth over my eyes, but not my nose. I needed air. She handed me a panic button. "If you have a problem, squeeze and I will get you out immediately." I nodded. She gave me ear plugs to lessen the noise, patted my hand, and left, closing the door behind her.

*I can do all things through Christ who strengthens me. I can't do this God, but You can.*

The slab slid under the alien space ship. With the cloth over my eyes, I couldn't see it, but I could feel the massive metal suspended in space just inches above my head, above my nose and mouth, stealing my breath. I began to pray.

I wiggled my toes. I could move! I slowly moved my left arm. I reached out beyond the confines of the slab. Air, I had plenty of air. My nose itched, and I could scratch it. The ear plugs muted the noise from explosions to knocks. "Knock, knock. Who's there?" I smiled. "Knock three times on the ceiling if you want out."

Bangs followed the knocks. Booms like fireworks, electrifying noise, not earth-shattering blasts.

I began to sing praise songs in my mind, wiggling my toes to the beat. I held the panic button in my hand—soothing, reassuring, pacifying.

And it was over. I survived the Monster MRI! *Thou prepares a table before me in the presence of mine enemies: Thou anointest my head with oil; my cup runneth over.*

"Thank you, thank you for being so patient and kind," I told the technician.

She smiled like Mother Theresa. "They put me here because I am a mother hen."

"God bless you!" I said, restraining the urge to hug her.

The increased pain in my shoulder following my ordeal wasn't too bad. It reminded me I am alive.

*Surely goodness and mercy shall follow me all the days of my life: and I will dwell in the house of the Lord forever. Amen and Amen.*

# Reflections on my Thirteenth Year

## by Robert C. Taylor

It has been said that a boy's thirteenth year is more often than not the most memorable year of his life. Caught in a void between early childhood and adolescence, he's excited about the prospect of adult life, while at the same time reluctant, or perhaps afraid, to shed the security and innocence of his youth.

I turned thirteen in nineteen-fifty-nine, a year that proved to be a most remarkable chapter of my life. It was the year I landed my first real job. In August of that year, my brother Jack and I were hired to sack groceries at Reese's Supermarket where my dad worked as night manager. I pulled in fifty cents per hour, not a shabby wage back then for a teenager. I worked all night on weekends, twelve-hour shifts, and enjoyed sacking groceries, stocking shelves, sweeping the floor and other necessary chores.

Milton Reese, the store owner, while having a reputation as a hard-nose, was also known as quite a practical joker. He loved playing tricks on people, especially his employees, and it became an obsession for my brother and me to beat him at his own game. We came up with the perfect plan a week before Thanksgiving, but we needed assistance in carrying it through. Our plan required someone with an adult voice. For this we turned to our Uncle Louie.

Louie, my dad's brother, was quite a character in his own right. He became known as the Black Sheep of the family, a drinker and a rover, never staying at one place for any extended period of time. He just seemed to blow into town from time to time, spinning exotic tales of his many exploits, which we learned to take with a grain of salt. My parents always treated Louie well, but I think it's fair to say that no one expected him to do anything worthwhile with his life.

269

But opportunity, it has been said, is no respecter of persons, and often appears in the strangest of guises. Louie's golden opportunity came about as a result of a broken neck. It happened during a barroom brawl in Houston, where Louie suffered that injury as well as other less critical ones. He spent a year, more or less, recovering from his wounds in a hospital in Galveston. After fully recovering, he rode the Greyhound to Fort Worth where he took up residence in our home. That was the first time we saw Louie with the big white brace around his neck, but certainly not the last. Louie would don the brace on the weekends, long after he had fully healed, take his cup of brightly colored pencils, and catch the city bus to the ritzy section of town. He would sit on the corner of the busiest intersection with his head bowed low, and a hang-dawg expression on his face. He perfected the art of looking pitiful and of preying upon peoples' sympathies. Every Sunday evening, he would come home with more money in that cup than my dad had made working all week long at the supermarket. Taking off the brace, he would stash it in the closet where it would stay until the next weekend. I always enjoyed seeing him come home on the weekends because he wasn't the least bit stingy with his ill-gotten gain.

Our plan to prank Milton Reese was a rather simple one, and quite harmless, or so we thought, compared to some of the pranks Milton had pulled on us, most of them involving food that wasn't exactly what the label claimed it to be.

Our plan involved Nettie Mayfield, an old crabby black woman, and a regular customer of Reese's Supermarket, albeit not necessarily a preferred one. Nettie was a pest and a grouch, as well as a constant complainer, and the employees of Reese's store, and even Milton Reese himself, or I should say especially Milton Reese, would cringe upon seeing her enter the establishment. She had been known to start fights with customers, as well as employees, and had been asked on several occasions to exit the premises.

Our plan was to call Nettie and inform her that she had won a twenty-five-pound turkey from Reese's Supermarket, and all she had to do was to come into the store at ten on the Saturday morning before Thanksgiving and claim her prize, no purchase necessary. But as I said, we needed an adult voice, and when we approached Uncle Louie, he proved more than willing to assist us with our diabolical scheme.

My brother and I, as well as Louie, made sure we were present that Saturday morning, a morning that will be forever etched in my memory. Pitting an old crab like Nettie Mayfield against a stubborn hard nose like Milton Reese is not unlike pitting Godzilla against King Kong.

Nettie raised Billy Hell that morning, but Milton was determined to stand his ground. "You didn't win no damned turkey!" he yelled, "because there was no such friggin' contest!" But Nettie was adamant about receiving the prize she had been promised. Their voices could be heard more than two blocks away, and the argument attracted a large crowd of onlookers, many choosing sides, and there were rumors of wagering among the crowd, with Nettie receiving the more favorable odds. It became painfully obvious early on that Milton didn't stand a chance against the mean old crab of a woman.

For a while the crowd appeared to be divided along racial lines, the black folks rooting for Nettie and the white folks rallying behind Milton. However, the longer the argument lasted the more the tide turned. More and more white folks, who didn't wish to wind up on the losing side, were deserting Milton and turning their loyalty towards Nettie. As the argument wore on, Milton could sense he was running out of support. So, bless his heart, he decided it would be better to give up a turkey rather than take a chance on losing a large majority of his customers. He sent Cliff, his meat market manager, to pick out the biggest bird in the store, and when they presented it to Nettie the first thing she did was check the weight, printed right there on the label— *fourteen pounds, eleven ounces.* Well, she would have none of that.

"I won a twenty-five-pound turkey, not this scrawny fourteen-pounder!"

"You didn't win a damned thing!" Milton countered. "This is the biggest turkey I've got and you didn't win it! I'm giving it to you so you'll get the Hell out of my store, and by God, this is all you're getting from me!"

Nettie informed him that it was too late anyway because the spirits, as she called them, were already angered against him.

"I won't be threatened," Milton told her, but when all was said and done Nettie left the store with her fourteen-pound turkey, a seven-pound cured ham, and four pounds of assorted luncheon meats.

\* \* \*

All in all, I loved my job at Reese's, but as they say, "all good things must come to an end." One night in the wee hours, my brother and I smelled smoke and heard the wail of sirens. Jumping onto our bikes, we followed the fire trucks, which led us to Reese's super market. Standing there among the crowd of onlookers, and watching the flames soar high into the night sky, I was certain I heard Nettie's name mentioned several times. We never knew who or what started the fire. To this day I recall Nettie saying to Milton, *"It's too late, the spirits have already turned against you."* Could it be that Nettie helped those spirits along by providing the gasoline and striking the match?

# The Phantom

## by Beverly Harrison

Daddy had a friend from high school, a running buddy as he called him, who loved to rebuild and sell old cars he found in the wrecking yards of Oklahoma City. John was the oldest son in a family that raised and sold cattle, but his first and only love was automobiles. He had rebuilt and sold cars since he was old enough to drive. That would be 14 years of age, but don't tell anyone.

When my dad and John were in their 20s, they hitchhiked from Oklahoma City to Chicago to see Sally Rand at the 1933 World's Fair. Sally Rand was an American burlesque dancer and actress, most noted for her ostrich feather fan dance and balloon bubble dance. She was arrested many times during her career for perceived nudity and lewd behavior. She was never nude. She was just very good at appearing to be nude.

And she was every healthy young man's dream. But that's another story.

After they returned from Chicago, Daddy and John took separate paths. Daddy got married and moved away, eventually moving to Dallas and going to work for North American building aircraft for the war effort. John remained in Oklahoma City and took over the family cattle business, but he continued his first love of rebuilding cars. He and my dad remained good friends.

John had specific requirements for a car from the wrecking yards. The body had to be in good condition without any major dents or other damage, all of the parts had to at least be in the car, and the price had to be affordable. So far, his hobby had made him enough money to live in a line cabin on the ranch and stay away from the cows. It wasn't he didn't like cows, but he preferred them one-inch thick and served on a dinner plate with a baked potato. After all, his family had been in the cattle business since the Oklahoma Land Rush of 1889. He just happened to like cars more.

On his 40th birthday, John found his dream car: A 1934 Rolls Royce Phantom. It was part of an estate sale, but no one wanted to buy the wreck. The body was in perfect shape with few dents, the bumper was in the backseat, and the other various accessories were in the trunk.

After he negotiated a deal with the owner of the yard, he brought the car to his cabin on the back of a wrecker.

This car he would keep. He nicknamed it 'The Phantom.'

For the next six months he spent every spare minute repairing it. He rebuilt the engine and the transmission, replaced the interior and the seat covers, created a new dashboard, and added five new tires with wide whitewalls. The results were perfection.

The finish was shiny black, the headliner and steering wheel were brown, the seats were brown leather, and the buttons and levers were gold.

At last he was ready to drive it around town.

After several months of successfully driving it farther and farther away from his hometown, he decided to drive across country to visit family and friends in Los Angeles. It's 1,328 miles from Oklahoma City to LA, and the trip would take 20-plus hours on Interstate Highway 40 West.

The weather there and back was perfect, and he spent a week in Los Angeles making new friends and renewing old friendships. Then it was time to make the trip back to Oklahoma City.

Just outside of Albuquerque, New Mexico, his dream trip came to a sudden stop. The axle on his car broke.

This was well before cell phones, so he walked the last three miles to Albuquerque and hired a mechanic to bring his car into town. That was the easy part. Finding a replacement axle was the showstopper.

Finally, he called the main headquarters of Rolls Royce

in London, England, and explained his problem. Was there a dealership in America that sold axles for his car? He finally had to order a new axle and waited in town for the axle and parts to arrive.

Two days later, a very large helicopter with the Rolls Royce logo carrying a mechanic and parts landed at the local airport, and repairs to the car began. It took the mechanic from Rolls Royce and the mechanic in town one additional day to replace the axle and return the car to John. Handshakes were made, paperwork with the mechanic from Rolls Royce was signed, and John paid the local mechanic for his part of the job. Then John was on his way back to Oklahoma City and the mechanic was on his way back to England.

Now came the hard part. Waiting for the bill. He knew it would be excessive—a new axle and parts to replace it; flying a mechanic on a helicopter across the ocean; housing and meals for the mechanic and pilot. He didn't look forward to seeing the total price.

One month came and went but there was no bill in the mail. Another month came and went and still there was no bill. By now John was concerned.

After the third month, he called Rolls Royce in London, and explained what had happened and why he was calling. When would he get the bill for the repairs?

The person on the other end of the phone call transferred him to his manager, who then transferred him to the District Manager. Finally, he was transferred to the Director of the International Division.

After he had explained his dilemma for the fourth time, a very patient Director gave him his answer.

"My good man, there must be some mistake. A Rolls Royce does not break an axle. Have a nice day, sir."

# Why's That Dog on the Bus?

## by Kathryn McClatchy

"Why's that dog in here? Shouldn't be no animals on the bus. He's gonna bite me! Bus Driver! You make her get that mutt off the bus. I paid my fare. I don't have to share this space with no damn dog."

"Ma'am, you need to settle down," said the bus driver, glancing up at his rear-view mirror as Gizmo and Kathryn settled in their seat three rows ahead of a very loud and irate woman in her mid-twenties. It was just past sunset. Most passengers were on their way home from a long day at work. Kathryn had had a long day also, wasn't feeling well, and dreaded the noise, smells, and jostling of public transportation which would surely turn her headache into a full-blown migraine attack.

Gizmo was doing as he had been trained. Sensing Kathryn was unwell, he was completely focused on her. He knew the routine for riding the bus. Stand close to Kathryn while she steps up into the bus and pays her fare. Walk up the aisle in front of or behind her, as she commands, depending on how crowded it is. When she points to a seat, Gizmo goes in before her and lies on the floor under her seat. No dog parts on the aisle or they might get stepped on. No begging for attention from strangers. This is the routine.

Gizmo assumed his usual position on the bus.

"You gonna let that smelly dog ride on this bus? Bus Driver! That dog is mean. He's growling at me."

"Ma'am, that's a trained service dog. He has as much right to be on this bus with his handler as you do. He's not even near you. Please stop disrupting the other passengers." The other passengers in question were trying their best to ignore the loud woman, or were rolling their eyes at their seatmates. Kathryn was grateful Gizmo was on his best behavior and had been recently groomed. It didn't hurt that they had ridden with this driver a number of times before.

Bus rides could be difficult at best for service dogs. Even at off-peak times without crowds, it was difficult for Gizmo to feel secure with all the vibrations of the bus. Every time the bus crossed a train track or pothole, it startled him, often causing him to bump or bang himself against the bottom of the seat. Since Gizmo relied on his nose to monitor Kathryn's health, and his nose picked up so much more than human noses, it was distracting to be so close to so many feet, backpacks, lunch bags, and grocery sacks—not to mention all the smells left by people who had been on and off the bus all day. How long ago was that baby with the dirty diaper on the bus?

"Bus Driver! I pay taxes. I don't have to ride with no damn dog in my face. Make him get off."

Before the driver was able to respond, and while Kathryn was trying to decide the best way to handle the situation, two other passengers came to Gizmo's defense. They both tried to de-escalate the situation by pointing out how well behaved he was, and how he wasn't anywhere near her. Kathryn chose to stay quiet and keep calm. If she got upset, Gizmo would sense her stress and try to help, and that might be perceived by the difficult woman as aggression. When logic failed, another passenger who was familiar with ADA rules tried to explain them to the woman. Instead of calming down, the woman got louder and more belligerent.

At the next stop, the bus driver stood up and turned around. "Ma'am, we've all tried to be patient with you, but enough! You are the problem here, not the dog. Your choice is to either sit and be quiet until we get to your stop, or you can get off here. You choose. Any more trouble from you and I'm calling the police to remove you." He glared at her, as did many of the passengers around her, until she slid down in her seat, mumbling a string of profanities under her breath. Gizmo kept focus on Kathryn.

Three stops later the young woman pushed the yellow strip by the window to notify the driver to stop, and gathered her belongings to exit. The bus jerked to a standstill. Kathryn kept eye contact with Gizmo, relieved this situation was about over. While watching Gizmo though, she didn't see the woman's next move. As she passed their seat, she side-stepped onto the floor under Kathryn's leg, and stomped on Gizmo's tail. Before she even removed her foot, she screamed and yelled, "That dog's attacking me!"

Kathryn silently thanked Mike Pugliese, Gizmo's first trainer, for making sure Gizmo could handle this abuse during puppy boot camp and repeated temperament testing. Rolling that shopping cart over his tail had seemed so cruel during Gizmo's Public Access Test, but now the long-suffering black Lab simply looked at Kathryn with sad eyes.

The man seated immediately behind Kathryn spoke up in Gizmo's defense. "Get yourself off this bus. That dog never did nothing to you! You just hurt an innocent animal that spends his life helping someone who can't help herself. And that animal has more sense than you. You stepped on him on purpose, and he just kindly moved farther out of your way. Girl, you need to learn some manners from that dog. What's wrong with you? Go on. Get!"

By now others were yelling at the woman, and she realized she had no recourse but to close her mouth and exit the bus. As the doors closed behind her, the passengers quickly settled down. A few asked if Gizmo was okay. Kathryn reached down and gently checked his tail. He flinched just enough to let her know it was tender, but not enough for her to suspect any serious damage.

Kathryn thanked those around her for their concern and support. A few people apologized on behalf of the woman. One person asked a couple of questions about Gizmo. An older man mentioned that he had worked with a military dog in the army— "just amazing what those dogs can do." Of all the times they had ridden the bus, this was the first time anyone had been openly hostile towards Gizmo. Hoping it would be the last, Kathryn pushed the yellow strip as her stop came into view.

# Four Guys in a Boardinghouse

## by Barna A. Richards, M.D.

Jimmy and I were friends and teammates, and we looked forward to football practice starting in the fall. We felt strong and healthy; both being outfitted in our farmer-tanned skin after working all summer in the oil fields. Along with the rest of the guys on the team, we thought we would have a good year, but about two weeks before practice started, we had a setback. Jimmy and I both learned that because his parents and mine had taken jobs in other towns, we wouldn't be playing.

Nothing could have affected him or me worse than this news. Football was what we lived for, and by moving to a new town, at best we would have to miss an entire year, and we wouldn't be with our friends whom we had played with since Junior High. The coaches wanted us to play also, and they began to brainstorm over ways we could stay. Between coaches, teachers, townspeople and businessmen, a solution was found: Jimmy and I would live with two of the school personnel, and the school would hire us to be janitors to allow us the money to pay rent and have a little to spend.

One of the men, Richard Owens, taught in the school, and the other, Harold Miller, served as an administrator. The two men shared a duplex where I would live with Mr. Owens, and Jimmy with Mr. Miller. These two brave gentlemen served as surrogate parents to two kids who were still wet behind the ears, as the old saying goes. That arrangement probably wouldn't be possible today, because someone would find a problem with it, but those were different times, and no one objected.

These two gentlemen tutored us in an informal way, even though they had no obligation other than to provide a place to stay, and Mr. Owens became a lifelong friend. He is now in his 90s, and I in my 80s, and we have recently reconnected; it is fortunate that we lasted long enough to accomplish that. Mr. Owens (quite a few years passed before

I could call any of my teachers by their first name) taught me some practical things of a social nature. Having lived in small towns, I had little sophistication, but my mother had taught me manners, and Mr. Owens helped me with social graces, of which I had little exposure. Well, I can call him "Richard" now. He seemed to really care about my welfare, and his tutelage was done without rancor or condescension. We also had a lot of fun; Richard played piano and organ, and when he did, a party many times happened, and he always seemed to have a pretty girl around, much to my liking. I am grateful for his influences on my life.

Mr. Miller possessed a more reserved persona and influenced Jimmy and I in other ways, exposing us to music, Broadway plays, and a little opera. He also chaperoned four of us—me, Jimmy, Bobby D. Crawford, and Danny Villarreal—to Chihuahua, Mexico over the holidays There we enjoyed the city's sights and their New Year's celebration, and boy, did they celebrate. Booze flowed like water, and we teenagers took full advantage of the chaperone's lack of attention to our imbibing, as he was engaged in lively conversation with the resident dignitaries. The attendees, they of upper-class Hispanic culture, were owners of land and some of inherited wealth. They loved a celebration, and New Years' seemed to be a special one for them. They dressed in fine clothes, with the men in tuxedos, and the women in long gowns and wearing their best jewelry. They impressed those of us who weren't accustomed to such elegance. They were gracious and welcomed us warmly, even though we were not equal to their level of opulent society.

The four of us, the oldest was 17, enjoyed the ambiance of the city, and while admittedly being somewhat impatient while visiting cathedrals, we had appreciation for the historical landmarks and the pleasant sensation redolent of life of an earlier time. We met some girls who were chaperoned by an aunt while we went to a bowling alley, much the same as a bowling alley at home, and had a good time. The chaperone was customary in both Spanish and

European cultures when young men and women were courting, and she sat a comfortable but watchful distance from us. We spoke no Spanish, except Danny Villarreal who translated. I felt I had gone back to a romantic and more formal era of civilization when higher morals were standard and good manners expected. The experiences we had in Mexico introduced me to a different culture. The affluence of the New Year's party-goers contrasted with the prevalence of overwhelming poverty, and made a lasting impression on me.

Back home, in the spring of that year, an incident occurred at our duplex when both of our benefactors were out of town, and some of our teammates came for a visit. Two guys decided to wrestle, not in anger, but vigorously, and, during the ensuing melee, one of the combatants hit a wall with good force, caving in the drywall. Whoops! Disaster. Jimmy and I expected we had just lost our home. We'd be expelled, kicked off the football team, woe was us.

A serious discussion then commenced. None of us could afford to pay to have it repaired, and on a weekend, no one would be available anyway. Panic, fret, worry, and fear were our lot. Mr. Miller always kept his apartment in meticulous fashion and would be very disappointed, if not terribly angry, and he was due home the next day. Then, innovation, necessity (the mother of invention), and an epiphany came from W. C. Herricks, one of the wrestlers. He had done work with his father, had learned some carpentry, and thought he could fix it. Miraculously, with some help from us amateurs, the wall became whole again. When Mr. Miller arrived the next day, we proudly showed him our handiwork, explaining how we thought a new wall would dress up his home, but Mr. Miller said in a very stoic and direct manner, "I liked it the way it was."

When all the smoke cleared, there were no terrible consequences. We weren't expelled, we stayed on the team, and Mr. Miller, after a period of penance on our part, forgave us. After one year, however, it seemed he had done all the surrogate fathering he could suffer.

The next year, 1952, there were four 'homeless urchins,' all of them teammates who needed succor, and Moore's Boarding house provided the solution. Everyone in town held Moore's Boarding House in high esteem as an eating establishment where real home cooking stoked the appetite for all comers. The clientele consisted of oil field workers in oil-stained coveralls, shop keepers in dresses, barbers, students, and an assortment of salesmen dressed in suit and tie. They all made a point of getting to town at lunch or dinner time to enjoy the offerings that Mrs. Moore prepared with loving hands. Very shortly, I learned what was meant by 'boardinghouse reach,' because if one was of a shy nature, the food would disappear right in front of his eyes when a hand on an arm as long as a giraffe's leg fetched it. This was because the meals were served family style on long tables, and, as Darwin might have said, 'survival of the fittest' prevailed. No one left hungry though, because Mrs. Moore always provided plenty of food.

Anyone of common sense would have predicted that four teenagers, with unbridled testosterone dictating much of their thoughts and actions, and living unsupervised in a boarding house, would result in chaos, if not disaster. Really, what could go wrong, or, more likely, what were the odds that something would not go wrong?

We weren't bad kids, and actually we were pretty dull, our days being spent attending school, followed by football practice, and later in the year, basketball and track or baseball. After practice, we did our janitor work and felt too tired to do much else, having put in a 12- or 14-hour day. Occasionally, we went to a movie or accepted an invitation to a friend's house, but our social life suffered because the lack of transportation hindered any possibility of making the drag or having a date. There were no TVs to entertain us then, probably a good thing! We shared one large room, Spartan, like a military barracks without the drill sergeant, or an orphanage without a house mother. We each had a bunk bed, but there were no frills such as desks, curtains, pictures, carpets, couches, or lounge chairs. One closet served to hold all our clothes, but since we didn't have many, the closet held all we had. When we first opened the closet in the middle of winter, about a million mosquitoes flew out, the little bloodsuckers having found sanctuary there.

Our pay for the janitor job barely covered room and board and didn't allow for many frivolities, but as kids of the depression, we didn't expect much more and felt happy for what we had. We took showers after practice, so bathing wasn't a problem, but we would have been stinky otherwise, with only one bathroom in the boardinghouse. Laundry presented another problem. I wore one pair of Levis for about four months, and I washed my white T-shirts and socks in the sink—sporadically. I didn't have the luxury of having my laundry done. Perhaps the most strikingly pleasant thing about living in the boardinghouse was to awaken each morning to the aroma of rising yeast rolls.

Speaking of the bathroom, one of the guys got a case of crabs (pubic lice). He related the story that he got the bugs from the toilet seat and blamed it on the housekeeper, but strangely, no one else got them. He initially didn't know what they were, and when he told the lady who ran the store across from the school, (who mothered us, the lady, not the school), that he had these little bugs crawling all over his pubic area, she laughed and told him what they were and what to do. He persisted in his story about the commode in the boardinghouse, but we still didn't get them.

The four guys included Bill, who came from Kansas by way of Strawn, Texas and exemplified the personality of the typical mid-westerner, laid back, non-confrontational, mannerly, and a good athlete. Jimmy, on the other hand, made wisecracks about almost everything and made a shamble of peoples' names. For example, one of the administrators whose middle name was 'Westproctor,' Jimmy called 'Eastproctor,' or 'Westschictor.' He had several names for me, also, but they aren't appropriate for publication. Jimmy also played tough football. Jerry never said much, in fact I can't remember having conversations with him, but he and I got along very well. I guess I fit in the middle, having opinions that I didn't hesitate to share, but I didn't like controversy either, even though I had a hot head on the football field and found myself removed from a couple of games for vigorously disagreeing with officials for their egregious calls.

Bill took a very popular girl to the movie one evening—think *The Last Picture Show*, and as he and she sat in the very back row, some other guys heard him singing the very popular song "Mona Lisa" to her. From then on, his name was Mona Lisa, later shortened to just 'Lisa,' a moniker he didn't like very much, but we were persistent with addressing him that way for the remainder of the time before he graduated.

The four of us who roomed in the less than opulent surroundings didn't have a free ride. We all had to work to pay our way, because if anyone paid for our upkeep, it would have been illegal with the UIL and could cause the team to forfeit all of its games. The previous year, during the school session, the school hired us to clean the building, and I experienced a disappointing revelation when I learned that the girls' rest room was always dirtier than the boys' rest room. 'Sugar and spice and everything nice' didn't seem very valid after that experience. We did our work after school and football practice, or whichever sport we played, after which activities we were expected to keep up with school work. I could have used this rather full schedule as an excuse for my not-so-good grades, but the truth lay in the fact that I thought it sissy and girlish to take books home, and thus my grades resided near the bottom of the class. In 1952, Stanolind Oil Co. hired us to do their janitor work, most likely after great pressure from coaches, city fathers, and fans. Could it have been possible the school was less than satisfied with our performance the previous year?

One evening Coach Barton loaned us his car. This came about because one of the guys convinced him we would all be very careful, but foolishly we went to the officer's club at Rattlesnake Air Force Base in Pyote, Texas a few miles away. We knew the bartender there would serve us beer, even though we were only 15- or 16-years old. It still is hard to believe that an air force base, a federal facility, would serve alcohol to teenagers, but it happened. We had a few beers— actually I think I took about three swallows to show my manliness, but I didn't finish the beer. We weren't drunk, at least in our adolescent brains, but on the way home, some guys in another car started fooling around and side-swiped Coach's car. Oh my! I was so scared I could have just jumped out and run into the mesquite bushes and hidden, but we had to face the music. When we told Coach what happened, he only said "I'm glad no one got hurt." Whew! What a relief. Coach Barton became a second father to many of us and a good one I still miss.

As predicted, our football team went to the state semifinals that year, having lost to a team from a town named Newcastle, about the same size as Wink and similarly, not an oasis in the desert. The team arrived in seven or eight cars, players, cheerleaders, fans, and all, and we were confident we would prevail over these pretenders to the throne. We lost and were devastated because we knew we were the best team, but they didn't agree, and neither did the score: 33 to 26, we on the low side. I had been a starter on defense and played sparingly on offense, but I don't recall contributing greatly in that game that ended in ignominious defeat. The next year there would be a different outcome.

The following summer we formed a loosely organized baseball team. I pitched one game and got bombed the first inning. I could throw hard and fast but had no movement on the ball, and the batters soon figured me out and had batting practice that sent balls at me like kamikaze bombers that caused me to duck after each pitch. That outing ended my very short pitching career that might have been better with some coaching, but I didn't have any prior pitching instruction.

One day we played a game up in Andrews—or Seminole, I can't remember which—and on the way home I decided to change clothes and took off my baseball pants. Since I had to pee, I had the driver stop and I got out, waited for cars to pass, and as I finished my business, the car sped off, leaving me only in my jockstrap with a bare butt and feet. The temperature scorched to about 110 degrees, and the asphalt highway was much hotter, and as I ran to catch the car, it sped off again. When I finally got back into the car, everyone had a good laugh except for me.

Later in the evening, my feet felt like they were in an oven, and my soles began to swell, looking like water-filled balloons. By the next day, the bottoms of my fluid-filled feet looked as though they might burst at any moment, and they hurt badly. I had to crawl to the bathroom and could not go to meals, as the swelling and pain continued, and I languished in bed almost two weeks before I could comfortably walk again. During that time, I felt alone and depressed and had a lot of self-pity, wondering if I had done permanent damage to my feet, and that scared me. I could have gone to my parents, but I didn't know how I could physically get to Odessa where they now lived, and I didn't want to worry them. Also, I feared they would insist I come home. No one came to check on me the entire time during my lonely and miserable vigil, and that further disappointed me. I guess my friends were embarrassed that they had caused me so much misery. My feet finally healed, and by football season they were no problem, a tribute to the healing powers of a youthful body.

We won the state football championship that year, 1952. A state championship anywhere, in any class, is a difficult achievement, and we were very proud. I made three interceptions in the final game against Deer Park, a town close to Houston. Deer Park is now a much more populated city and in the highest class of Texas sports. It was a town that was growing rapidly even then, which gave them an advantage over us, with new kids and athletes coming in to their schools, while our little town continued to lose population. It seemed strange then, and still does, that I felt no elation at the end of the championship game, the most coveted goal in high school football. Later in life I have become more appreciative.

The doldrums characterized life after football season—school bored me, and I didn't have a real girlfriend. Quail season lasted until the end of February, and that gave me some pleasure, but shotgun shells were expensive, and I had limited funds. I didn't like basketball—the gym always felt cold, taking a shower was an ice bath, the locker room smelled of athlete's feet and body odor, and I didn't like the coach. Jock itch and athletes' foot plagued me, and I scratched until the skin bled. Once, I peeled skin off the ball of my foot about the size of a quarter and a fourth of an inch thick, and the underlying skin caused me much pain.

One might imagine how well I performed in school—not well. If not for quail hunting, that time of year was nearly a total loss, and I can't recall a single thing I accomplished. Actually, after careful consideration, I can't remember accomplishing anything at all in high school, but working in the oil fields provided me with a better real-life education in many ways.

> *"Life's but a walking shadow, a poor player,*
> *That struts and frets his hour upon the stage,*
> *And then is heard no more; it is a tale*
> *Told by an idiot, full of sound and fury,*
> *Signifying nothing."*
> *Macbeth, Act V, Scene 5*

This famous quote by Shakespeare about sums up life in general, doesn't it? —unless one is a narcissist and believes he or she is a very special individual, of which there are very few. After practicing medicine for over 50 years, I'm sure my 'strut across the stage' will not have changed the world for either better or worse, but it was done with good intentions, honesty, and fairness.

Finishing the school year offered the opportunity to work more in the oil fields, in jobs that would be considered terrible by some of today's teenagers. Back then we sought them eagerly, cherishing a paycheck earned by hard work, and enjoying a sense of accomplishment in having provided for our spending money.

We would arrive at the contractor's office at 6:00 a.m., our sack lunch in hand, waiting on the porch for a foreman to tell us if a job was available that day. If so, we went out in a truck and did whatever was needed. I learned very soon that digging ditches in caliche rock gave me a pain in the back, blisters on my hands, and a sunburn from the west Texas heat that often reached 110 degrees, or more. We used a bar weighing 15 to 20 pounds to break up the caliche, and a day of lifting it up and down numerous times made for a sound night's sleep. Digging in sand didn't offer any great advantages either, for although the sand was easier to dig, it fell back into the hole as soon as it was shoveled out.

If we didn't get work on a given day, we took our lunch to Charley's pool hall and played pool or dominoes, thus furthering our real-life education among the spit-and-whittle gang of old guys who were full of advice for us 'young bucks.' These old men played dominoes and seemed psychic in their ability to know what everyone had in their hand, never hesitating to chew our butts out when we didn't make the right play.

"Damn Bronc (Charley called all of us kids Bronc), didn't you know Hahd had the double six?" No, Charley, I didn't. 'Hahd' had come from Massachusetts, where 'Rs' are as rare as Republicans in New York; his nickname was 'Hard Boil,' thus 'Hahd.'

It might seem strange, and almost criminal to today's parents, that we spent a lot of time in the pool hall, but this place wasn't in the inner city where the mob might've hung out. Oh, it is true that some unsavory characters called it their second home, and a few might have shot a gambler (or someone who stole his girlfriend) back in the old oil boom days, but they weren't a threat to us, primarily because we played football, which made us immune to violence, at least off the field. Later in my medical practice, it occurred to me that my work in the oil fields and my acquaintances in the pool hall taught me that ordinary men, many who hadn't finished third grade, were pretty sharp fellows. They had suffered through the great depression, and most had served in WWII. Knowing these men made me a better doctor, because I understood what a hard day's labor meant, and my working-men patients seemed to appreciate the fact that I didn't look down on them when they came in sweaty and dirty, straight from working all day.

While my education suffered from a lack of interest and a paucity of effort toward academics, later reflections on those scholastically barren years bring to mind that not all was lost. Does a Harvard graduate know the difference between a tool pusher and a roustabout, a drill stem from a Hughes bit, a Mexican drag line from a Ditch Witch, a vinegaroon from a butterfly, a pulling unit from a drilling rig, an electrical floor polisher from a wet mop, snooker from eight ball? I learned those things the hard way. I worked, or sometimes played, to gain such knowledge.

Graduating from high school scared me and offered some uncertain and uncomfortable choices: go to work; go to college (and work); or go in the military. The military probably offered the best choice, but to remain home never entered our minds. Many of today's youth have more comforts, less financial concerns, and more opportunities, but there may be something lacking that might never be replaced: self-reliance. Maybe that's why so many youths seem to be enthralled with socialism, sadly believing someone else will take care of them. What a rude awakening they have awaiting them.

# POETRY

# The Old Home Place

## by Dan Vanderburg

*The Christmas season always makes me think about home and family. In 1918 my grandparents bought acreage in northeast Texas and built a large, country home for their family. At the time, their family consisted of one son and four daughters ranging in age from Mother's eldest sister of 14 years to my mother, who was an infant. I believe Grandad may have experienced something like this when he found the land to build his new home.*

### Grandad's Dream

He searched all through the countryside
To find the perfect site
To build a great-big family home
To suit his family right.

He led his horse through native grass
And smelled the sweet, fresh air,
And climbed the hill to sit awhile
To see the beauty there.

He reached and took a big handful
Of rich earth at his feet,
And dreamed of crops that he would raise
And garden's bounty treats.

He took a while to walk around
The hill all lush and green.
The barn goes here, the garden there,
The house goes in between.

The visions came to life for him.
The country home would be
A joyful place to make a life
For his big family.

He couldn't wait to show his wife
What he had found that day,
And bring her back to let her see
Where all their kids would play.

He dreamed of that big house up there
With porches front and back,
Two floors high with gabled roof,
There's nothing it would lack.

The water well, with bucket close,
And outhouse built for two.
They'll have lots of coal oil lamps,
And stone fireplaces too.

With that house built and family in,
They'd never want for more.
They'd have everything right there
That they'd been working for.

Smiling as he turned to go,
He mounted up to leave.
"Pretty ain't it?" he nodded to himself,
And whispered to the breeze.

*As a child, I enjoyed the many happy days at Grandmother's and Granddad's old, two-storied farm house, and went back time and time again, each time to a new adventure. It was the perfect place for a kid to play and spend time with such loving people in those important, innocent, carefree years.*

*Time slipped away. I grew up and saw my grandparents less as they aged, not because I loved them any less, I just had other teen-age and young adult priorities. Old age and infirmity took their toll with my grandparents. Many years after they both passed on, I visited their old home place again. It had been uninhabited for over fifteen years. I was inspired to write:*

## Nostalgia

Driving up the hard-packed lane
It finally came to view.
Memories that had dulled with time
Began to stir anew.

I saw the yard where I had played
Now high in Johnson seeds.
My climbing tree, once large and proud,
A skeleton in the weeds.

The porch, the walls, the gabled roof,
The weather's done its work.
The wind and rain and sun and snow,
Their duties did not shirk.

I went inside reluctantly
To see what time had done.
I brushed away the spider webs
That spiders once had spun.

The gaily printed paper hung
With aging, toil-worn hands
Now hangs forlornly from the wall
In faded, ragged strands.

The railing's gone forever
That gave me so much joy,
Running up and sliding down
When I was just a boy.

The laughter's gone forever too
As are the sounds and scents.
All that's left are echoes
Of those truly sweet events.

The elements of time have caused
This old house to age.
But I no longer mourn its loss.
My mind's a history page.

*Quite a few years after the visit that inspired the above poem, I returned once again to the old homeplace while in the area for a Memorial Day visit to the country cemetery where the grandparents were buried. My cousins and I once more went to visit the home place. We found the current owner had torn down the house and scraped the ground smooth and disposed of the debris where the grand old house, smoke house, water well, and well-tended garden once proudly stood. The land had been returned once again to natural prairie with nothing to indicate there had ever been a home or family there.*

*Years later after reminiscing about my last visit to the old home place, I wrote this poem about that memory.*

## Nostalgia II

So many years have come and gone
Since I last saw that place.
But sitting here, and thinking back,
A smile just crossed my face.

I think of what I saw that day
When driving up that lane.
I thought that I'd be sad to see
That things were not the same.

The big old house I knew so well
Forever gone to me,
But in its place a change had come
That I was glad to see.

I saw that day what Granddad saw
When he first found the land,
And why he fell in love with it
And built a home so grand.

I stood and looked out o'er the fields
As he had done also,
And with my eyes saw what he'd seen
A hundred years ago.

I saw with every sense I had,
To know the land as he.
I think I knew just what he felt
As those thoughts came to me.

The lush green grass and bright wildflowers
Gave promise of rich earth
With crops to feed a family
And profit of good worth.

I felt warm sun upon my skin,
The cool wind brushed my face
Bringing with it all the smells
Of lush grass on that place.

I reached down then as he may have
To pluck a tender blade
And put it 'tween my lips to taste
What that rich earth had made.

I heard the bees and mockingbird,
The Bob White's call so clear.
All the country sounds around
Were music to my ear.

The house is gone, and prairie's back
Like when Comanches roamed.
Now I know why Tom Bell chose
This place to be his home.

Smiling as I turned to go,
A zephyr whispered by.
"Pretty ain't it?" the light breeze said,
Almost as a sigh.

# A, B, C, D

## by Connie Lewis Leonard

A, B, C, D,
Read To me.

Come and sit
Upon my knee,

Let me hold you
Close and tight,

Before this day
Turns to night,

My dear little one,
Son of my only son,

I cherish each day
We have to play.

My little boy grew
Up much too soon,

An athlete, a graduate,
A teacher, a coach, a groom.

Too busy with life,
Day-to-day strife,

I failed to cherish
Each moment we had,

Now my little boy
Is your big, strong dad.

I can't turn back the clock,
But wisdom demands I stop,

Put aside the trivial,
Strive for the eternal.

E, F, G,
How I love thee

Son of my son,
My only grandson.

# What Have You Done?

## by Donna Pierce

I look at your picture, what have you done?
Where have you been, and how far have you run?
So many hard times now show in your eyes,
I wish I had saved you from all the lies.
The world is cold, but for you to survive,
You must have God's grace and faith on your side.
Don't hold in your sorrow just let it go,
For there is a tomorrow, don't you know?
Deep down in your heart, there's a will to win,
So reach down inside for it and begin.

# The Pageturner's Pen

## by Jonathan Mathews

Pages yet turning are filling with ink.
Do ever we pause, can you consciously blink?
What will be written of time we have past?
How long before our next page is the last?

What is the legacy left to remain?
Reading our story, what is there to gain?
What would be found if we took time to look?
Have we yet to realize our life is a book?

We each are a person, of what are we made?
The pieces of past circumstances arrayed.
So which are your pieces and what have you kept?
Do you in your thoughts your own story accept?

What have you learned in the trial and test,
And thinking back now, do you trust it was best?
What of your character would not have been?
Had you not have conquered the struggles within?

What of the good you have seen as you go?
Which of the wonders of life do you know?
How do you help people, what do you give?
What in your life gives you reason to live?

What of the heartache, and what did you learn?
Which of life's many deceits made you turn?
There must have been sorrow, misery, pain.
Everyone suffers, but was it in vain?

Who in the future will, reading you, find
Someone inspiring, loving, and kind?
Why in the future could somebody fail;
Learning your evil by reading your tale?

Which of your lessons, once learned, have you taught?
Some teaching purposed, but most teaching not?
Why, of your lessons, are many hid deep,
Burying secrets in turbulent sleep?

All has a reason while each has a cost.
Some step out surely, but many are lost.
Why keep your silence with others in need,
When your story's moral could help them succeed?

Whatever is written, it always is read,
So write your own pages, for then you are dead.
But one thing remember, as all authors do,
Whatever you write is the image of you.

When your life is over and new lives have come,
Your work will be seen, if not many, by some.
So, knowing your influence, this I would ask:
Please, write a good story, do well in your task.

We each have a purpose, one part of the whole.
Just give the first push, watch life's carpet unroll.
Together we'll make it, this, surely, I know,
But never we get there if we never go.

We each have a story, but stories have passed.
So what of our future, which pages will last?
We're here to help others, to graciously give,
So go with a purpose, and consciously live.

# Grampaw, Was That You?

## by Dan Vanderburg

Grampaw, was that you back then
Playing with that toy?
How cute you were so long ago
When you were just a boy.

Grampaw, was that you back then
With that old jalopy car?
That was just the first you owned
And they would take you far.

Grampaw, was that you back then
Wearing soldier's clothes?
That foreign war, so far away.
That road—you freely chose.

Grampaw, was that you back then
Dancing the night away?
Oh my gosh, that's Grandma!
It's on your wedding day.

Grampaw, was that you back then?
That very special guy?
Working hard for family
As years went flying by?

Grampaw, was that you back then
Who showed your grandkids fun?
You made me feel in my own way
I was your special one.

Grampaw, was that you back then
That held me in your lap,
And listened to my secrets
Before I had my nap?

Grampaw, was that you back then
That took me out for treats,
Then fibbed to Mom back home
That supper, I would eat?

Grampaw, was that you back then
That taught me things to know
To be a better person
And do well as I grow?

Grampaw, was that you back then
That showed me how to see
That if I just try hard enough
Dreams could come true for me?

Grampaw, was that you back then
That gave this place such worth?
This world's a better place right now
'Cause your feet have walked this earth.

Grampaw, was that you?

# Perspicere

## by Jonathan Mathews

I feel all around me the gentlest plea
To share hidden beauty that only I see.

We call ourselves poets, but what does that mean?
Our minds are as wanderers ever between.

The sure of reality, sequence and end,
And pure possibility. These edges blend.

At points of convergence of hoping and time
We artists of words author paintings of rhyme.

We write for reality, masked as pretend,
And weave the true fables that fiction has penned.

Where thoughts are as currents in culture the stream
We plait the dry rushes of life in with dream,

And ask what could ever not possibly be
By lighting another's desire to see.

I work from a quiet place poorly defined
Which helps me write freely when life is confined.

Here I keep memories, wishes and dreams,
Some dear conversations, quotations and schemes,

Collages of people, and words short and long,
With feelings to match, whether weak, whether strong.

I keep trails of logic with argument cues,
And several perspectives I frequently use.

But prized of my treasures are paintings and scenes.
They serve as my windows for practical means.

I look through a piece as it hangs on my wall,
And I enter its world as a door in a hall.

Our lives can be binding, the facts tend to lead.
A mind when exploring a picture is freed.

I meet people, go places, see things and learn.
I write my own stories and live them in turn.

Here words can show beauty and phrases can speak,
And heartfelt encouragement carries the weak.

But living is choosing, and fiction a guise,
For life is my painting, those windows my eyes.

I'm not quite as absent as absent may seem.
I simply wake up and continue to dream.

The real world inspires me, day after day,
But real worlds and fiction do oft overlay.

There nothing around you is set as it seems
To a teller of tales and a weaver of dreams.

# Friendship

## by Donna Pierce

I passed by the place where you died today.
It was quite sad, I have to say.
We were great friends at one time,
but my husband you thought was fine.
For if you knew him, you wouldn't have blinked,
I tried to tell you to make you think.
It was not that I was afraid to lose the man.
It was your betrayal I guess, and who I am.
You see, your friendship was more important to me,
than the man who saw himself as someone he couldn't be.
Sleep soundly in that bed beneath the tree.
Know my poor friend, that I forgive thee.

# The Last Dance

## by Dan Vanderburg

Hello out there! I'm here at last
To show myself to you.
I waited till the rest were gone
So I'd stand out, all fresh and new.

I'm tall above the dying stalks
All bright and at my best.
I'm all alone in my grandeur,
In my best red, velvet dress.

High above the ground I hear
The whisper the breeze brings,
And sway with music in the air
Brought forth by angel's wings.

I bend and swing and move just right
And add a dip or two.
I'm glad to give this one last show.
I know it pleases you.

All through spring and summer
Your yard had every hue.
Brown leaves now hide the grass,
I'm all that's left for you.

I waited till the rest were gone
To push my stalk up high.
For one last blast of color
And dance against the sky.

Soon I'll fade and be no more
When autumn days get colder.
But I must dance this one last time.
I know I'll not grow older.

I take great pride in giving you
This one last dance my dear.
But wait till spring, I promise you
Much more again next year.

# AUTHORS

# Rick Anderson

Being born in Seattle, Washington in 1949 to a career Air Force officer and his wife, Rick led a nomadic military dependent's life before finally settling in Southern California upon his father's retirement from the service.

Shortly after graduating from Redlands High School, Rick enlisted in the Marine Corps, serving as a combat "grunt" during the Vietnam War.

Upon completion of his enlistment, Rick returned to college, completing both an Associate's degree in Business Administration at Orange Coast College, then a Bachelor of Science degree in Entomology at the University of California at Davis. Graduation brought a career in the food industry first at Del Monte Corporation and then at Miller Brewing Company in Fort Worth, from which he retired after almost 30 years of service.

A relative newcomer to writing, he began his writer's journey as a path to share his service experience in the Marine Corps with his current wife, Donna, and sons Eric and Ryan. One story led to another, then another, and a newfound passion was born.

Rick's other interests include fishing, metal detecting, water color painting, and photography. A resident of Granbury for over 25 years, Rick now splits his time between Florida in the winter and New York during the summer.

# Gail Armstrong

Gail was born in Brockton, Massachusetts, grew up in Connecticut and attended Peter Bent Brigham School of Nursing and Boston University.

She married her husband John 57 years ago this April. Together they raised two sons and two daughters, who gave them 12 grandchildren. Their children were raised in the same home she and her husband own today.

Gail is a classically trained pianist who has played professionally and sung at area restaurants and at family weddings. She recently performed a concert for friends and family with plans for another one soon.

Music is not her only love. She adores drawing, painting, gardening and people tell her she is a great cook.

Gail and her husband enjoyed boating for many years until last year. They sold their boat to have more time for family events and land travel.

At any time, you might see her writing a poem. Something will trigger her muse and she sits down to write. Poetry is her first love in writing. Anything that touches her senses, nature, children, the sunset, an event, etc.

She loves to dabble in writing children's stories and has a talent for being able to look through the eyes of a child and see things not normally noticed by adults.

Since she started writing short stories for Granbury Writers' Bloc last year, Gail says her life has taken on new meaning. She knows short story writing is an art and she works at perfecting it. Writing is interesting, exciting, fun and she looks for inspiration for good plots constantly.

Inspirational books and novels, such as books by Deepak Chopra. Dr. Wayne Dyer. M. Scott Peck M.D., Ayn Rand, Jon Meacham and Mary Higgins Clark are a few of Gail's favorites.

"At 80 I've only begun." She says.

# Gary Christenson

Gary Christenson is a new fiction writer with much to learn. He began writing fiction after several years of writing non-fiction for his precious metals educational blog *deviantinvestor.com*.

He authored several books on gold and silver in the past five years. Christenson self-published *Buy Gold Save Gold! The $10K Logic.* He also self-published *Gold Value and Gold Prices From 1971 to 2021*, which was translated into German and traditionally published in hardback in Germany. His articles are published on *deviantinvestor.com* as well as other popular sites such as *321gold, Peak Prosperity, Goldseek, and Dollarcollapse.*

Christenson is a retired accountant and business manager who has studied markets, investing and trading for 40 years. Fifty years ago he did graduate work in physics, but did not complete his Ph.D. dissertation.

# BJ Condike

Brian arrived in Texas as soon as he could after growing up and attending school in Massachusetts. An avid and lifelong reader, his first interest in writing sparked when minoring in English as he studied chemistry at UMass Amherst.

Brian began writing fiction only a few years ago. He has won several local short story contests, and recently placed in the top 1% of a Writer's Digest national short story competition. He is currently attending the Writers Path program at Southern Methodist University, and has completed the first draft of his mystery novel, *Wrongful Death*. His ultimate goal is to traditionally publish one or more novels.

Brian has pursued several personal interests, including community theater, photography, woodworking, home improvement, fishing, and bowhunting. He is proud of his daughter Meridith, his son Curtis, and his two granddaughters Emily and Ava. Brian looks after his 102-year old father, and enjoys living in Granbury with his loving wife Mary Lou and their Welsh Corgi Lucy.

For more information, see www.BJCondike.com

# ML Condike

Mary Lou grew up in Massachusetts and graduated from Worcester State University with a BS in Mathematics, and Worcester Polytechnic Institute with Masters in Business Administration.

Since high school, she has aspired to become a writer. After a career in business, she retired and began her dream. She has two unpublished books, a novel, and a nonfiction. Her ultimate goal is to write a series of mystery novels.

Recently, her short story *Until Your Better Is Best* was published in *Boundless, Stories by Authors Destined to Soar, A Vinculinc Anthology*, Vinculinc, Inc., 2017. The story is available on-line. Vinculinc has accepted a second story (*Sacrifice*), also available on-line, which is a candidate for a future anthology. She has recently placed in the 2019 Kathryn McClatchy Flash Fiction Contest. She also freelances for Redfin Publishing.

Mary Lou is participating in Southern Methodist University's Writer's Path in Dallas. She is a member of Mystery Writers of America, Sisters in Crime, and the Granbury Writers' Bloc.

Contact Mary Lou at MLCondike.com

# Peggy Purser Freeman

**AKA** Meg Arlen. Award-winning author, novelist, editor, journalist, and motivational speaker, Peggy worked for twelve years as editor of Granbury Showcase Magazine. Currently, she writes for ten different magazines across Texas and edits books on a limited basis.

Peggy's inspirational stories are published in numerous Chicken Soup for the Soul titles, including *Happily Ever After -101* best stories on love and marriage chosen from a wide variety of past Chicken Soup books. Two have been chosen as stories of the day on Chicken Soup's national podcast.

She taught writing classes at Continuing Education at UT Arlington and Tarleton's Langdon Center in Granbury. She wrote and presented *Kid Talk*, for 620 AM Radio Disney's public affairs show and produced a *Kid Talk* series for DCTV.

As a motivational speaker, Peggy encourages others to write their stories. Her Student Writing Workshop uses games and activities to improve student test scores and shares her personal experience with dyslexia with students.

- *The Coldest Day in Texas*, (TCU Press) one of three finalists for The Texas League of Writers Teddy Book Award, presented by First Lady Laura Bush.
- *Swept Back to a Texas Future* – a historical play for children, depicting an overview of Texas history.
- *Cruisin' Thru Life~Dip Street and Other Miracles,* inspires family values.
- *Spy Cam One* – (3-6 grades), Digby defends the First Family.
- *Teach Writing Without a Pencil*, offers fun-filled games and activities to help teach writing.

Peggy's books are available on Amazon.com and on her website PeggyPurserFreeman.com. Follow her on Facebook, Twitter, Pinterest, Instagram and Good Reads.

# Beverly Harrison

Beverly joined the Writers' Bloc about five years ago when a clerk at the now closed Blockbuster told her about our group of writers. Almost immediately, she stepped in to support the club and accepted the position of Treasurer. She has looked after the club finances ever since.

In her youth, Beverly attended the Grand Prairie schools and studied at the University of Texas at Arlington. For the past 35 years she has worked at a company in Fort Worth.

Beverly moved to Hill City about fifteen years ago where she resides with her husband and daughter Holli. She also has a daughter Jaime who lives in Azle. She has no siblings and her parents are deceased.

When Beverly isn't working, she writes fan fiction. Fan fiction stories are published in a private library. She also has stories published in the Granbury Writers' Bloc anthologies.

Beverly has provided guidance and support to her daughter Holli, a young writer who is coming into her own.

# H. M. Harrison

H. M. was born and raised in Arlington, moving to the Granbury area with her family in 1991. This was also the year she started writing story snippets. Already an avid reader from her mother's influence, this was a natural progression. Her writing began with fan fiction for *Xena: Warrior Princess*.

Her mother then encouraged her to try writing things she might do something with, like publishing. This proved a fun journey exploring worlds untouched by anyone and seeing where her characters led her next.

Her strongest genre influences can be summed up in three movies: *Return of the Jedi, The Lost Boys, and Return of the Living Dead.* She has carried a love of both sci-fi and paranormal permanently due to their impact. Although *Return of the Living Dead* gave her a lifelong case of the creeps regarding zombies. Except she has enjoyed *The Walking Dead*. Go figure.

# William "Bud" Humble

William "Bud" Humble is a native Texan who's been writing for over 25 years. Though he's tried other things, his love of speculative fiction keeps drawing him back. His desire to help others achieve their literary dreams has led to him becoming the W.O.R.D. Director of Operations, a co-founder of Writers in the Field, and this year, he's also the driving force behind the WORDfest SW in Burleson.

# Connie Lewis Leonard

Connie Lewis Leonard is an accomplished novelist and active journalist. She has been a member of the Granbury Writers' Bloc since 2002, serving as an officer for most of those 17 years.

She writes Christian fiction and devotionals and has published four books with a fifth book currently in draft form. Her latest Christian romance, *Light up My Life in Texas,* was released in March 2018. Other books by Connie include *Somebody Somewhere in Texas*, released in November 2016, *A Psalm a Day*, released in 2015, and *Big C, little c,* released in 2014.

As a journalist, she regularly writes inspiring personal interest stories about people who make a positive difference in the world. Her articles can be found in regional magazines including Lake Granbury Living, published by Green Fox, and numerous other magazines published by With You in Mind Publications and RedFinn Publications.

A retired, public school teacher, Connie shared her passion for writing with her students, encouraging many young writers. She has a Master of Arts from Midwestern State University and a Bachelor of Science in elementary education from Angelo State University. Connie lives in Granbury with her husband and three rescue dogs.

Connie's books can be purchased on Amazon.

ConnieLewisLeonard.webs.com

GoodReads.com

Facebook.com/ConnieLewisLeonardAuthor

# Jonathan Mathews

Jonathan Mathews, an 18-year-old poet and scholar, has taken life itself to be a writing prompt. Drawing from both his small town, Texas childhood and the unforgettable diversity of extensive international travels, he writes both philosophical and natural beauty poetry, considering the human situation and environment in which we live.

Throughout his childhood Jonathan had considerable experience with crafting arts like pottery, basket weaving, sewing, and leather/woodwork, and suggests such things, as well as writing, as practices in creativity. Although he severely disliked English as a subject when he was younger, he remembers specifically a poetry writing assignment in 9th grade, the product of which inspired his entire writing career.

Growing up a homeschooler with a computer engineer and a marine biologist for parents, and deeply involved in Boy Scouting, 4-H, and church for over ten years, he loves to apply adventure and morality concepts through the lenses of service and science. Having recently moved with his family from his home town of Granbury to Gilmer, Texas in order to help their grandparents build and start a farm, he enrolled in LeTourneau University in Longview, Texas.

Now he is finishing his Sophomore year as he pursues a Bachelor's Degree in Biology with minors in Chemistry and Psychology. Upon graduation, he plans to attend medical school where he will fulfill his childhood dream of delivering emergency aid to victims of traumatic circumstances by becoming a surgeon. Though schooling takes most of his time, he remains an avid reader and would happily suggest Dickens, Twain, Lewis, Snicket, Paine, and Adams to anyone who asks. Although his writing may slow during the semesters, college has given him many new prompts, and he looks forward to continuing it wherever the road of his life may take him.

# Kathryn McClatchy

Kathryn started her career in marketing and advertising, then segued into academia teaching literature, composition, research skills, and rhetoric.

In 2006, as she was finishing her Master's degree and preparing to start her PhD, Kathryn suffered the first of many strokes—one day she was a college professor, the next day she was having to relearn to read, write, talk, walk, and pretty much everything else again.

In the last decade, she has applied her education and experience to reinventing herself as a writer and public speaker.

In addition to writing thrillers and creative nonfiction, Kathryn has created and/or managed social media campaigns for three non-profit writing organizations, created and facilitated a flash fiction contest that has since been named after her, and coaches writers and businesses on platform building, productivity, ADA Compliance, and developmental writing.

Learn more about Kathryn at KathrynMcClatchy.com.

# Donna Pierce

Donna grew up in Wyoming riding her horses and playing in the imaginary world of cowboys and Indians. She moved to Billings, Montana to attend college. Donna's background is in finance and marketing. Most of her life has been spent writing business plans, policies, and procedures. Now she wants to write the fun "stuff."

She is the mother of two grown children and has two little granddaughters.

Donna lives on a small farm in Weatherford with her three dogs and three horses. She enjoys making story books and art with her granddaughters and working cows with her horses. She also enjoys shooting and has been involved with a gun club. Donna has been providing weekly jail and prison ministry over the last year.

She enjoys writing because it "allows her to dwell in other worlds while creating the course of what goes on around her." Donna is looking forward to this new path in her life and hopes that she will be able to put a smile on a few faces and also be able to take some readers down these paths with her.

"Now that I am retired, I can be a kid again." ~ Donna Pierce

# Barna A. Richards, M. D., FACEP

Dr. Barna Richards' first Book, *44 Years in the ER* documents the evolution of the ER, its history and its heroes from the 1960s to the end of the century in the Dallas/Fort Worth area. That history documented change, progress and finally a specialty arm of medicine.

Born in 1935 in Weatherford, Texas, Barna Richards grew up in Ranger and Wink, Texas. He attended Wink High School, played on the 1952 state championship football team and graduated in 1954. His career began at North Texas State College (now UNT) in pre-med and he graduated in 1959 with a BA in biology. Dr. Richards received his MD at the University of Texas Medical Branch, Galveston, Texas.

He received an internship and family practice residency at John Peter Smith Hospital, Fort Worth, Texas, from 1963 until 1965. He worked in solo private practice, in family medicine from 1965 to 1991. He worked in the ER during these years, nights and weekends.

Dr. Richards served as Medical Director and staff physician of the emergency department at Arlington Memorial Hospital, Arlington, Texas, 1987 to 2006; Medical Director, EMS, City of Arlington, Texas, 1987 to 1997; Medical Director, EMS, City of Pantego, Texas where he monitored and taught cardiac and trauma care to paramedics, 1988 to 1996.

Find Dr. Richards' books on Amazon.

GranburyWritersBloc.com/authors-page/barna-richards-m-d-author

# R. L. Sykes

At the age of 12, Rebecca's mother handed her a *Reader's Digest* condensed book, *Octavia's Hill*. She was immediately hooked on mysteries. Mary Higgins Clark, Linda Castillo, Lee Childs, Lisa Gardner, and John Grisham have become some of her favorite authors. Once hooked on a story, she has been known to stay up all night to finish it!

During college writing intrigued her, but with no time to write between studying and working, her writing collected dust.

Rebecca joined SMU Writers' Path in 2016, which provided the structure she needed for her mystery/romance stories. Granbury Writers' Bloc has been the experience she needed to learn and grow in the writing world. Her goal is to find an agent and to be traditionally published.

Rebecca is married and has 2 children who keep asking Mom who the killer is and she won't tell them until they're old enough to read her book.

Rebecca's pen name is: R.L. Sykes

Twitter: @rlsykesauthor

Facebook: @rlsykesauthor

www.rlsykesauyhor.com

"Who doesn't like a lightning filled, heart-pounding Texas thunderstorm with a killer on the loose?"

# Robert C. Taylor

Robert Taylor writes incredible and entertaining fiction and poetry. He has been a member of the Granbury Writers' Bloc since 2004 and served as president for several of those years. He has written more than 150 short stories and completed two novels, *Laughter and Tears* and *Feeding the Wolves*.

Many of Robert's stories were gleaned from his childhood while others are pure fiction. He leaves it up to the reader to guess which is fact and which is fiction. When asked about his subject matter he responded, "At my age, I've got a lot more material if I write about my past."

Robert attended Texas Wesleyan University and worked in management at Dillard's Dept. Stores for 27 years.

He is married with five children and resides in Granbury Texas.

Now retired, he spends his time golfing, fishing, writing, and enjoying his grandkids.

# Dan Vanderburg

After attending schools and colleges in the Dallas, Texas area, Dan enlisted in the U. S. Navy during the Vietnam War. Later, he spent his working career in management in the computer industry.

As a sixth generation Texan, Dan loves researching Texas history and writing about its exciting past.

He started his first novel, *Legacy of Dreams*, an action/adventure Texas pioneer story, in 1990. It took twenty years of honing his writing craft a few hours a week while working in his primary career to publish that first book in 2010. Dan's second novel, *Trail of Hope*, was published two years later. His third book, *Freedom Road*, was released a year after that, and completes the action/adventure trilogy, the Texas Legacy Family Saga Series.

*The Littlest Hero* was published in 2016. The next year he published his first fantasy novel, *The Extraordinary Adventures of Max Malone*.

Dan started writing poetry and humorous short stories well before he ventured into novels. His book of humorous short stories and poetry, *Happy Sounds*, was published in 2016.

Besides writing, Dan enjoys speaking to groups about the hard life on the Texas frontier. He also enjoys gardening, cooking, remodeling his home, volunteering, and hanging out with family and friends. He is the proud father of two adult daughters, Tina and Shannon. He lives with his dog, Stormy, in Granbury, Texas.

Learn more about Dan Vanderburg and his books at his website, DanVanderburg.com.

Made in the USA
Columbia, SC
03 November 2022

70386332R00189